FALLING ANGELS

THE SEDONA FILES: BOOK 5

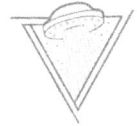

CHRISTINE POPE

DARK VALENTINE PRESS

FALLING ANGELS

ISBN: 978-0692627754

Copyright © 2016 by Christine Pope.

Revised version copyright © 2019

Published by Dark Valentine Press

Cover design by Lou Harper

Book formatting by Indie Author Services

CHAPTER ONE

Twenty-five years from now....

THE ROOM WHERE MY EXTENDED FAMILY—BLOOD relations or not—had gathered pulsed with a kind of shocked silence. I think we were all still trying to piece together what we'd just seen on the TV screen before someone had blacked out the transmission. I knew I was. Who—or what—had those dark, looming shapes actually been? They'd moved faster than any human being I'd ever seen, that was for sure.

Because of my family's history, I assumed the worst. Not all visitors from beyond the stars were benign like my father and grandfather.

Otto, who had made himself scarce for the past quarter-century or so, now blocked the screen and regarded us calmly, perfect features impassive, arms crossed. Or rather, he seemed calm enough, although I noticed that he wouldn't look directly at anyone. Maybe he wasn't happy about having to address such a large crowd all at once—my aunt's family room had been filled to capacity, couches and chairs crowded with my cousins, my aunt and uncle; my parents; the Olivers and their children, Michael and Taryn.

My mother was actually the first person to speak. She rose from her chair, fine brows pulled together, full mouth compressed into a taut line. Otto, who had once been the spirit guide of our long-time family friend and my sort of adoptive aunt Persephone Oliver, was probably number one on my mother's list of people she couldn't stand, so I understood her anger. After all, it was Otto's fault that my father's powers had been stripped from him and he'd been exiled here on Earth, forever unable to go back to his life among the stars.

Anyway, I didn't question her anger. I might have even felt an echo of it myself, although my resentment was by nature secondhand, a grudge born from her and my father's pain, and not because of any loss I'd personally experienced.

Hands on her hips, which were still as slim as they'd been in pictures of her when she was my age, my mother glared at Otto and said, "Oh, *we* need to talk? What happened to not interfering in matters that don't have anything to do with us? You seemed to be pretty strict about that, once upon a time."

"Kirsten—" my father began, but Otto only shook his head.

"Circumstances have changed," he said, his tone cool enough, although something about it seemed to cut right through my father's protest. Our unwelcome visitor's gaze swept the room, and once again it seemed to rest on me for a second longer than it should.

Despite the situation, and despite knowing that— well, according to my parents, at least—Otto was possibly the biggest asshole this side of Alpha Centauri, I couldn't help feeling a little flush rise to my cheeks as I stared back at him. Jerk he might be, but he was also absolutely gorgeous. His were the kind of dark, exotic looks you didn't get a lot of here in Sedona, with those chiseled features and long-lashed brown eyes.

The silent connection between us was broken as soon as he turned to look back at my mother. In a way I was glad; no one had been paying much attention to me, but I knew a flush had risen to my cheeks, and that wasn't something I really wanted to try to explain…especially since I wasn't sure I could explain it even to myself.

"I understand you are upset," Otto said calmly, "but I had hoped that tempers might have cooled after more than twenty-five of your years had passed."

His reply only seemed to irritate my mother further. Scowling, she opened her mouth to speak, but Persephone, who was wearing a somewhat resigned expression, cut in before my mother could say anything else.

"Maybe if you could just tell us what's going on, Otto."

For some reason, he frowned. Then he said, his tone sharp, "Please, we are far past that particular subterfuge. 'Otto' was only a persona and a name I took on to make you believe I was someone from your world's past. My true name is Raphael."

Well, I had to admit that "Raphael" did suit him a lot better. Nothing could be further from the sixteenth-century Turkish eunuch he'd pretended to be than the godlike person standing in front of us, so "Otto" had seemed like kind of a ridiculous name for him.

Persephone shrugged, the metallic threads woven through the scarf she wore glinting a little with the movement. "All right, *Raphael*. Whatever makes you happy. I'm guessing what we just saw on TV was interference of some kind by our old friends the Reptilians?"

"Precisely," he replied. "When Martin and Kirsten drove the Reptilians from this place, they did not go all the way home. Instead, they—"

"So where exactly *is* 'home'?" Paul asked. That was probably a question he'd been pondering for longer than I'd been alive, and I could tell he'd been itching to ask it.

Otto's—that is, *Raphael's*—mouth thinned. I got

the impression he wasn't too pleased by the interruption. "What your people refer to as Alpha Draconis, if you must know."

Paul, in contrast to the gorgeous but scowling Raphael, looked like someone who'd just won a bar bet. "I knew it," he muttered under his breath, but he settled back against the back of the couch, apparently content to let Raphael continue with his story now that his question had been answered.

"As I was saying," Raphael continued, now sounding as tetchy as someone with such a warm tenor voice could, "after their defeat, the Reptilians did not return to their home system. Instead, they set up a base on Mars, where they could continue to monitor your world from a safe distance."

"Only now it's not so safe, is it?" Lance put in.

"No. Neither safe for you, nor for them."

"Who attacked the astronauts?" The words were out of my mouth before I even realized I was going to ask the question. So far, this discussion had included only the grown-ups in the room, and I'd gotten the impression that the younger generation was supposed to stay out of it. But all of us "kids" were in fact adults, even my cousin Melissa, who at nineteen wasn't old enough to drink but was definitely an adult in the eyes of the law. Anyway, I figured we had just as much right to be involved in the conversation as anyone else. "Are they dead?"

Raphael's dark gaze slid back toward me. If I hadn't known better, I would have said he was wearing mascara or something. I didn't think I'd ever seen a man with lashes that thick and black. Then I wanted to shake myself, because what the hell difference did it make anyway? I shouldn't be focusing on trivial details like that, not when something so much more important was going on.

"No, they're not dead," he replied, and a sort of collective sigh of relief filled the room. "But do not think the Reptilians saved them out of altruism. Since being banished to Mars, they have been unable to collect any human specimens. Now several humans have fallen into their hands."

"My God," Persephone said, while my friend Taryn shot a frightened look at her mother. I could only imagine how hard this must be for the two of them—both psychics, both probably being bombarded from all sides by the worry and fear and confusion flying around the room.

Even I could almost feel it, and I definitely wasn't psychic. Yes, I'd inherited a few peculiar talents from my parents, along with their alien blood, but reading minds wasn't one of those gifts. At least, not in the way Taryn could. I knew my parents shared a special kind of psychic link that allowed them to communicate without speaking aloud, but that was because of their soul bond. I'd only be able to read the thoughts of my soul mate, and so far he didn't seem to be in too much of a hurry to appear.

My father stood up then. He was dressed casually, in jeans and a sweater and his favorite pair of scuffed lace-ups, the ones my mother had been bugging him to get rid of forever, but in that moment, I could see how he was clearly of the same race as Raphael, tall and perfect and somehow ageless. I'd sort of taken his appearance—and my mother's—for granted, since they were my parents and I looked at them every day. Seeing them now, though, I realized how much they really did stand out from the rest of the group who'd gathered at my Aunt Kara's house, and wondered why I'd never noticed before.

I supposed I should count myself lucky, since I'd inherited those same looks, thus guaranteeing that I'd probably get carded into my forties the way my mother still did, but that was a story for another day. In the meantime, I wanted to hear what my father had to say.

"You said, 'circumstances have changed,'" he reminded Raphael. "How so?"

For a second, Raphael hesitated. I could almost see him running over possible answers in his mind, wondering how much to tell us. After all, my father and my mother and I were of his race, or at least partially so, but everyone else there was just a mere human in his eyes. Well, except for Grace and Logan, who were Reptilian/human hybrids, even though they didn't look it. Anyway, I guessed that Raphael didn't want to reveal too much in front of any of them, even if he had come to us for help.

At least, I assumed that was why he'd appeared

out of the blue like that. Why else would he show up after so many years?

"It is…possible," he began, sounding somewhat hesitant, "*possible,* I'll admit, that perhaps we were somewhat too strict when it came to interpreting our rules about non-interference."

My father's eyebrows lifted, and my mother frowned, then said, "Seriously? That's what you've decided, after taking Martin's powers away and making sure that neither I nor my daughter were ever able to explore a universe that should have been ours?" She sounded bitter, and I couldn't blame her. Not that I really wanted to have grown up anywhere except Sedona, since it was what I knew. Some people might have thought it was exciting to be three-quarters alien, but I didn't know if I possessed the courage to leave the world where I'd been born and travel among the stars the way my father had.

Not that I'd ever been given the option, of course.

"It is not what *I* personally have decided," Raphael said, that waspish note back in his voice. "Rather, after certain other events transpired in the interim, many members of the Assembly realized that we might have underestimated the ambitions of the Reptilians."

"I thought you said they just went to Mars and set up shop there," I said.

"The group that had its base here in Sedona, yes," he replied. "But of course, they were only a very small fraction of the total Reptilian population.

Perhaps spurred by their defeat here, they have expanded more aggressively in their own sector of the galaxy, and subjugated many who did not have the fortune to be protected by those such as your mother."

At those words of praise—indirect as they were— my mother sent a startled glance in Raphael's direction. Probably, the last thing she'd expected to hear him say was anything positive about the way she'd managed to call on her powers to drive the Reptilians out of Sedona. She'd had to summon a strength she didn't even know she possessed to prevent those hostile aliens from gaining access to the peculiar energies at work here.

"At any rate," he went on, "we did nothing to dislodge them from their base on Mars, since it seemed that they were only observing and not taking any direct action against your people."

"Until now," Paul said, his voice grim. "What we just saw on TV looked like pretty direct action to me."

"It was," Raphael agreed, "and in doing so, they have opened themselves up for retaliation. We had hoped to avoid such an eventuality."

"But what can any of us do?" Persephone asked. She pushed back a few strands of curly hair and added, "After all, it took five months for that expedition to get to Mars…."

Raphael and my father exchanged a glance. I thought I saw amusement in Raphael's eyes, while my father—his expression was a little more difficult to parse. Eagerness...worry...maybe a tinge of excitement?

"Our technology is advanced far beyond yours," Raphael said then. "From here to Mars is a trip of only a little more than an hour."

Paul's eyes looked like they were going to bug out of his head. "'A little more than an hour'?" he repeated. "You can't use FTL for intra-system travel, can you? Is it some form of gravity drive?"

Holding up a hand, Raphael said, "The technology involved is of no concern right now. What does matter is that we reach those prisoners before the Reptilians can do anything to bring them harm."

"'We'?" my father inquired, again with a lift of his eyebrow that I knew all too well.

"Yes," Raphael replied, apparently ignoring the sarcastic edge to the question. "You and Kirsten and"—he paused for a moment, gaze traveling to me for a second or two before moving back toward my father again— "your daughter Callista."

Shock coursed through me, even as my mother burst out, "Are you insane? Do you think I'm going to let you drag my daughter off-planet on some sort of insane rescue mission? She's just a kid!"

"Thanks, Mom," I remarked sourly. All right, I knew she was only speaking from a place of worry and fear. But she didn't really think I was a child... did she? I could vote, drink, get married, or start my own business if I wanted to. At the same time, I was almost glad of her protective mama-bear attitude. I might have been three-quarters alien, but up until that point in my life, I hadn't done anything more dangerous than attempt some ultralight flying over the red rocks of my hometown.

"She is almost the same age you were when you defended this place against the Reptilians," Raphael said calmly.

"That was different!"

"How?"

"Well—" She flailed for a few seconds, then sent a pleading look in my father's direction. "Martin, tell him how crazy this is."

He was silent for a long moment while everyone else looked on. I wouldn't say the rest of the group were holding their breaths, exactly, but it was obvious that they could all tell this decision was something my parents would have to agree on, and so were trying to stay out of it—even my Aunt Kara, who wasn't exactly known for her hands-off attitude. Maybe the decision to go also lay between me and Raphael, too, since he wanted the four of us to make up the rescue party, but it was clear that the human contingent, or even the human/alien hybrid contingent, hadn't been included in this particular invitation.

Then my father looked over at me. His eyes, the same smoky gray-blue as mine, were troubled. "Raphael is right in that. You're an adult. You have to decide what you want to do."

I swallowed. What the hell was I supposed to say? Never mind that I didn't know how in the world I'd be of any help in rescuing a bunch of kidnapped astronauts from the hands of some particularly nasty aliens. If I'd been invited to do some power shopping down in Phoenix, maybe then I would have been of some help. Yes, my Uncle Lance had made sure I knew how to shoot a variety of guns and maneuver a 4x4 up a rocky cliff face, but those skills, useful as they might be down here in Sedona, still didn't seem quite what was required for a rescue mission to Mars.

Then I sent a quick glance over at Raphael, trying to gauge what might be going through his mind. Did he think I was weak for not immediately volunteering? But his face was impassive. He waited there in those white robes of his, which should have looked foolish in the prosaic surroundings of my aunt's family room but instead only made the rest of us appear woefully underdressed. I still didn't understand any of this, not really, and I could tell from the way my mother's brows were drawn together that she was also having a hard time figuring out what this all meant.

That decided it, really. As frightening as what Raphael was asking might be, I couldn't quite feel all that scared, not when I knew my parents would be going along as well. And maybe if we did as he asked and were successful, he'd ask the Assembly— whoever they were—to lift my father's exile and return the powers that had been stripped from him.

That would be worth whatever risks I might have to take.

I lifted my chin and asked, "And my father? I assume you're going to restore his powers, or what would be the point in his going with you?"

A flicker of something I couldn't quite read passed over Raphael's perfect features. "You are correct in that assumption. I have been given the ability to return those powers to him, if he agrees to help."

Well, that decided it. Not that I'd really seriously considered leaving the Mars mission's astronauts to their fate when I apparently had the ability to do something about it, but if this expedition meant that my father would once again have the powers which had been stripped from him before I was even born, then I knew there was only one thing I could say. He was watching me closely and gave the slightest shake of his head, as if to say, *Don't do this on my account.*

But I'd already made up my mind. I didn't exactly know what my father had been missing all these years, but if I had a chance to put things right….

"Okay," I said. "Tell us what we have to do."

CHAPTER TWO

"We must go now," Raphael said. "I understand that this discussion was necessary, but we have already used up too much time."

To my surprise, Logan spoke next. He'd been sitting quietly next to my cousin Grace during the entire exchange, listening to the back and forth, but then he said, "I want to go with you."

Grace went rigid with shock. Then she immediately shook her head. "Oh, no. No way. Not when we've just worked things out between us—"

"I'm a soldier," he argued, although I noticed the way he reached over to take her hand, as if to reconfirm the bond between the two of them. "They could use my help."

Raphael said, "You would do this, working against those who created you?"

Sparks seemed to flash in Logan's gray eyes.

"They might have bred me. But they did not create me. I am my own man."

I had to admire the way he'd spoken, calm but with an undercurrent of steel to his words. It hadn't been hard for me to guess why Grace was so attracted to him, despite his being a human/alien hybrid—the man was smoking hot—but right then, I could also see why she loved him. He had integrity, even if the aliens who'd first cooked him up in a test tube obviously did not.

A nod from Raphael. "It is true that it would be helpful to have someone with your skills."

"Logan—"

The despair in Grace's voice was so obvious, it nearly broke my heart. My Aunt Kara shifted her position where she stood, as if she wanted to say something but then realized it wasn't her place to interfere right then. This matter was between Grace and Logan.

And Uncle Lance—his mouth was pressed into a hard line, and I could see the way his fingers tapped at his hip, as if longing for the holstered gun that had hung there in his former life. He probably wished he could come along with us, but I knew Raphael would never think of him as a qualified addition to the party, even though Lance had once been an Army Ranger and probably knew more about actual combat than anyone else in the room. Problem was, to Raphael, Lance didn't count, because he was only human.

Logan lifted Grace's hand to his lips and kissed it gently before placing it back in her lap. "This is something I can do, Grace. Please."

A long, long moment, during which she stared down at her hand, almost as if she was expecting to see the visible print of Logan's lips there. Finally, she gave a very small nod. "All right. I don't understand, not really, but—okay."

"Good," Raphael said. "Then let us go."

I shot him a puzzled look. "Just like this?" I asked, glancing down at myself. I hadn't really dressed to impress, since I knew I'd just be spending the evening with the family, but even so, I wasn't sure if jeans and heeled boots and a tight sweater really comprised the best ensemble for staging a commando raid on an alien outpost.

"Anything you require can be procured on my ship," he replied, and I couldn't help experiencing a little shiver of anticipation. I was dying to see the inside of that ship.

"We'll need to stand close together," my father said. Clearly, he knew the drill.

I got up from where I'd been sitting on the love seat, then walked over to my father. My mother did the same, and Logan pressed Grace's hand one last time before coming to assemble with our little group. Raphael moved closer to us as well. His hand went to a spot on his hip, not all that different from the place where Uncle Lance had been itching for his sidearm. For the first time, I could see that Raphael wore a silvery belt underneath his voluminous outer robe, and from that belt hung what looked like a strange, opalescent jewel encased in silver.

His fingers moved over the surface of the jewel. I barely had time to catch a final glance of the group gathered in my Aunt Kara's family room—for some reason, Persephone's daughter Taryn looked the most troubled—before a brilliant white light surrounded me, my parents, Logan, and Raphael.

My entire body felt as if it was breaking out in the world's worst case of the goosebumps. The skin at the back of my neck prickled, and it seemed as if my hair was trying to stand on end, which would've been quite a feat, considering it fell most of the way down my back. I wanted to reach out and grab my mother's hand for reassurance, but I couldn't seem to move, couldn't do anything except let that strange white light wash over me and move through me. At least I was still breathing normally.

I couldn't tell how long it all lasted—much longer than I would have liked it to, that was for sure—before the light suddenly disappeared, and I felt my feet hit a hard surface. A stumble before I recovered my balance, and then I blinked as I tried to focus on my surroundings.

We stood in a large room with walls of curved metal. Lights that shimmered along the entire spectrum and back again formed long, arched bars between the metal panels that made up the walls. And immediately ahead of us was a huge window, and framed in that window was a blue-green disk, one edge beginning to fall into shadow.

Earth. We weren't in a room, but standing somewhere on Raphael's spaceship. Even though he'd told us that was where we would be going, the scene took my breath away.

I swallowed and looked over at my parents. My mother's eyes appeared just as wide with wonder as mine probably were, but my father only gave a single thoughtful nod, as if reacquainting himself with something he hadn't seen in a long time. And Logan —I could tell from the way his gaze flicked from place to place that he was taking it all in as well, but he remained silent.

"Welcome aboard," Raphael said. He moved away from us to a tall pedestal of dark gray metal. Lights surged across the top of the pedestal, and he ran his finger over its surface. At once, the view of Earth outside the windows—or view-screens, or whatever they were—began to shift. The pedestal must have been attached to the ship's navigational system, and Raphael had just given the command to leave orbit. "We will arrive at Mars in approximately one point three of your world's hours. In the meantime, we'll need to outfit ourselves for the mission. This way."

He gestured toward one of the metal walls, which slid out of the way when he pointed to it. The seamlessness of it all was a little disconcerting. All right, intellectually I understood that the alien race Raphael and my father belonged to had technology that was far more advanced than what I was used to down on Earth, but it still jarred me to see it in action.

As we followed Raphael down a corridor, also of metal, with those shimmering, soothing lights set at regular intervals, my father asked, "Your crew?"

"I have none," Raphael replied. "You know that it is not strictly necessary on a vessel of this size, and we preferred to put as few of our people at risk as possible."

That remark made me think that he—and his masters, whoever they were—had to have known in advance that things were going to head south with the Mars mission, and that Raphael would need to bring in some Earth-based backup.

"Oh, so it's okay to put us at risk, just not your own people?" I asked.

He shot me an irritated glance. "There are reasons why you are far better suited for this task than anyone I could have brought along with me."

"Oh?" I challenged him. "Like what?"

"Callista," my father said, his tone a warning. All right, maybe I was pushing things, but I really didn't like the idea of being considered expendable.

"It's fine," Raphael broke in, sounding uncharacteristically mild…for him. "If I were in her position, I would be asking the same questions."

Both my parents looked somewhat astonished by that reply, probably because they'd had previous dealings with Raphael/Otto and therefore knew he wasn't generally the type to let things roll off his back.

He flickered a quick glance at them. "Have you spoken much of how you drove the Reptilians out of Sedona?"

My mother lifted her shoulders. I could tell from the way she wasn't exactly looking at anyone that his question had made her uncomfortable. And yes, she had talked about her showdown with the aliens, but in roundabout ways, saying that it had been the energies of Sedona, of the Earth itself, that had been just as much a factor in defeating the Reptilians as her own powers.

"A little," she finally admitted.

"They've taught me," I told Raphael. My tone might or might not have been a touch belligerent. "Trained me to use the powers I inherited." Eyes narrowing, I added, "At least you didn't take away the ability for my father to pass his power on to his child, even if he couldn't use it himself."

Raphael didn't reply immediately. Something of a frown pulled at his brows, but he only waved a hand near one patch of wall, and a doorway appeared there. Weird how that worked; it was almost as if the metal had a fluid quality that allowed it to melt out of the way when a door was needed and then flow back into place afterward.

Beyond that strange doorway was a circular room with small bays placed at regular intervals around it, eight in all. "Step into one of these," he commanded.

"You will be properly outfitted for the mission ahead."

My mother didn't move. Arms crossed, she surveyed the bays, a skeptical expression on her face. "Why do you have eight of these things here if you're the only person on board?"

I'd been thinking more or less the same thing, but I had to keep from grinning at the pained look that passed over Raphael's features. It was kind of funny to watch someone so inhumanly gorgeous try not to grimace. Or maybe I was just attempting to find the humor in the situation, because that way I could try to avoid thinking about the nervous butterflies that kept fluttering around in my stomach.

"The ship was designed to carry up to eight crew members, but it can be piloted solo," he replied, tone remarkably even, all things considered. "Is there anything else? Would you like an explanation of the propulsion system, or perhaps the sanitary facilities?"

"No," she said, not bothering to hide her own grin. "I suppose I'll get to figure those out on my own eventually."

He didn't rise to the bait. "Then please, get in a bay. If it makes you feel any better, I will also be using one."

"It does, actually," she said, and my father only shook his head. I supposed he was probably used to that sort of thing. My mother never had been exactly the reverent type.

"What's it going to do?" I asked as I stepped into the person-sized divot in the wall. The metal was featureless, completely smooth and cool to the touch, and I couldn't begin to figure out how the whole thing operated.

"As I said, it will see you are properly outfitted for the mission that lies ahead."

"What will happen to my own clothes? I like these boots."

His jaw set, and I got the distinct impression he was trying to prevent himself from rolling his eyes. "They will be stored safely."

I supposed I had to take his word for it. Maybe worrying about my boots was kind of stupid, considering what was at stake. I swallowed, doing my best to ignore the sour taste of fear in my mouth.

As soon as my head touched the back of the bay, an opaque, glassy film covered the opening, obscuring my view of everyone else in the room. That is, I could see vague shapes, could tell that everyone else was also getting into their own bays, but I couldn't make out anything more than that.

Light flashed all around me, blue-white. I shut my eyes against the glare, felt once again those strange tingles and pinpricks all over my body. Was this Raphael's version of a practical joke? Were these bays actually some kind of transporter devices, instead of the "outfitters" he'd claimed they were?

Well, I couldn't do anything about it now, since it seemed I was basically glued in place and couldn't have moved even if there was someplace for me to go. A few more seconds passed, and then the light dimmed and I was able to open my eyes.

My sweater and jeans—and yep, the high-heeled designer boots I'd scooped up at an after-Christmas sale at Nordstrom Rack—were all gone. Now I wore a dark gray jumpsuit made of a fabric that didn't quite feel like cotton or silk or even microfiber, although it gave the impression of being incredibly soft and incredibly sturdy at the same time. My long hair had been pulled back into what felt like a tight braid that fell down my back, although since I couldn't see myself, I couldn't say for sure exactly what the hairstyle looked like. I was wearing boots, but low-heeled ones that seemed to have been designed to fit my feet perfectly. It was hard to tell I even had them on, they were so light, although as soon as the opaque film disappeared and I stepped back out onto the floor of the changing room, or whatever you wanted to call it, I could feel the way the boots both cupped and supported my feet.

Like the world's best foot bra, I thought with a mental grin. Speaking of which, my undergarments felt subtly different as well, although I certainly wasn't going to open up the jumpsuit to take a peek inside. Not that I was sure how I'd even be able to accomplish such a thing. That jumpsuit didn't have a single zipper, button, or snap. It almost looked as if it had been grown around me, which might present some problems when it came time to go to the bathroom.

All those worries about logistics went right out of my head, though, when I glanced across the room and caught sight of Raphael.

He also had on the same dark gray type of jump-suit I wore, which I wouldn't have normally thought of as figure-flattering. But with those sweeping robes of his gone, I could see how broad his shoulders were, his lean long legs, and, well—

Your mother will freak if she catches you stealing a peek at Raphael's ass, I scolded myself. Somehow, I did manage to tear my gaze away, but not before I'd gotten enough of an eyeful to confirm that he did in fact have a very stare-able butt.

By that point, everyone had emerged from their respective bays. My mother's hair had also been braided out of the way, and she and my father and Logan all wore the same gray jumpsuits as well. Logan brushed a hand over one sleeve of his suit, his expression troubled. Was he remembering wearing something similar, back when he'd been "hatched"— or whatever you wanted to call it—at the alien base?

It wasn't the sort of question I would've had the guts to ask even under normal circumstances, and I certainly wasn't going to ask now.

"In approximately forty-five of your minutes, we will reach Mars orbit," Raphael said. Had he noticed the way I'd been staring at his body? From his matter-of-fact tone, I had to guess not. Thank God.

My mother wore a worried from. "Won't they be able to tell we're coming?"

"Neither the Reptilians nor your own space agency's sensors will be able to detect this ship, so you need not worry about that."

My father didn't appear too surprised by that revelation. Well, why would he? Once upon a time, he'd been surrounded by this same technology. Logan nodded, and my mother also remained quiet and stood there with her arms crossed, clearly expecting Raphael to go on with his briefing.

"The Reptilians have also captured the crew members who stayed back with the landing module," he went on. "They are all being held now at the base the Reptilians constructed in the crater on Utopia Planitia. That is our destination."

"How many of the enemy?" Logan asked. His gray eyes were intent, focused. It looked to me as if he'd clicked right back into soldier mode. In a way, that was reassuring; he definitely gave the impression of someone who knew what he was doing. On the other hand, something about him had altered subtly, making him seem far less approachable than I'd originally thought. I wondered what Grace would have thought of the change in him, if she'd been around to see it.

"The number on active duty at these bases can vary, but generally it falls somewhere between forty and fifty."

That reply took a moment to sink in. *"Fifty?"* I repeated, the word coming out in a nervous squeak.

One corner of Raphael's mouth lifted. "I suppose you think that ten to one is not very good odds?" His attention shifted to my mother. "How many did you vanquish, all those years ago? Two hundred?"

"I really didn't stop to count," she said. Her voice sounded calm enough, but from the way she cast a worried glance toward my father, I could tell she didn't much appreciate having to revisit that particular memory. "A lot."

"Well, then. You and Martin and Callista possess those powers—as do I—and Logan is, as he claimed, trained for combat and reconnaissance. There really is nothing to worry about."

Easy for him to say. I swallowed, trying to figure out the best way to ask the question. Oh, well, I'd just let him be condescending and make me feel like an idiot, and then maybe after he got that out of his system, he could give me an answer I'd understand.

"About those powers," I ventured. "I'm not saying I'm an expert or anything, but everything my parents have taught me so far has been about tapping into the power of the Earth, using the energies in Sedona to either reach out with or to turn inward to protect myself. How is that supposed to help me on another planet like Mars?"

Raphael didn't smirk the way I'd been expecting him to. Instead, he steepled his fingers under his chin, then narrowed his eyes as he appeared to consider my question. "All worlds have their particular energies. Those in Sedona are very powerful, which is why the Reptilians sought to exploit them. Even so, you can tap into the energy from any other world, even Mars. All you have to do is learn how to access it. When you work with the power of your home world, what do you do?"

"I—" It was hard for me to explain, just as I supposed it would be hard for someone with perfect pitch to explain how they knew to always hit the right note. "I guess I can just feel it. I go still and breathe it in, sort of."

I stopped there, expecting him to mock my vague reply. But he didn't. Raphael nodded and said, "It is no different when you go to another world. You simply need to reach out and let the energy come to you. It is part of the harmony of the universe, and the force that gives us our advantage. You see, the Reptilians are always working against the natural order of things, and that is why they bring discord and destruction wherever they go. We can use their very natures against them."

Logan didn't look too thrilled by that particular revelation. I couldn't really blame him; it had to be hard to realize such toxic DNA was part of your genetic makeup. Not for the first time, I wondered how the Reptilians had managed to make someone so human-looking when Logan was actually anything but human. But, from what I'd heard, genetic manipulation was one of their strengths...

and their obsessions. So was Logan one of their successes, or their failures?

"And that's why you want Kirsten and Callista here, isn't it?" my father asked. "They're of our race, and so can access those powers, but they're of Earth as well, and will have an easier time accessing the energies of a world from their own system."

"Precisely," Raphael replied, then directed his next words to my mother and me. "Deep within, you two are made of the same elements that make up your solar system. Martin and I have a great deal of training in these matters, and so of course we will be able to assist you, but our chances of success are much greater with you two on the team."

I wanted to be reassured by his confidence in me, especially since it was one of the last things I'd been expecting, but right then, all I could do was hope his belief in my so-called powers wasn't misplaced. After all, it was one thing to go through the exercises with my parents, sitting at one of Sedona's vortexes and allowing myself to sense the way its energies ebbed and flowed, and how I could lace them through my fingers like ribbons of light if I wanted to. Taking those ribbons of energy and turning them into a weapon was something entirely different. I'd never done anything like that before. If I couldn't manage the task, I would be risking the lives of everyone on our team.

"What is the plan, exactly?" my mother asked then. From the way she'd been watching me, I knew she could tell how nervous I was. She'd asked the question because she knew the thing I hated the most was uncertainty. I'd rather hear the worst than have some nebulous fate hanging over me.

"In a way, the Reptilians have made it easier for us by bringing the entire crew of the Mars mission together in one place," Raphael said. "We will energy-jump into their base, and then—"

"'Energy-jump'?" I asked.

"Just the opposite of how we got up into this ship," my father said gently.

"Oh, like in *Star Trek*." There was the franchise that wouldn't die. Last I heard, they were in the middle of filming sequel number eighteen or something. But at least it meant I knew what a transporter was, even if Raphael called it something different.

"It's actually not like it at all, but we don't have time to worry about the particulars now." Raphael didn't look terribly thrilled by the interruption, but seemed ready to forge ahead once he'd determined that my father and I weren't going to contribute anything else to the conversation—at least, for the moment. "At any rate, we should be able to catch them by surprise. And once we're inside their base, the four of us will be able to deflect their attacks by using the planet's energy as a shield. Then we will bring your astronauts back to their ship and get them headed home."

Well, that sounded simple enough…except for the fifty or so things I could think of that might go wrong, starting with "energy-jumping" right into the middle of a group of Reptilians and going from there. And what about the astronauts themselves? Did Raphael think they were just going to keep their mouths shut about the little assist they got from a bunch of strangers in gray jumpsuits? They'd certainly have to file a report about what had happened to them, how they'd been rescued.

I asked as much, and Raphael responded, "They'll have no recollection at all of seeing any of us."

His reply made me want to laugh. "Oh, so you're going to use that old 'Men in Black' memory-wipe trick."

"It is not a trick," he said, dark eyes glinting with disapproval. And yet, they held mine for a second or two longer than they should, and a little shiver went through me. No, I had to be imagining things. There was no way in the world that he could be looking at me like…well, like *that*.

Luckily, my mother didn't seem to have noticed our strange little exchange of glances. "Okay, leaving that aside for now, how are the astronauts going to explain away what we saw—what the *world* saw—on that news feed a few hours ago? And what about the little fact that they weren't supposed to head back to Earth until six months from now? All of the data that's been programmed into their guidance systems to get them home is going to be completely incorrect."

"What did you see, precisely?" Raphael returned

calmly. "A dark blur rushing at the camera. A screen that went black. These phenomena are easy enough to explain away. Equipment malfunctions, the same reason why they aborted the mission and returned to Earth. As for plotting their return trip, any mission such as this has backup plans. Contingencies. They came home early because a malfunction bled away most of their oxygen supplies. Problem solved."

There had to be about a million ways to poke holes in his plan, but as I was not a mission specialist at NASA, I didn't really know what any of those ways might be. Besides, the important thing was to get the astronauts out of there, wasn't it? We could worry about explanations later. It would be pretty hard to point a finger at any of us, since the astronauts wouldn't be able to remember who their rescuers were...or even what they were being rescued from. I had to assume they'd be given false memories to cover up the ones Raphael erased.

All of us—Logan and my parents and I—shared troubled glances, but it didn't seem as if anyone was inclined to argue with Raphael. Not even my mother. She was quiet, turning the platinum wedding band on her ring finger around and around, a nervous gesture she seemed to resort to whenever she wasn't quite sure what to say.

"Very well," Raphael said then, once he seemed to realize no one was going to contradict him. "We're now less than fifteen minutes out from Mars. Let us return to the viewing station."

We all followed him, obedient little ducklings trailing their momma, back to the room where we'd first appeared on the ship. Now the disk that filled the forward-facing window—view-screen, whatever —was sandy orange, not blue green, although it also had white caps at its poles.

I stared at it, my pulse beginning to speed up. Despite my mostly alien blood, I'd never thought I would ever set foot on another world. And, unlike some of the UFO hunters my family hung out with— or real astronomers like Paul Oliver and his son Michael—I was okay with that. I'd never been the type to wish for an existence other than my own.

Well, now it looked as if I was going to get it, whether or not I wanted anything other than my humble terrestrial life. My mother's eyes were wide with awe as Mars grew closer, my father almost eager, as if he'd just begun to realize he was coming back to the life that had been denied him a quarter-century earlier. Something about him appeared even taller and straighter, and I wondered if his powers had been restored during the time we were all in those outfitting bays. Raphael hadn't mentioned anything, but….

As for Logan—well, he was just the opposite. His jaw was set, mouth pressed into a line. Yes, he'd volunteered for this mission, but it looked like he wasn't overly thrilled about confronting the beings who'd once been his masters, now that the time had come.

Just when it appeared as if our ship was about to start falling right into the planet's surface, we began to slip sideways, orbiting the ruddy-hued world. I couldn't relax, though. Sure, Raphael had said the Reptilians wouldn't be able to detect our presence. But if we were in orbit, that meant the time of reckoning was just about here. Once again I swallowed, forcing back my fear. I needed to take a cue from my father and Logan and stay cool.

"I will bring us in as close to the base where the astronauts are being held as possible," Raphael informed us. For the first time, I noticed that the opalescent jewel he'd worn beneath his robes now hung from the belt at his waist. His fingers hovered an inch or so away from it, but he wasn't yet touching its surface.

"What about the guards?" Logan asked.

"We must be prepared to meet them," Raphael replied. "I could bring us in farther away, but that would only provide more opportunities for the Reptilians to attack. This way, we will surprise them, and have more chance of performing a fast, surgical strike."

A pause, and then Logan nodded. His mouth was still set, but his eyes looked far away. Was he thinking of Grace in that moment?

In direct contrast, my father appeared more focused than I'd ever seen him. Yes, he glanced from me to my mother, but I think that was more to confirm to himself exactly what was at stake here. He would do whatever he needed to in order to keep us safe.

I could only hope I didn't look as nervous as my mother. Not that I could blame her. However, I really wanted Raphael to think that I was on top of things and ready to go, and that a little interplanetary raid was all in a day's work for me.

Yeah, right. About the biggest challenge I'd faced so far in my life was choosing which dress to wear to prom. Or coming home after I'd gotten my degree instead of staying in Flagstaff and getting an apartment the way my cousin Grace had. Maybe that had been a stupid decision on my part. Maybe I would be feeling a lot more confident and secure in my abilities right now if I'd spent the last year living on my own, rather than in the guesthouse at my parents' place. It was a little better than staying in the room that had been mine ever since I could remember, but in terms of striking out as an independent young adult…not so much.

"Can you feel it?" Raphael asked then, his gaze shifting toward the reddish disk in the view-screen, then back to me.

I didn't have to ask what he meant. For a few seconds, I said nothing, only reached out with the part of my mind that I used to sense the energies back home, where I could feel them like warm currents through the still waters of a pond.

And I did feel it. Different from the energy flows back in Sedona—dull copper rather than bright gold

—but in that moment, the power pulsing within the red planet was a tangible thing, one I could use to wrap around myself...or push outward if necessary. Sedona's powers always made me feel strong, rejuvenated. Would I experience the same thing here, or would tapping into the energy of an alien world drain me, make it harder for me to fight?

Pushing back my anxiety, I nodded. "Yes. It's definitely there."

He glanced over at my mother. "You?"

"Yes," she replied at once. No hesitation at all. I'd never been able to tell for sure whether our powers were on a par, or whether mine were slightly stronger because I had more alien blood than she did. Right then, though, it seemed as if she was able to access those energies just as easily as I could.

"Weapons?" Logan asked then. "I don't have the same abilities as the rest of you."

There wasn't a trace of accusation in his tone. He was just being factual. I didn't know if I would have been as unruffled in the same situation.

"Of course," Raphael said, fingers moving over the surface of the jewel he wore. In that same instant, a belt with two silvery pistols appeared on Logan's waist. At least, they looked like pistols to me, although so sleek and smooth and featureless I wasn't sure I could have figured out where to load them or even how to pull the trigger.

Logan didn't seem to have that same problem, though. He unhooked one of the pistols from the strap that held it in place, then lifted it toward him, turning it over so he could inspect it closely. Apparently satisfied by what he'd seen, he gave the smallest incline of his head.

"They'll do."

"I should hope so." The note of irritation had returned to Raphael's voice, but he seemed to leave it aside as he transferred his attention from Logan to the rest of us. Once again, it seemed as if his gaze lingered on me for a second longer than it needed to, but then he went on, tone brisk, "Time is wasting. We must go now."

CHAPTER THREE

A<small>T ONCE, WHITE LIGHT WASHED OVER ME, AND THE</small>
room where we'd all been standing disappeared.
This time, I'd known more or less what to expect, but
even some foreknowledge didn't make the experience any less disconcerting. Or maybe I was on edge
because I knew something of what waited for us at
the end of this particular "energy jump."

We materialized in a dark corridor. Since we were
going straight into the base, and it seemed that the
Reptilians breathed pretty much the same
atmosphere we humans did, no one had mentioned
needing any kind of breathing apparatus. Even so, I
blinked, trying to get my eyes to adjust to the
dimness, then took a single cautious breath. Everything felt more or less normal, although the air had
an acrid tinge to it that burned the back of my throat.
The gravity seemed to be Earth-normal, too, which

made me think the aliens must have some kind of artificial gravity generator running.

Lights had been placed at regular intervals along the hallway, but the illumination they gave off was reddish and dull, and just barely enough to keep yourself from tripping over any obstacles. I guessed the Reptilians must have very different eyesight from us humans—or human-like aliens, in the case of Raphael and my father—and so the muddy lighting was perfectly adequate for their needs.

Logan had one of the pistols Raphael had given him gripped in his right hand, and I drew on the energy of the planet where I now stood, raising it around me like a shield. Although I wasn't directly in contact with any of them, I could still sense my mother and my father and Raphael doing much the same thing, although my father's manner seemed hesitant. No big surprise, really; Raphael might have returned his powers to him, but my father still hadn't been able to use them for longer than I'd been alive. He was bound to be a little rusty.

Despite my misgivings, it appeared we were the only living beings in the corridor. True, Raphael had assured us that the Reptilians couldn't detect his ship, or the way we'd energy-jumped in here. In the back of my mind, though, I'd half expected to get dog-piled the second we showed up. But that didn't seem to be the case...at least, not at the moment.

"Here," he said, moving a few paces down the hall to a door with some kind of lighted panel next to it. Presumably, the panel was the Reptilians' version of a locking mechanism, and I wondered how in the world Raphael intended to get past it. Yes, the technology he appeared to command was so far advanced it might as well be magic, but—

He unclipped the opalescent device from his belt and passed it over the lighted panel. At once, the door retracted into the lintel with a hissing noise that made me want to wince. No sleek liquid metal here, it seemed; the Reptilians might be technologically superior to mere Earthlings, but they clearly weren't as advanced as Raphael's—and my father's—people.

As soon as the door was out of the way, Raphael went into the room beyond, Logan right behind, while my mother and I were sort of in the middle of our group and my father brought up the rear. We'd only gotten a foot or so inside the chamber before a shaky voice said, "What the *hell?*"

I peered past Logan's shoulder to see a man in his late forties with short-cropped dark hair staring at us in shock. He wore a pale blue jumpsuit with a patch depicting a yellow and red flag on one arm, and in the spot right above his heart was another patch that read "Cruz." So this must be Gonzalo Cruz, the Mars mission commander.

Standing next to him was another man, younger and Asian, whose name was Leung, according to the patch on his jumpsuit. Right behind them were two more men, both Caucasian, although I couldn't see the names on their jumpsuits. If I'd been more interested in the Mars mission, I probably would have known their names without having to look for them, but I wasn't rabidly into space and space exploration the way Paul and Michael Oliver were—or the way my cousin Kelsey was, mostly because she had such a massive crush on Michael that she sort of automatically adopted his enthusiasms, whatever they might be.

But even though I hadn't really studied the Mars mission, I did know enough to recall that there were also supposed to be two women on the expedition. Alexis Cheng, who'd been driving the rover the Reptilians had captured, and another one whose name I couldn't remember. I did think she was the expedition's geologist, or something like that.

Logan said, "We've come to get you away from here. Where are your two other crew members?"

Clearly, he knew enough to know that the crew's current head count was off.

Commander Cruz's jaw tightened. "They took them."

"The Reptilians?" Raphael asked. His tone sounded almost too neutral, but from where I stood, I could see the way his shoulders and back seemed to stiffen.

"Yes," Cruz replied. His dark eyes were haunted. "They didn't say anything, just came in a while ago and hauled them off somewhere." He stopped then, gaze roving over our little group, and I saw the way he gave a half-shake of his head, as if trying to figure out who we were and how in the world we could have gotten down to the surface of Mars when there wasn't supposed to be another ship in the system capable of making such a voyage. Unfortunately, I knew we couldn't explain. Not really. We weren't there for explanations, but only to get Gonzalo Cruz and the rest of his crew away from the aliens who had kidnapped them.

"Logan?" Raphael said then, although he didn't change his stance, kept gazing forward at the captive crew members.

Luckily, Logan seemed to know what Raphael was asking. "If this base is anything like the one back in Sedona—and I have a feeling it is, since the Reptilians tend to stick with what works for them—then the women would have been taken to the bio-labs, which should be a few levels below where we are now."

"How can you know that?" the younger man, Leung, broke in. "And why take the women and not the rest of us?"

An expression of pity moved over Logan's face. Quietly, he said, "I don't think you really want to know the answer to that."

A complete non-reply, but his meaning seemed to sink in nonetheless, judging by the looks of horror that Leung and his fellow crew-members gave one another.

I swallowed. My mother had done her best to shield me from some of the more unpleasant truths about the Reptilians, but even so, I knew that the leader of the base she'd finally destroyed had managed to invade her mind several times, had made it clear enough what he intended to do to her once he and his people were victorious. That day had never come, thank God. All the same, I'd gotten the distinct impression that the Reptilians were sometimes a little more hands-on about their genetic experiments than any of us had wanted to believe. It didn't take a huge leap of the imagination to guess what their captors had planned for the two female astronauts.

"We'll get them," my father said, his voice grim but determined. "How long since they were taken away?"

"Not too long," Commander Cruz said. "The aliens took our chronometers, but best guess is half an hour or forty-five minutes ago."

"Then we should still have time," Logan put in. "They are...deliberate."

The commander raised an eyebrow.

"A victim's fear is something to be savored," Logan told him. "At least, that's what I have known of them."

"Jesus Christ," said one of the other crew members, the man who was standing directly behind Commander Cruz.

"We will not let it come to that," Raphael said then. His gaze flicked to my father. "Martin, take them up to the ship. There is no reason for them to remain here. The rest of us will go to secure the two remaining crew members."

My heart seemed to drop somewhere into the vicinity of my stomach at those words. What, was Raphael actually asking my father to leave the rest of us behind?

Apparently so...and apparently neither of my parents was any more enthused about the idea than I was. My mother snapped, "Are you out of your mind?" even as my father said,

"If you think I have any intention of leaving my wife and daughter down here—"

"Do you doubt my ability to look after them?" Raphael interjected. He didn't raise his voice, but something about his tone seemed to cut through both my parents' protests. Still calm, still unruffled, he went on, "You are the only other person here who knows how to operate the energy-jump device. Take these men out of harm's way, and I will contact you when we have the women."

A long silence as my father appeared to digest those instructions. He shot a single worried glance at my mother and me, then another over at the men from the Mars expedition, all of whom were also quiet as they waited to hear what their fate might be.

Then, at last, "All right. But if anything happens—"

"Nothing will happen," Raphael said.

"I'll make sure of that," Logan added.

Something in the way the hybrid soldier stood

there, pistol in hand, face somehow intent and still at the same time, seemed to reassure my father. He nodded. "Okay."

"Are you crazy?" my mother burst out. "You're just going to leave us down here?"

A wry smile touched his mouth, and he bent and kissed her on the cheek. "From what I recall, Kirsten, you're not exactly lacking in defenses."

"That was different—"

"No different," Raphael broke in. "Or rather, different only in that this time you have your daughter to help you, and me, and Logan here. And far fewer of the enemy to face. So I believe the odds are rather better now."

Commander Cruz spoke up. "We can help."

But Raphael shook his head. "No. You cannot help us in this fight, and we cannot risk you being recaptured. The best thing for you to do is go with Martin here. That way, you will be safe."

The men all exchanged glances, but none of them appeared inclined to argue. That remark about being recaptured seemed to hit home.

Even though I was scared shitless—more or less— at the thought of having to go after the two captives without my father around as backup, I couldn't help smiling a little at the look of consternation on my mother's face as Raphael's words sank in. She didn't seem to notice my reaction, though, since she was busy staring up at my father, as if seeking her own reassurance in his features.

Apparently, she found it, because a second later she said, "All right. Get them out of here. I don't want to think of what could be happening to those women while we're standing here arguing."

He touched her cheek. "Give 'em hell, sweetheart."

Then he moved toward the Mars mission crew members, saying, "This might feel a bit strange — "

And a white light surrounded them, and swallowed them, and then they were all gone.

Raphael wore a look of grim satisfaction. "Good," he said. "Let us go."

Logan took the lead, since he seemed to have the best idea of where to take us. Raphael walked beside him, while I followed behind, my mother next to me. From the glitter in her eyes, I could tell she was still angry with Raphael for separating us, even if she understood why he thought it was necessary to do so.

For me—well, I did the best I could, keeping the energy of the red planet close at hand, not knowing when I might need it. We went down a very ordinary-seeming stairwell, with metal steps and gray-painted walls and those same reddish lights everywhere. Logan did appear to know where he was going, although with every step I could feel the tension in my neck ratcheting up that much further.

Where the hell were all the Reptilians? All right, so Raphael had said they wouldn't be able to detect our presence. Still, why hadn't we encountered any so far? Surely they had to go on routine patrols or whatever. Or maybe not. Was there much reason to keep an eye out for intruders when, at least in their own minds, they thought they were the lords and masters here, and anyone who might come to rescue the Mars crew millions of miles and many months away?

That thought reassured me somewhat, although I knew there would be plenty of the aliens concentrated at the bio-labs. For all I knew, that was where all the Reptilians were currently gathered, gloating over their captives. Raphael had sounded confident in our ability to go up against them, but I'd never been in an open confrontation with anyone in my life. Well, unless you counted the time Leisha Pendleton blocked me in the locker room and called me a boyfriend-stealing skank. For the record, I absolutely did not steal her boyfriend. I wasn't interested in him, and even if I had been, I would never have gone after someone I knew was already hooked up. But I guess Leisha had heard him telling a friend that he thought I was hot, and she'd flipped out.

Anyway, using the teeniest smidgen of my other-worldly powers to push Leisha against a bank of lockers while I made my escape wasn't quite the same thing as facing down forty or fifty rapacious Reptilians.

We descended two levels, but Logan stopped at the third one, one hand pressed flat against the door.

"What is it?" I whispered.

"I can sense them," he said. Although his complexion was fairly tanned, something about it looked grayish and pale right then.

Raphael didn't blink. "How many?"

Dark lashes swept down as Logan closed his eyes. His brows pulled together—in concentration, I thought. After several long, agonizing seconds, he said, "Can't tell for sure. At least ten."

Well, ten wasn't so bad. Four against ten sounded a lot better to me than four against fifty.

"Where?" Raphael asked.

What a cool customer. He sounded as if he was asking Logan where to meet for lunch, not the location of a bunch of hostile aliens.

"Down…to the left. About fifty meters."

"Any closer than that?"

"Not that I can sense. They seem to be concentrated in one location."

Which made sense, if they were all gathered around the women, drawing straws to see who got to play with them first. I swallowed the sudden rising bile in my throat and forced that mental image away. Despite the whispers and rumors, I didn't know for certain that was what the Reptilians were up to. They could have been prepping their captives for their first round of experiments. It was a bio-lab, after all.

Okay, that didn't sound much better.

Raphael turned slightly so he could look back at my mother and me. She'd been quiet the whole time, listening to the exchange between the two men, but her chin went up as she locked eyes with the alien man who had once been her adversary.

"You and Callista will need to shield us," he said. "Can you manage that?"

She nodded, then sent a faint questioning look in my direction.

"Sure," I told him. Surprisingly, I sounded calm and confident, the exact opposite of how I was feeling right then.

"Good." I thought I heard approval in his voice, and flushed faintly. Good thing it was way too dark in there for him to notice. He went on, "I need you to concentrate on our shielding, because I'm going to be focused on obscuring our presence."

"How can you do that?" My parents had never mentioned that particular ability to me. But then, maybe they'd thought it wasn't the best thing in the world for their daughter to know how to come and go without anyone noticing.

For a second, he looked annoyed, as if he was thinking that he really didn't have time for these sorts of explanations. But then his shoulders lifted, and he said, "It's simply a matter of bending light around you, of pushing the perception of others in your vicinity away from you. Not difficult, precisely, but if you haven't been trained in it, the technique can be tricky."

I shot an accusing look at my mother, and she frowned, saying, "I'd never heard of it before now, either. So you can take this one up with your father, Callista."

Maybe I would…if I survived the next few minutes. Right then, though, I knew it was best not to argue. "Thanks for explaining."

"You're welcome." Raphael inclined his head at Logan, who nodded and opened the door with the hand that wasn't clutching a pistol.

I found myself holding my breath, but in reality, nothing happened. Our little group stepped out into the corridor, which again seemed way too prosaic for a Reptilian base to me, with its gray polished concrete floor, gray walls, and reddish lights at regular intervals along the hallway. Inventive interior decorators they were not.

Beside me, I could feel my mother gathering the planet's energies around us, weaving them into a lattice of protection. I joined in, taking the flows of power and intertwining them with the barrier she had created, making something that felt impenetrable enough to stop a bullet.

If the Reptilians even used bullets, which I somehow doubted.

We moved down the corridor. The farther we progressed, the more I could see Logan tensing up, even though the hand holding the gun never shook. I guessed he must be sensing the presence of the aliens growing ever stronger. What that could do to him, I didn't know for sure. Both he and Grace had made it sound as if he'd broken completely free of their control, but how could they know for sure when there hadn't been any Reptilians left on Earth to bend him to their will?

Finally, he said in a hoarse whisper, "There."

The doorway set into the wall looked exactly the same as the other doors we'd passed. Another one of those lighted panels was embedded in the concrete, same as the one Raphael had opened earlier, using that strange opalescent stone of his. Only he'd given it to my father to get the Mars crew members back up to our ship, so I wasn't sure what Raphael had planned here.

We all stopped, clustered around him. I couldn't keep myself from glancing up at the ceiling and at the walls, worried that I'd see some kind of surveillance equipment catching our every move-ment. But both the ceiling and the walls looked blank and smooth, except for the doors with the locking panels next to them. Which didn't mean a whole lot; even on Earth, our surveillance tech-nology was so sophisticated that it was almost impossible to detect unless you really knew what you were looking for, and so I had a feeling whatever the Reptilians had set up here to keep watch over their labs was light-years beyond that. It definitely wasn't the sort of thing you'd be able to see with the naked eye.

Even though he was without his little miracle

device, Raphael didn't look worried. He began to lift his hand toward the panel.

Keeping my voice low, I asked, "How is that going to work? You gave your stone to my father."

He didn't look back at me, only kept his palm hovering over the little rectangle with the lights that seemed to flicker from deep within it. "Yes, but using the stone that one time gave me the knowledge necessary to break any of their codes." A pause before he added, his tone laced with amusement, "Do you really think I would have handed it over to your father if I needed it for this mission to succeed?"

"I guess not," I said, feeling foolish—but not so foolish that I let myself release my grip on the energy fields swirling around us.

No reply, but I thought I saw him incline his head slightly before he moved his hand over the panel in a strange pattern—down, then up, then from right to left. As soon as he completed the final pass, the door hissed upward, and a whole lot of things happened at once.

Logan surged forward, gun up, while Raphael stayed parallel with him. My mother followed, and I couldn't do anything except remain lined up with her as best I could, since I knew that our proximity only helped to strengthen the protective energy fields we'd been maintaining the whole time.

There were—well, I'd hesitate to call them people, since they certainly weren't human. Tall, and covered in shimmering dark bronze scales, and with eyes that glowed dull red. At least ten of them, although my shocked brain wasn't really up to the task of keeping an accurate count at that particular moment. As soon as we entered, they moved toward us, calling out in a sibilant language that made me want to cringe the same way that listening to fingernails dragged down a blackboard might.

A flare of blue-white light from Logan's gun, and two of them were knocked down immediately. The loss of their comrades didn't appear to deter the ones remaining, however, who continued to advance. Raphael raised a hand, and a wave of that same bluish light seemed to erupt from his palm, pushing outward in a wave that knocked down the approaching aliens the same way a shockwave from a bomb blast would flatten anyone in its path. They collapsed onto the concrete floor and didn't move.

As I stared in surprise, trying to reconcile what I thought I'd known about Raphael with this decidedly more warlike incarnation, he strode forward, going to a set of long metal tables at the far end of the room. On two of those tables lay the limp forms of a pair of human women. They were still clothed, thank God, although it looked like the zippers on the front of both their jumpsuits had been yanked down, exposing the thin white T-shirts they wore underneath.

"Dr. Cheng?" Raphael said, bending over her the younger and slighter of the female crew members.

Eyelids fluttered, and she stared up at him with unfocused dark eyes. "Wha—"

"You're safe now." He gestured toward my mother, and she hurried forward to the other astronaut.

"Marta? Dr. Levin?"

The woman, who looked to be about ten years older than Alexis Cheng, fair hair escaping the braid that confined it, put a hand to her forehead. "Who—"

"No time for that now," my mother said briskly. "Can you stand?"

Marta Levin nodded, then pushed herself up to a sitting position. She didn't appear to have been restrained in any way, but her expression was as bleary as someone who'd been bar-hopping for the past few hours. The Reptilians must have drugged her or used some kind of mind control on her.

Looking wobbly, she lowered herself to the floor and then held on to the table for a few seconds to steady herself. At the same time, Raphael helped Alexis Cheng, who seemed even shakier, get up from her own table.

I was so preoccupied with watching them that I wasn't paying any attention to the felled Reptilians, probably because I figured they were down for the count. But then I heard a scraping noise from behind me and whirled just in time to see one of the aliens pull a gun of his own from his belt and point it directly at Logan, who had turned away briefly to scan the opposite side of the room, in case any more enemies might come through the door set into the wall there.

"Logan!" I cried.

He turned so fast that he was almost a blur—but not quite fast enough. A pulse of reddish light flashed across the space that separated him from the alien, and then it caught him high up in the chest, almost at his shoulder. He let out a shocked grunt and crumpled to the floor.

A scream of denial burst from my throat, and, without thinking, I gathered up the energy I'd been using to protect us—to no avail, apparently—and thrust it outward the same way I'd seen Raphael do, in a shocking flare of light and pressure, fueled by a pulsing anger that they'd hurt one of our own. The Reptilian who'd shot Logan went down, and the ones near him, who'd begun to stir as well, also were flattened.

I didn't waste any more time on them, however. Instead, I went straight to Logan, just as my mother did the same thing, abandoning the astronaut she'd just rescued so she could kneel on the floor next to our wounded companion.

He wasn't bleeding, exactly, but had a huge area of smoking, blackened flesh where the pulse from the alien's gun had penetrated, burning the fabric of his jumpsuit entirely away. His eyes were shut, his face moist and pale.

"It's bad," my mother said.

For some reason, I couldn't look at her. I could

only stare down at Logan, willing him to be okay. He had to be okay. He and Grace had been through so much together. I didn't want to think about what she would do if she lost him. It would destroy her.

Raphael, shockingly, didn't seem all that worried. "We'll get him to the ship. The medical bay will take care of it."

Considering everything I'd seen on that ship so far, I guessed he wasn't exaggerating about its medical facilities. We still had to get Logan there, though.

"Well, I think it's time you beamed us up, then," I snapped.

A frown pulled at Raphael's brows, but he didn't answer me, instead telling the two astronauts, who were staring at the rest of us in shock, "Move closer to them. We need to all be transferred in a group."

I doubted they had any idea what he was talking about. Luckily, though, they did as he said, limping over to us. I noticed that their feet were bare, and wondered what the hell the Reptilians had done with the women's shoes.

Not that it probably mattered all that much. The important thing was that they were with us, crowding around Logan's limp form, Raphael only a step or two behind them.

As he moved, though, I thought I saw one of the Reptilians stir, the ominous glint of metal in his hand. A gun, pointed at Raphael. For a split-second, I wondered why the alien would be aiming at him when I was the one who'd just knocked them all off their feet. But then I realized that of course they'd prefer to avoid harming me. With Raphael out of the way, there would be only women left.

I didn't stop to think. I just pushed myself to my feet and reached out and grabbed him by the arm, yanking him toward the rest of us. As my hand closed around his wrist, a tingling warmth moved up my arm, a rush of—

No, that wasn't possible. Because what I experienced right then was a sort of need that seemed to cramp my entire body with its intensity. For the space between one heartbeat and the next, all I could think of was Raphael—the strength of the arm beneath my fingertips, the warmth of his flesh. The lab, the women we'd rescued, the Reptilians, my mother...all of that was washed away, replaced only by him.

His dark eyes met mine, despairing. Behind that despair, however, was a certain resignation. He'd known this moment would come, and had dreaded it.

And then I didn't have time to think anymore, because once again, the white light came up and surrounded us, blazing through our bodies, taking us away from the Reptilians and their base.

But it couldn't burn away the knowledge of what I'd just seen.

CHAPTER FOUR

I HEARD MY FATHER'S VOICE, SAYING, "WHAT happened?"

I shook away the tingling after-effects of the energy-jump, but it wasn't so easy to shake off the way I'd reacted to Raphael's touch. Somehow, the jump had separated us, thank God; he was standing a few feet away when the real world solidified around me.

Or maybe he'd done that on purpose as soon as he reached the bridge of his ship.

Logan lay on the floor, my father kneeling next to him. The two women we'd just saved from the Reptilians looked on, still a little shaky. Well, I supposed they could be excused for feeling some-what off-kilter after being taken captive by aliens and then suddenly whisked away by a beam of light right before they were about to suffer a fate worse than death.

"I'll take him to the medi-bay," Raphael said. He wasn't looking at me. Just as well, because I needed a chance to recover from what I'd just experienced.

My father nodded, then handed Raphael the opal stone in its silvery housing. As soon as Raphael had it in his hand, he bent over Logan, the two of them disappearing in a flash of white light.

"Is someone going to tell us what the hell is going on?" came a man's voice, and I looked up to see Commander Cruz approaching, the other three men in his crew directly behind him. As they came closer, both Alexis Cheng and Marta Levin appeared visibly relieved, stepping away from us so they could be with the rest of their fellow astronauts.

Judging by Cruz's angry tone, I got the feeling that my father hadn't spent the time alone with them here giving them a briefing. He got to his feet and faced them, but not before he sent both my mother and me a quick, appraising look, as if he wanted to make sure that we hadn't suffered any harm while down at the aliens' base.

I was glad he didn't have time for more than that one swift glance, though, because I really didn't want him to take a close look at my face. Right then, I was feeling more than a little shell-shocked. My body still seemed to thrum with the resonance of Raphael's touch.

"You're safe," my father said, his voice as

soothing and friendly as only he could make it. I'd be lying if I said that particular tone hadn't driven me nuts a few times during high school, but it seemed to be having the desired effect right now. Commander Cruz didn't back away, but something in the tense set of his jaw seemed to relax slightly. "I know this is a lot to take in," my father went on. "But please believe that we only have the safety of you and your crew in mind. As soon as our own crew member is stabilized, we'll return you to your ship and make sure you're headed safely home."

"That's not possible," Leung—whose first name I recalled right then was Troy—protested. "We weren't set to go home for six more months. The positions of the planets are all wrong. We won't have a window until those six months have passed."

"It's not a problem," my father replied. "It will be taken care of."

A long silence, during which the members of the Mars mission crew gave one another some very pointed looks. Even Alexis Cheng and Marta Levin looked disconcerted. I could tell that whatever the Reptilians had drugged them with was wearing off, because the two women's eyes grew clearer and sharper with every passing second, which meant they probably intended to start asking questions at any moment as well.

Then Gonzalo Cruz asked, "Who are you people?"

"Friends," my mother told him.

Cruz shook his head and opened his mouth to reply, but was forestalled by Raphael's reappearance. At least this time, he walked onto the bridge—or whatever you wanted to call it—more or less normally, rather than appearing in a flash of light. The men and women facing him didn't look particularly reassured, however.

Ignoring them, he addressed his first words to my parents and me. "Logan is resting, and is out of danger. He will need to remain in the pod for some twenty-four of your hours for the healing process to be complete."

Relief rushed through me, although I still wasn't looking forward to telling Grace what had happened to her lover. Not that my parents would even allow me to take on that task. Yes, Grace and I were cousins, but they were her aunt and uncle, and Logan had been wounded on their watch.

Then Raphael turned toward the assembled group from the Mars mission. I was glad he did so, because that meant he was looking at them and not me. All the same, it was harder than I thought it would be to direct my attention anywhere other than his rear end in that form-fitting jumpsuit.

"We are friends," he said. "Unfortunately, I cannot say more than that. You've all had a narrow escape, but you will return safely to your home world."

Marta Levin stepped forward then. I'd never been that good at guessing people's ages, partially because my own parents were so damn ageless-looking, but I thought she might be in her early forties, attractive and blonde…and now beginning to return to a self-assurance that in most cases was probably second nature to her. "And who were *they?*" she asked, with a small tilt of her head toward the reddish disk of Mars that filled the view-screens.

"Enemies," Raphael said shortly. "That is all you need to know." His eyes narrowed as he appeared to take in the way the third male crew member, the one whose name I still couldn't recall although he had an American flag patch on his jumpsuit, glanced away and seemed overly interested in a single point on the shining metal floor. "But I would hazard a guess that some of you know more than you wish to reveal."

Commander Cruz flickered a suspicious glance at his compatriot. "Anything you want to tell us, McKenzie?"

The other crewman, who looked to be about the same age as Marta Levin, shook his head. "I have nothing to say, sir."

"Mm-hmm."

"I suppose you can work that out amongst your-selves," Raphael said. "In the meantime, we do need to make sure you get safely on your way." His hand went to the stone at his belt, and before any of us had time to blink or do much of anything else, all of the Mars mission crew had disappeared in another of those flashes of white light.

"What the hell?" I demanded before I could stop myself.

Raphael turned back toward us. The merest flicker of those dark eyes toward me, and then he said, tone casual, "It was time they were sent on their way. We could give them no more explanations—or rather, it would have been a waste of time to have done so, considering I have made sure that they would have no recollection of what happened to them after the Reptilians attacked."

"Just like that?" my mother asked. She sounded skeptical.

"Just like that," he replied. "You may ask your husband to explain the mechanics of the procedure once you are home, but I find such explanations tedious. It's enough to know that they will all find themselves returned to their own ship, heading back to Earth on a trajectory that will get them there in approximately three months' time."

My eyebrows lifted, even as I pushed back my annoyance at his refusal to explain how he'd altered the astronauts' memories. "I thought it was a six-month trip."

"I may have made some adjustments to make their journey more efficient."

I didn't know why that should have surprised me. After all, the Mars mission might have had some of the world's greatest minds behind it, but even they weren't any real match for a civilization thousands of years ahead of them.

"Okay," I said. I wasn't sure why I was continuing to engage with Raphael, when really it would have been safer for me to keep my mouth shut until I could get away and process what that micro-burst of desire actually meant. Maybe I just wanted to reassure myself that I could hold it together around him and not arouse my parents' suspicions. "So somehow you managed to do all that in the blink of an eye, so to speak. What's to keep the Reptilians from attacking the Mars crew as they travel home?"

That question made both my parents send questioning glances in Raphael's direction. Apparently, they'd been wondering the same thing.

However, he didn't appear at all disturbed by my query. With no change in inflection, he replied, "The Reptilians attacked Alexis Cheng and her companion because they encroached on the Reptilian base in Planitia Utopia. If her team had landed in a different location, they would most likely have been left to carry out their mission unmolested."

I planted my hands on my hips and stared up at him. "So you're saying it's the astronauts' fault?"

"Not at all," he replied, apparently unruffled. "I am by no means an apologist for the Reptilians. However, they prefer to work in secret whenever possible, and therefore an open attack on your people's spaceship—unless the Reptilians have no other choice—is not in their best interests."

"They weren't being that secretive back when I had to force them out of Sedona," my mother said then, her tone sour. A few strands of pale hair, the same shade as mine, had begun to work themselves out of their braid and fall around her face.

"Actually, they were." A slight smile touched Raphael's lips, and I had to force myself not to stare at his mouth, had to keep myself from wondering what those lips would feel like pressed against mine. "I am not saying that they didn't plan to come out into the open, once they had the upper hand by securing Sedona's energies for their own use, but until that happened, they did their very best to make sure no one else knew of their existence."

My mother crossed her arms. "Their presence there wasn't that big a secret."

To my surprise, it was my father who spoke then, not Raphael. "It wasn't a big secret to you, or to your sister and Lance and to some of the other members of your MUFON group. But think about how one of your neighbors would have reacted if you'd turned to them while you were in line at the grocery store and asked for their opinion about the alien base hidden out in Secret Canyon."

"Okay," she said, grinning but shaking her head at the same time. "I get it. I would have loved to have seen Mrs. Martinez's reaction to that one. She already thought I was half-crazy anyway."

"So you see," Raphael put in, "the aliens made their move on Mars because their hand was more or less forced, but I very much doubt they will interfere further." He stopped then, appearing to decide whether or not he should say anything else. I thought I saw the faintest lift of his shoulders before he added, "If they do, they know they will have to answer to the Assembly."

"Because that's always stopped them in the past," my father remarked, tone dry as the Arizona desert.

"Perhaps not, but I know my presence with the rescue party will have given them some pause."

I could see his point. For whatever reason, Raphael and this "Assembly" he represented seemed to have changed their tune when it came to interfering in human affairs, and so seeing him in their base on Mars had to have been something of a shock for the Reptilians. Maybe that was enough to make those hostile aliens think twice about any kind of retaliation. One could hope, anyway.

We all fell silent then. By that point, Mars was long gone from the view-screens. The star field shifted around us, but I had no idea how fast we must be traveling, only that it was fast enough to get us home in less than a couple of hours.

I let out a sigh, but a small one that no one else would be able to notice. Raphael had said Logan was on the mend, but I knew we still had a rough few hours ahead of us.

Going home wasn't going to be easy.

"Where is he?" Grace demanded as soon as we

appeared in the family room at my Aunt Kara's house. Everyone was still congregated there, and as my eyes strayed to the old-fashioned wooden clock on the mantel, I realized that only a little more than three hours had passed since we left. It was now a hair after midnight. Strange how your life could change in such a short amount of time.

Raphael said calmly, "He was injured. But he is healing now in the medi-bay on board my ship. He—"

"Take me to him," she cut in. Her blue eyes flashed. I knew when my cousin Grace got that look on her face, you might as well give in then and there.

But apparently, Raphael hadn't gotten that particular memo. "He is resting. He will not know you are there. It is better for you to wait until the healing process is complete, and then he will be able to rejoin you here in Sedona."

She crossed her arms, her expression pure challenge. "I don't care. I want to see him now. Got it?"

"Might as well do as she says," my Uncle Lance drawled. He'd been sitting next to my aunt on one of the couches, but he got up then. "Unless you think standing here and arguing about it is easier than just letting her see the man."

For a few seconds, Raphael hesitated, his gaze sweeping the room. But he had to have realized that everyone was pretty firmly on Grace's side—the Olivers looked concerned, my cousin Kelsey almost eager, as if she knew that all the exciting things happened to everyone else, and so she might as well just sit back and watch the show. And of course, my aunt and uncle were going to side with their daughter.

"Very well," Raphael said at last. To his credit, he sounded only slightly grudging. "If it is your wish to sit there and watch him sleep for the next twenty-two of your hours, so be it."

"It is my wish."

"Well, then."

He came up to her, and without saying anything else, laid his hand on the opal jewel at his hip. The two of them immediately vanished, and a collective gasp swept through the room, even though everyone there had to have seen Raphael and my parents and me do basically the same thing only a few hours earlier. I got the distinct impression that he'd initiated such a precipitous departure because he was annoyed with Grace and didn't intend to give her the courtesy of any kind of mental preparation.

With the two of them gone, everyone more or less pounced on my parents.

"What happened?"

"Where did you go?"

"Are the astronauts safe?"

My father held up a hand. "Yes, they're safe. They're on their way home."

"That's not possible," both Paul and Michael Oliver said at more or less the same time. Trust the two scientists to seize on the impossibility of my father's reply.

My parents exchanged a weary smile. "It's possible if you're dealing with a highly advanced civilization," my mother told them. "Not that I pretend to understand any of it myself. But hasn't there been anything on the news?"

It was Paul's turn to offer a tired smile. "Of course there hasn't. If what you say is true, and Raphael and his people have somehow managed to work it so the astronauts can come back entirely off-schedule and not run out of fuel, then I have a feeling that the spin doctors are in the process of coming up with some sort of plausible story that can deflect the inevitable questions. Which won't be easy."

That made sense. Yes, at some point, they'd have to release the information that the mission hadn't ended in complete catastrophe, that the astronauts were safe even if they hadn't been able to stay on the planet's surface and carry out all their carefully planned observations and experiments. In the meantime, though, NASA and the other agencies involved in the joint mission would have to come up with a cover story, one tight enough that it couldn't get too many holes poked in it.

"Is Logan going to be all right?" My Aunt Kara this time, her features drawn with worry.

"Yes," my father said immediately. "The Reptilians got a good shot in, but it's nothing that the ship's healing facilities can't handle. He won't even have a scar."

That reply caused another murmur to go around the room. "So they really do have a base on Mars," Lance said, eyes narrowed.

"Yes," my father replied. "A fairly large one, from what I could tell. But Raphael seems to think the Reptilians don't have any immediate plans to come back here and cause trouble, and I'm inclined to believe him. There's too much risk of retaliation."

Lance didn't look all that convinced, but then, he'd never had too high an opinion of Otto/Raphael, either.

"It's late," my mother said then. "I don't know about the rest of you, but I feel like I'm about to keel over. How about we all regroup in the morning?"

Persephone Oliver nodded. "I think that sounds like an excellent idea. I know we're all worried about Logan, but if Martin thinks he's in good hands, then it's probably best to let things run their course."

Everyone appeared to agree with her statement— some more grudgingly than others, in my Uncle Lance's case—and the Olivers got up from where they'd been sitting so they could go collect their coats and jackets.

As Taryn passed by me, she murmured, "So you really were in a spaceship? What was it like?"

Good question. For all I knew, she could have pulled the images right out of my head if she'd wanted to, but she was far too polite to do anything like that. "It was beautiful. Elegant. And fast. We went from here to Mars in less than an hour and a half."

Her eyes widened, but she didn't have much of a chance to say anything after that, since her parents and brother came by and scooped her up. And after that, it was time for my parents and me to go, my mother promising Kara that we'd be back the next morning, and maybe we could discuss all this over breakfast?

My aunt appeared relieved by that suggestion. I could tell she was bursting with questions. Also, she seemed to be happiest when she was feeding her family, extended or otherwise. Getting debriefed over pancakes and bacon was probably her idea of heaven.

Even as we left the house, though, and headed out to the car, I couldn't stop thinking about Raphael, somewhere thousands of miles above me, in a ship that no sensor on the planet could detect. Was he staying with Grace to make sure she didn't wander off and get herself into trouble, or had he left her to maintain a lonely vigil at Logan's bedside?

I had no idea. I also had no way of knowing if I would ever get a chance to speak to Raphael away from everyone else.

Even so, the mere thought of being alone with him both excited and terrified me.

CHAPTER FIVE

MY MOTHER WASN'T THE ONLY ONE WHO WAS DOG-tired, because, even with everything that had happened earlier in the evening, I basically passed out the second my head hit my pillow. When I woke up, bright morning light was peeking past the edges of the blinds in my bedroom, and I cast a bleary look over at the clock on my bedside table.

Nine-fifteen.

Could have been worse, I supposed. I'd heard Kara say something about ten-thirty or thereabouts to my mother, so I knew I had a little time, even if I didn't have the luxury of letting myself fall back asleep for another hour. But time enough to get ready.

The bathroom in the casita I'd called home ever since I turned eighteen had great hot water, so I took as long a shower as I dared, letting the water pour over me and wash away any residual weariness. It also helped to get rid of any lingering feelings of ickiness I had from being in the Reptilians' base. Something about the very air there seemed to cling to my skin and the sensitive tissues of my throat, making me feel as if I'd been coated in a thin, oily film.

Since I really had no idea what the day might turn into, I dressed casually but nicely, in one of my newer pairs of jeans, and the high-heeled boots I'd honestly thought I'd never see again but which were sitting on the floor of my closet when I opened it that morning. Likewise, the sweater and jeans I'd been wearing had been left folded neatly on top of my dresser. People could say what they wanted about Raphael, but the man clearly had an eye for detail.

Thinking about him got my pulse racing all over again. Unacceptable. Seriously, I had no idea what was going on with me. Scratch that. The real problem was that I actually *did* have a pretty good idea—and the mere notion was enough to scare me shitless.

All right, focus. Soft blue knit top to match my eyes, slim black leather jacket over that. It was cold enough that I'd still need an overcoat, but I was feeling much better about facing the world once I was dressed and had some makeup on.

I crossed the courtyard and winced at the chill, but I was inside the main house before the cold could get to me too much. While the casita provided me the privacy I wanted, the closet space there wasn't exactly

what you'd call adequate, so I still kept my outerwear
and some off-season items in the bedroom that used
to be mine. My parents hadn't changed it, either, even
though it hadn't been my room for more than three
years; there was the same washed-pine furniture, the
same quilt in shades of blue and green on the bed.
Really, I wished they would make it over into another
office or something. Maybe then they'd realize I didn't
plan to move back in there, that in my mind, the casita
was my steppingstone to moving out entirely.

Not that I'd had the guts to do anything about
that yet.

Because we were going to eat at Aunt Kara's, my
father had only made coffee. He raised an inquiring
eyebrow at me as I entered the kitchen, and for the
umpteenth time, I shook my head. No matter how
much I tried, I just couldn't make myself like coffee.
Instead, I went to the kettle, which still had some
water in it, and turned on the gas so I could make
myself a cup of tea.

"You're sure she's our daughter?" he asked my
mother, who looked like she was already on her
second cup of Italian roast.

"Last time I checked, yes."

I made a face at both of them and got the box of
Darjeeling from the pantry. But once I'd fetched my
favorite turquoise-glazed mug from the cupboard
and set it down on the counter, both their expressions
had turned somber.

"I called Kara," my mother said. "She told me she still hasn't heard anything from Grace or Raphael."

At the sound of his name, I could feel myself stiffen, but I forced myself to turn back toward the stove as I said, "Well, he did say twenty-four hours. It hasn't been that long yet. If it gets to be past noon and he still hasn't gotten in touch, I guess that's when we should start to worry."

My father nodded. "That's what I said, too. But we all know that Kara thinks something's wrong with the universe if she doesn't have something to worry about."

That remark earned him an icy, blue-eyed glare from my mother, but she didn't say anything, only sipped at her coffee. I knew she would have loved to argue the point with him but realized he was only pointing out the obvious.

The kettle whistled then, and I busied myself with pouring hot water into my mug and then dunking the teabag into it. It just seemed safer to avoid eye contact. Maybe I was overreacting. After all, absolutely nothing had happened, except that I'd touched Raphael's arm and felt...something. All right, a whole lot of somethings. Surely just feeling something shouldn't be enough to arouse any suspicions, though. In a normal family, that could very well be true. But when your parents were alien or at least part-alien, and shared an uncanny form of mental communication, in general it was safer to assume that they could sniff out secrets that would sail right over the heads of regular humans.

As I blew on my tea to cool it down, my father said, "Well, Paul was right. News about the Mars mission was being broadcast this morning, and they're saying just about exactly what we thought they would say. Catastrophic malfunction of the landing module, immediate recall to the ship, emergency rerouting and return to Earth."

"What else could they say?" my mother asked reasonably. "'Oops, our landing party ran into some bad-guy aliens and we had to rely on some friendly strangers for rescue'? That wouldn't go over very well, would it?"

He grinned. "Probably not."

From there, they headed into a discussion as to whether Raphael's assessment was correct and that the Reptilians really would keep their hands off the Mars expedition ship and its crew as they made their laborious trip back to their home world. Too bad Raphael couldn't have lent them some of his own ship's super-duper propulsion systems so they could get back more quickly, but I supposed that would have raised even more eyebrows, not to mention giving our scientists access to technology I was pretty sure Raphael's bosses didn't want to end up in the wrong hands.

And then I was done with my tea, and my parents with their coffee, so we put our mugs in the dishwasher and went to gather up our coats. New Year's

Eve had been clear, but overnight, clouds had swept in, muting the bright colors of the red rocks. I wasn't sure if the weather would be cold enough for snow or not, but it felt that way.

As we headed out to the garage, something compelled me to say, "I think I'm going to take my own car."

My father paused, gloved fingers resting on the handle of my parents' Mercedes sedan. "What for?"

I shrugged, hoping I looked casual. "Oh, I was thinking about doing some shopping on the way home."

"On New Year's Day?" he asked, and my mother shot me a narrow look, half concerned, half puzzled.

"Sure," I replied. "You know almost everything in Uptown will be open because of all the tourists being in town for the holiday."

Neither of them could really rebut that statement, because it was the simple truth. Yes, those same stores were always closed on Christmas Day, but New Year's didn't have that same significance when it came to spending time with your family.

To be honest, I wasn't really sure why I'd made the request, except some pricking of my thumbs or my spider sense or whatever you wanted to call it was telling me that I needed to be free to travel on my own and not be tied to my parents' schedule. Yes, my aunt had said we were all getting together for breakfast, but those gatherings tended to turn into all-day affairs. Once that group started talking, it could be pretty hard to shut them up.

"Okay," my father said after a long pause, during which I purposely thought of nothing except the amethyst necklace I'd spotted in one of the Uptown shops and had been secretly coveting for nearly a month. I still didn't know for sure if he could actually read my thoughts, but I figured I might as well be careful.

Then both he and my mother got in their car—the sedan, not the 4-matic they used when they were planning to head out into the wilderness that surrounded the town, or when they drove up to Flagstaff. I climbed into the BMW SUV that had been my high school graduation present, then said, "Aunt Kara's."

Of course, the vehicle knew exactly where to take me. After my parents had backed out of the garage, the BMW did the same thing, following at a safe distance as we came down the winding road from our hilltop property and into the town proper before heading up toward Oak Creek and the big house Kara and Lance shared, and which Grace had once called home.

Usually, I would have taken control of the SUV, because I liked to drive myself rather than have the car do it for me, but right then my thoughts roiled just enough that I thought it was probably better to have the onboard computer handle driving duties. Instead of the road before me, all I could see was

Raphael's face, the despair in his eyes. He'd known. He'd known there would be this strange, impossible attraction between us.

I recalled then the way his gaze had rested on me when he first appeared in the family room at my aunt Kara's house. At the time, I hadn't thought anything of it, except that possibly he was curious about me, the offspring of the man he'd exiled here a quarter-century earlier. But now I realized his interest was probably much more complicated than that. He'd known he would have that reaction to me, if we were ever to touch.

My parents had spoken of it a little. That was the way of my father's race, and of the blood my grandfather Gabriel had passed down through my mother. Those star-folk always recognized the mate of their soul, even if it took centuries to find that one particular person. Not that they were completely celibate up until that moment, but the parties involved always knew those liaisons were temporary, and only existed to release some biological backpressure. They didn't marry, or have children, until they found their one.

So did this mean I was Raphael's "one"? It was entirely possible I'd read things into my reaction— and his—that weren't even there. On the other hand, I knew I hadn't imagined the heat that had flooded through my body, or the sorrow in his expression before he pushed it away and went blank-faced again.

I needed to talk to him. How I would manage that feat, I had no idea, since I didn't even know if he would bring Grace and Logan back here with him once Logan was done healing, or whether he'd simply beam them back to Earth and stay safely away.

But then, there had been the impulse that had driven me to take my own car this morning. Maybe that had been the universe telling me I needed to have the opportunity to get away from my family.

Any such escapes would have to wait a while, though, because my car was already headed down the winding lane that led to my aunt's house. Soon afterward, I pulled up next to my parents' car and shut down the Beemer. I got out just a few seconds after they did, and the three of us headed into the house, not bothering to stop and knock. They'd been expecting us, after all, and Kara preferred family to simply go on in, even though I knew Lance wasn't exactly thrilled about the lax security. Sometimes I wondered how those two had ever ended up together, they seemed so opposite in personality.

I'd spotted the Olivers' Range Rover out front, too, so it seemed our group was now more or less complete. No sign of Grace or Logan or Raphael when we made our way back toward the kitchen, although there was still time yet.

After that ,I didn't have much time to think about whether I was relieved or saddened that Raphael wasn't there, because everyone started talking at once—about when we thought we'd see Logan and Grace, and whether people were really going to believe the "official" story about a malfunctioning landing craft. In the end, that explanation would probably be hashed out on a thousand separate conspiracy websites, but that was NASA's—and the other space agencies'—problem. We'd saved those astronauts, and that was the most important thing.

Breakfast was served buffet-style in the big dining room at my aunt's house, with eggs and bacon and sausage and homemade biscuits and waffles and fruit and just about anything else you could think of to make the meal complete. I would have asked how Kara had managed to pull all that together, since the plans for this breakfast had been made only the night before, but she'd been a field marshal in the kitchen ever since I could remember, so the spread wasn't quite as astonishing to me as it might have been to an outsider.

I didn't want to completely stuff myself, so I had to pick and choose, which was hard. Everything looked delicious. As usually happened at these gatherings, I ended up sitting near the foot of the table with the other "kids"—my cousins Kelsey, Kevin, and Melissa; Taryn Oliver. Apparently, her brother Michael had been graduated to big-boy status now that he was in the middle of getting his doctorate.

Sitting that close to Taryn worried me, though. That's not to say we weren't friends, because we were, but when you were trying to hide something, being next to someone with demonstrated psychic abilities could be a matter for concern. I did notice the way her eyes narrowed as I sat down and then took a bite of eggs, but she didn't say anything.

My cousin Kelsey wasn't nearly as reserved. I could tell she was annoyed she couldn't sit closer to Michael, but that would have required some obvious jockeying, and she didn't seem quite ready to make her crush on him so obvious. Too late, in my opinion; I had no idea what the man himself actually thought about the situation, or of her, but it was clear enough to everyone else in the family that she was completely gone on him.

But that was their problem, not mine. I had enough to worry about.

Anyway, Kelsey didn't even wait for me to finish chewing before she asked, "Aren't you going to tell us *anything?*"

"Anything what?" I picked up my glass, glad that Aunt Kara had furnished the makings for mimosas. That little bit of champagne would help to take the edge off.

"About what happened! You and your parents just took off last night, and that Raphael person left with Grace, and the rest of us have just been sitting around, playing guessing games."

She sounded irritated—and a little frightened— and I couldn't really blame her. I probably would have felt the same if our situations had been reversed. Yes, it seemed as if the older generation was covering basically the same ground at the other end of the table, but when you've got twelve people sitting down together, it gets hard to overhear the conversation when you're separated by such a distance.

So I took another swallow of my mimosa, then gave her and Taryn and Melissa—and yes, my cousin Kevin, although as usual he looked as if he was supremely bored by everything going on around him—a carefully edited version of what had gone down the night before. Not that I tried to hide much, except my reaction to touching Raphael, and the way he'd looked at me afterward. Our exchange was private, and besides, it didn't have all that much to do with the way we'd rescued the astronauts, or how Raphael had sent them home afterward.

Once again, I got the impression that Taryn knew I was leaving something out, but along with her psychic gifts had come the sort of discretion you usually didn't expect from someone who was barely twenty-one, so she didn't say anything. Kelsey was full of questions—she wanted to know what Raphael's ship looked like, what it felt like to be on another planet, whether we could see anything while we were traveling in that strange white light with its power to move people almost instantaneously from place to place.

I dutifully answered everything I could, but when she asked what the Reptilians looked like, I shook my head. "Sorry," I told her. "That's not the sort of thing I really want to talk about while I'm eating."

There must have been something quelling in my tone, because she backed off and didn't push the issue. Taryn looked thoughtful, though.

"It's too bad," she said quietly.

"Too bad what?"

"It's too bad we're always fighting with them," she replied. She'd been holding a half-eaten biscuit, but she set it down then. "I mean, clearly they're not the good guys, but they're sentient beings, just like the rest of us. There's got to be a way to communicate with them, make them see our side of things. There has to be a reason for what they're doing. Has anyone tried to find out what that reason is?"

"I don't think they're big on talking," I replied, my tone sarcastic...mostly because I doubted she would have said such a thing if she'd seen them in action. Taryn did tend to think the best of people— which surprised me, considering she could read minds—but even she really needed to draw the line at Reptilians. "And I'm pretty sure that if there was a way to negotiate with them peacefully, then my father's people would have already tried it. I mean, they were pretty hands-off with the Reptilians for a long time, but it sounds as if even they're getting fed up."

She didn't say anything, only fiddled with the stem of her glass, turning it this way and that. From her expression, I could tell she wanted to argue with me but wouldn't, partly because she didn't want to cause a scene, and partly because she knew she didn't possess all the facts. Well, neither did I, but I knew enough to understand that the Reptilians weren't the type of beings to be swayed from their path, once they'd started down it.

It would have been nice to think that if the rest of the galaxy could only come up with the right negotiating strategy, then maybe they'd have a chance of getting the Reptilians to behave themselves. Unfortunately, I had the impression that just about every diplomatic angle had been tried already, to no avail.

Kelsey broke the silence by commenting that she wished she knew what was going on with Grace and Logan. I wished for the same thing, because now it was getting close to noon, and still no sign of her or her boyfriend, nor of Raphael. Maybe that was a good thing. Over the years, I'd gotten fairly good at hiding my emotions when necessary, just because having two quasi-psychic parents could be challenging, but having to conceal my reactions to Raphael when in the presence of such a large group of people might prove to be problematic.

I'd just opened my mouth to tell her the same thing I'd told my parents earlier, that it wasn't quite noon yet, and besides, it was very possible that Raphael had given the number of twenty-four hours as an estimate, not an absolute, when a flash of bright light reflected off the dining room walls. Almost as one, we all turned toward the hallway.

Standing there were Grace and Logan. Only the two of them, and I had to push away my disappointment. Really, if I thought I'd have a difficult time keeping it together around Raphael, then it was better that he wasn't there. Or so I tried to tell myself. It wasn't until that moment that I realized how much I really did want to see him again.

My aunt got up from the table at once and went to Logan and Grace. They were both looking a little pale, but otherwise, it seemed Raphael had been right—Logan appeared more or less returned to his old self.

"I'm fine," he said, just as Aunt Kara opened her mouth to speak. Grace was hanging on Logan's arm, and she nodded.

"That medi-bay is pretty impressive. He doesn't even have a scar."

Part of me wanted to ask him to show us his chest and shoulder to prove it, but I figured that request probably wouldn't go over too well with Grace.

"And once the healing process was done," she went on, "Raphael sent us back here."

"He could have come with you," my aunt said. "We've got plenty of food."

Although she was clearly tired, Grace still shot her mother a grin. "I don't think Raphael is too much into the whole 'family togetherness' thing. Anyway, he made it sound as if he had someplace he needed to be."

"Oh?" Lance asked. "Where?"

Grace's mouth twitched. "Like he'd tell me. But I didn't much care. I was just glad that Logan was all right. And now I think we'd both like some of that bacon."

Her request made pretty much everyone chuckle, easing the tension in the room. Well, everyone's tension except mine, I supposed. I felt fidgety, restless. So Raphael had someplace he needed to be? Maybe that was my signal to get out of there.

Easier said than done, unfortunately. It would look strange if I took off in the middle of the meal, especially since Logan and Grace had just shown up. Kara had set places for them, so it was a simple enough matter for them to sit down and play catch-up on their eating. In between bites, Logan offered some information—and berated himself several times for letting the Reptilians get the drop on him. Both my parents told him that was ridiculous, that there wasn't anything he could have done to anticipate the attack, but I could tell Logan wasn't convinced.

I agreed with them, although I doubted Logan would care all that much what I thought. He'd have to work through his perceived "failure," which probably rankled all the more because he'd been created to be a soldier. I was sure Grace would probably point out that he hadn't gotten all his training, since the Reptilians had bailed on the Sedona base before that training could even take place, but the two of them would have to work that out on their own time.

Eventually, the meal wound down enough that I

thought it was safe to get up and take my plate to the kitchen. While some of the others were doing the same thing—over my aunt's protests that she could manage just fine—I went over to my parents and murmured, "I'm going to head out. I'll see you back at home after I run some errands."

They didn't look too thrilled by my defection, but neither of them tried to stop me, either. I waved goodbye to everyone, thanked Kara for the breakfast, and then got the hell out of there. Good thing, because even though people were clearing away their plates, afterward they went to get themselves more drinks—coffee or tea or mimosas—which signaled to me that they planned to hang out there for some time.

I slipped away, retrieved my coat from the rack in the entry, and headed out to my car. It started up once I was within a foot, the door opening and letting out a welcome waft of warm air. I took manual control of the vehicle again—after blowing into the built-in breathalyzer and confirming that the one mimosa I'd drunk wasn't enough to put me at even half the legal blood-alcohol level. Then I guided the SUV back out to the highway, heading toward town, although right then I still wasn't sure of my destination.

Once I reached Uptown, I hesitated, but something didn't feel right about stopping there. So I kept driving, negotiating the traffic circle where Highways 89A and 179 joined before heading south. Just as I was approaching the Tlaquepaque North shopping center, I felt it—a distinct tingle at the back of my neck.

Because of the center divider in the road, I couldn't just pull into the parking lot. I had to head a little farther south to slingshot around the next traffic circle and come back to the shopping center, where I pulled into one of the few remaining parking spaces. It seemed I wasn't the only one who'd decided to get in a little New Year's Day shopping.

However, none of the shops appeared to be my destination. I passed them all by, wandering between the buildings and the bare sycamores on the property, my feet taking me along a path that led down toward Oak Creek. I'd walked here before, but not for some time. Still, even with the bare trees, it was a pretty spot, the creek flowing fast because of the runoff from the snowpack in Flagstaff.

I stopped near the bank of the creek and looked around. No one else appeared to have ventured down here, probably because the air was fairly chilly. I tucked the wool scarf I wore a little more securely into my coat and shoved my hands into my pockets. What the hell was I doing here? If I had any sense, I'd be up in one of the shops, trying to decide what I wanted to spend my Christmas money on.

A crunch of dead leaves made me turn.

Standing there in the middle of the path was Raphael.

CHAPTER SIX

My mouth went dry. The robes were gone, as was the jumpsuit I'd last seen him wearing. Now he had on a long wool coat over a dark suit and white dress shirt, although he wasn't wearing a tie. Even so, the ensemble was about as out of place in casual Sedona as a pair of board shorts would have been on Wall Street.

Regardless, Raphael looked the most human I'd ever seen him—and the most amazing. Anyone else who'd seen him right then might not have mistaken him for a godlike alien, but definitely a vacationing actor or model.

Somehow, I found my voice. "Hello, Raphael."

A grave nod. "Callista."

An awkward silence fell after that exchange. He seemed content to merely stand there and look at me, and I had to resist the impulse to reach up and smooth my hair, or touch a finger to my mouth to make sure the lip gloss I'd hastily reapplied after breakfast hadn't gotten smeared out of place.

I cleared my throat. "So…I have a feeling that my impulse to come down here really wasn't an impulse at all."

"No." Even though the day was cloudy, the light here was still bright enough that I was able to see his eyes clearly, their brown a few shades lighter than I had previously thought, striking against his black, black lashes. "I hope you don't mind, but it was the simplest way to get you here so we could speak to one another."

Did I mind? It was odd to think that he'd been exerting some kind of outside control over me, making me think that driving over here and then walking down to the creek had all been my idea. Harmless, I supposed, but I couldn't help but wonder how much influence he really did have on me. "I don't mind," I said, then added, "as long as you don't do it again."

"I will not. After we have spoken, then I think many things will have changed."

"About that…." My words trailed off as I tried to figure out the best way to proceed. Even standing this close, with only a few feet separating us, was enough to get my heart racing again. He seemed so much more real in that moment, with the heavy dark wool overcoat hanging from his broad shoulders and the warm-toned skin of his throat contrasting with the bright white of his shirt front. A normal man would probably have worn a scarf or muffler against the cold, but Raphael didn't seem to have any need for one.

Damn, he was making it awfully hard for me to concentrate.

I found myself clearing my throat again. "You knew, didn't you?"

He didn't ask what it was that I thought he knew. Warm brown eyes fixed on mine, he said, "I had an idea. I don't know how much your parents have told you about me, or about my abilities, but—"

"They told me a few things," I broke in. "Most of which you probably don't want to hear."

Surprisingly, he smiled. "I suppose that is to be expected. We did not exactly part on the best of terms. Anyhow, the main reason I was assigned to Persephone Oliver—although of course she was Persephone O'Brien back then—was that I have a keener sense than many of my people as to how the time streams may slip. It is not exactly what you would call precognition, but it did enable me to advise her with more accuracy than others might."

"So you knew about" — I made a sort of half-hearted flapping gesture between the two of us —"this thing we both felt?"

"'This thing.' Yes, that." He hesitated, finally glancing away from me and up at the bare trees that surrounded us, as if looking for enlightenment in the patterns their branches made against the gray sky.

"That is to say, I didn't know exactly what was approaching in my future, only that it would change my life irrevocably. And when I could see that the patterns were once more converging on this place, I guessed it must have something to do with your family. But when I came to your aunt's house and saw you, I knew."

"You did a pretty good job of hiding it."

His left eyebrow took on an ironic tilt. "We were all rather occupied at the moment. But I knew this connection between us was not something I could avoid indefinitely."

Not much liking the clinical tone he'd adopted, I crossed my arms. "So would you have preferred to avoid it if you could have?"

"That's rather a loaded question."

"Maybe. But, considering the things I've heard about you, one that I sort of needed to ask."

From the way his face went still, I could tell he didn't much like my reply. He looked as if he was about to say something else, but I heard more leaves crunching, followed by the high-pitched, excited voices of a couple of small children. A second later, a family with two kids who looked like they were maybe around four and six came down the path toward the creek. Their mother, who didn't seem to be that much older than my cousin Grace, paused when she saw Raphael and me standing there, but the kids were already running toward the water, and the woman and her husband had to hurry to catch up with them.

So much for privacy. Gathering a breath, I went over to Raphael and took his hand in mine, saying in a carrying voice, "Come on, sweetie. I want to show you that one necklace I saw in the shop back there."

Startled, he allowed himself to be led away. Once again, I'd felt that pulsing heat go through my body the second I touched him, but this time around it seemed muted somehow. Maybe because we were both wearing gloves?

After we were out of eyeshot of the family, though, he looked down at me and said, "'Sweetie'?"

"Well, I had to do something to get us out of there gracefully." As much as I really didn't want to, I let go of his hand. "Privacy is going to be a problem, you know. I live at home, and when you grow up in a town this small, *everybody* knows you."

"I don't think it will be as much of a problem as you think," he replied, a small smile playing around his mouth.

And in the next second, we were standing on the bridge of his ship.

I gasped. Had there even been a blue-white light? I couldn't recall for sure. One minute we'd been standing in the shelter of a wall overgrown with frost-brightened ivy, and the next we were here.

"You might want to warn a girl when you pull something like that," I told him, my tone almost but not quite scolding.

"My apologies." But he didn't sound at all contrite.

I pulled my hand from his. Nothing seemed to have changed up here, except the planet filling the view-screen was a serene blue-green Earth and not warm-toned Mars. "All right, it's private. I'll grant you that."

And much warmer than the chilly forty-something degrees we'd been standing in a few minutes earlier. I drew off my gloves and stuck them in my coat pockets, then unbuttoned the coat and unwound the scarf at my throat.

"If you'll come with me," Raphael said, "I'll take you someplace where it's more comfortable to talk."

That sounded...problematic...because being alone with him in more intimate surroundings might do a real number on my self-control. But we really did need to talk, and I'd much prefer doing so in a place where I could sit down and focus. That view of Earth was gorgeous, but also distracting.

"All right."

He took me from the bridge and down the same corridor I'd traversed previously, with its gleaming walls and oddly soothing banks of lights. If I was counting doors correctly, then we had already passed the room where we'd all been outfitted with jumpsuits for our rescue mission on Mars. It seemed as if we were going some distance, and I wondered why Raphael hadn't simply energy-jumped us to our destination. Maybe he wanted me to become more familiar with the ship, but as far as I could tell, one section of hallway looked just about the same as any other.

At last, we did come to a room where the door opened before us. Inside, I got a brief impression of cool shades of blue and green, seeming to mimic the planet we now orbited.

"Please," Raphael said, indicating that I should go inside.

I went in and found myself in what looked like a lounge of some sort—chairs and couches were organized in the kind of groupings intended for conversation, although I wondered what the point was when the ship only had one crewman. But then I remembered how Raphael had said the ship could have a crew of up to eight. Even so, the vessel seemed awfully large for a crew that small.

"Some refreshment?" he asked. "I have several types of mineral water, or there are fruit juices—"

"Water, please," I said. "Whatever you think I'll like best." I noticed that he hadn't mentioned anything alcoholic, which was probably just as well. I needed my wits about me. Anyway, did his people even drink? My father certainly did, but maybe that was because he'd spent decades here on Earth and had "gone native," so to speak.

Raphael went over to a space on the wall that opened up to reveal a refrigeration unit. He extracted one of the bottles—which was tall and thin and squared off—then poured its contents into a set of matching glasses. Or at least, they looked like glasses, albeit ones with subtle glowing patterns apparently embedded into their material. They didn't feel exactly like glass, or plastic, but something somewhere in between.

I took the glass from him and murmured a thank-you. Then he pointed toward one of the couch groupings. "Is that acceptable?"

"Sure," I replied, although I wasn't sure if he intended to sit next to me or on the couch across from the sofa he'd indicated. Only one way to find out, though.

I seated myself, and he took the couch across from mine. It would be easier to talk this way, facing one another, although I did wonder what it would have been like to have him sitting beside me, with the possibility that our legs might brush against one another. A little shiver went over me, but I made myself sip from the water he'd provided, telling myself that I needed to listen to what he had to say and not allow myself to get distracted.

When I looked up from my water, I saw that once again his gaze was fastened on me, dark, intent. "You asked me a question a few moments ago."

"I did."

"May I speak honestly?"

I wasn't sure I liked the sound of that. On the other hand, we needed to clear the air between us before we could progress any further. *If* we progressed, that is. I was still trying to process the very visceral reactions I kept having to him, trying to reconcile this handsome, solemn man sitting across from me with all the negative things I'd heard about him over the years. He hadn't behaved very well, as far as I could tell, but then, I'd only heard my parents' side of the situation.

"Of course, I want you to be honest with me," I told him. "What's the point if we're going to start off by hiding things from one another?"

"Thank you," he said. "I do appreciate that. Let me begin by saying that I certainly never thought I would find myself in this position. I had long ago resigned myself to living this existence alone. It happens to us occasionally."

"Why?" I asked, truly curious.

"We still don't know for sure. Something in our DNA gone slightly awry, an opportunity missed…it could be one of any number of reasons as to why one of our people finds him- or herself leading a solitary life. But I had my work, which seemed to be enough at the time."

I wanted to ask if he'd had any of those casual relationships my father had mentioned, but that seemed like too personal a question for the current stage of our relationship. Although maybe "relation-ship" was pushing things a bit, considering this was the first chance we'd even had to talk alone, and before this we'd only shared a few bits and pieces of conversation.

Somehow, though, I got the impression that

Raphael had kept himself severely alone, that if he couldn't have the match of his heart, then he wouldn't have anyone at all. From what my parents had said about him, it sounded as if he didn't have much patience for people and their various romantic entanglements. Sour grapes?

Fumbling for what I hoped might be a safer topic, I asked, "How many people were you 'assigned' to before Persephone?"

His face went still again, remote. "A good number. But I don't see how that has any bearing on what you and I are experiencing now."

He was right; it really didn't. To tell the truth, there was something surreal about sitting here on this graceful ship of his, with its feeling of a high-end hotel, and discussing our strange connection or attraction or whatever you wanted to call it as calmly as someone sitting down to have a consultation with their interior designer or something.

No, that wasn't right. No interior designer I'd ever met had sent my heart racing the way mine did every time Raphael's eyes locked on me.

I blurted, "So, how old *are* you?"

Surprisingly, he didn't look offended. "Does it matter that much?"

"Shouldn't it?"

"Did it matter to your parents?"

"Well—" I broke off and shook my head. My mother must had had her misgivings at the beginning, but clearly, they hadn't deterred her from marrying my father, or having me. "I guess not. But they don't talk about it, either."

Raphael sipped from his glass, then set it on the table before us, which looked like a large piece of stone extruded in an organic, flowing shape. Threads of bluish material ran through the beige and white matrix, reminding me of the boulder turquoise stones I'd seen in some Native American jewelry. Just like everything else I'd seen on the ship, it seemed designed to be graceful and lovely and unobtrusive.

I wondered what his people's cities looked like.

"It is different for us," he told me. "At two decades, our people reach their majority, and after that, they are free to search for their soul mate, who may be only a year or two older than they, or many centuries. We live so long that these differences in age matter very little as time wears on. Didn't your father speak to you of this?"

"Not really. That is…." I paused, trying to think of a way to phrase what I needed to say without sounding as if I was criticizing what Raphael had done when he exiled my father to Earth. "I guess he didn't talk too much about it, since it seemed obvious to all of us that we would be living our lives here, and that whoever I did end up with would be from here as well. He probably didn't see the point."

"I understand why he would think that way." Raphael leaned forward slightly; even that small alteration in the distance that separated us was enough to make my breathing quicken.

Could he tell? Probably. But he already knew a strong attraction existed between us. In a way, that was a relief. I didn't have to hide my reactions from him or pretend to be coy.

"He probably thought he was doing you a service by avoiding the subject, if he thought you would never have the opportunity to enter the world where he'd been born. But I am sure he explained our people's customs to your mother, made her understand it truly did not matter that so much time lay between them."

Obviously, she'd come to terms with the situation. But even though I was beginning to understand how such an age difference didn't matter, it didn't change the fact that I still wanted to know how old Raphael was. Just to satisfy my own curiosity, if nothing else.

"You didn't answer my question," I said.

For a long moment, he didn't respond, only sat there and watched me. He didn't look angry, or annoyed. If anything, another one of those faint Mona Lisa smiles was playing around his lips. But I couldn't look at his mouth for too long, or I'd definitely be getting myself into trouble.

Then he said, "By your people's reckoning, I am a little more than two thousand years old."

I'd been bracing myself for something like that. Even so, hearing him state the number so matter-of-factly startled me. To look at him, you'd have guessed he was in his late twenties, thirty at the most. Older than I was, sure, but not so much that it would raise any eyebrows if we were seen in public together.

Two thousand years. I tried to wrap my head around that number, but couldn't. All right, intellectually I could just barely grasp that he was an alien and so not bound by the same biological rules as the people who called Earth home. And I'd already seen how my parents seemed to age very slowly. But....

"This startles you?"

"Just a little," I said wryly.

"But is it really that much of a surprise? Martin has changed hardly at all since I left him here twenty-five years ago, and your mother clearly takes after her father Gabriel in this, since she also appears more to be your sister than your mother."

Well, that was true enough. Strangers were always shocked to discover that she was my mother. It wasn't that she hadn't aged at all; from what I'd been able to piece together, members of my father's race had some control over their appearance, could allow themselves to age to a point where they felt comfortable. That was why my grandfather did appear to be in his late fifties, and my father somewhere in his late thirties or early forties. My mother still looked like she was barely thirty, although I didn't know whether that was on purpose or because, being half human, she didn't have as much control over the process as a full-blood Pleiadian.

There had been some conversations on the topic, discussions I really hadn't wanted to hear, that at some point my parents' apparently ageless qualities would become just a little too glaring, and they'd have to move away and start over in a place where no one knew them. I hated to contemplate the possibility, but I understood their reasoning. Really, they probably should have moved on a few years ago, although I knew my mother was loath to leave her sister and extended family behind.

The one thing neither of my parents had ever brought up—probably because they didn't want me brooding over my future before it had even begun—was that someday I'd have to face that same eventuality. And what if I'd fallen in love with someone, knowing they would age while I didn't, or at least did so very slowly?

No wonder my love life was such a wasteland.

"It's all right," I said at length. "That is, I know we're working with a completely different set of rules here. It's just—you don't *look* two thousand years old."

He chuckled. "Well, I should hope not."

Something about that laugh...it was low and warm, strangely intimate. Definitely not the sort of sound I would have ever expected Raphael/Otto to make. I also could never have predicted what it would do to certain portions of my anatomy.

Once again, our eyes met. A shiver passed over me, even as a not entirely unwelcome heat began to churn low in my belly. And then Raphael got up from where he sat and came over to me, one hand extended.

I couldn't do anything except take it. The heat that had started to pulse in me felt as if it was traveling down to my fingertips, passing to him. A single shudder wracked his body, and then he pulled me to my feet and cupped my face in his hands. Just the sensation of his fingers against my skin was enough to make me run hot, then cold, as if my body couldn't figure out how to handle the overwhelming sensations now pounding through it.

But he didn't kiss me. He held me like that for a long moment, staring down into my eyes as if desperately attempting to find an answer he didn't even know he'd been seeking until that moment.

Then he whispered, "Callista, I have never—" The words stopped abruptly there, and a look of agonized hope passed over his face.

He could have been about to say almost anything, but in that moment, I thought I understood. His entire life had been spent alone. He'd long ago given up hope of ever finding the match for his soul.

Which meant he had never been with anyone. Not even once.

The thought sent a shiver of fear through me, because it seemed to mean that he'd decided I truly was his one, the echo of his heart he'd been looking for throughout the centuries. How could I possibly measure up to that? Despite my unusual parentage, I still thought of myself as an ordinary enough young woman. I hadn't done anything all that special with my life. Someone like Raphael should have a partner who was talented and brilliant and sophisticated. My test scores might have indicated that I was brilliant, but about the only out-of-the-ordinary thing I'd ever accomplished was to get my bachelor's degree in three years instead of four.

Also, I'd had no idea any sort of otherworldly match awaited me. I'd tried to live my life like a normal girl—or as normal a life as it could be, with a half-alien mother and fully alien father. I certainly hadn't thought I should be "saving" myself for anybody, and even though I knew I wasn't in love with him, I'd lost my virginity to a guy I'd been dating for a few weeks during my senior year of high school, mostly because I figured it had to happen sometime, and I didn't see the point in holding out for no reason.

Now, though, I wished I hadn't been so careless. There had only been two other guys after Seth, neither of them serious, which wasn't exactly a large number for a twenty-two-year-old who didn't have any moral or religious reasons to abstain. But even those three were more than Raphael had ever experienced.

"It's all right," I told him. Sooner or later, I'd have to tell him about my sordid past, but right then I only wanted to focus on making this as easy as possible for him. "I want—"

I'd been about to say, "I want you to," but I

wasn't able to get that far. My reassurance had apparently been all Raphael was looking for, because in the next instant his mouth was on mine, sweet with the taste of the mineral water we'd been drinking. And oh, God, no kiss had ever made it feel as if every nerve ending in my body had been lit with delicious fire, a heat that seared but did not burn. Our tongues touched, and I was melting into him, feeling his arms around me, so strong, so perfect. Somehow, I could hear how his heartbeat synchronized with mine.

Only a kiss, and yet it was enough to make me realize that there could be no one else except him.

After an endless, eternal moment, he pulled away. But one hand reached up to smooth the hair away from my forehead, then drifted downward to trace a fingertip across my cheekbone and down to my mouth. I trembled at his touch, marveling that such a whisper of sensation could evoke so much of a reaction in me.

To my surprise, when I looked up at him, his eyes were clouded with pain. "Raphael? What is it?"

He shook his head. "Nothing. Or rather, only the realization of how very hollow my life has been until this moment. I thought I was doing good work, making as much of a difference as I was allowed. But now I know how empty all my efforts truly were."

I couldn't let him think that about himself. Already everything I thought I'd known about him had been turned on its head. I knotted my fingers in his and pulled him toward me. "Don't say that," I told him. "I know it was because of your help that Persephone was able to drive the aliens from the base that first time. You did make a difference...and you saved Paul's life. And that's only the one instance I know of. There must have been hundreds more throughout your life." No reply, and I tightened my grip on his hands. "Shouldn't you be glad that at least we've found each other now? Everyone has regrets. We just have to learn to move past them."

A faint ghost of a smile pulled at the corners of his mouth. "I rather doubt that you have much to regret, Callista."

"Oh, yes, I do." I hesitated, then reminded myself I had told him only a few minutes earlier that we couldn't hide things from one another, not if we intended to have any kind of a future together. "I wish I'd known about you, because then I wouldn't have wasted myself."

"'Wasted'?" he repeated, brows drawing together slightly.

"There were...others," I said. "Only a couple, and nothing serious. But I didn't know there was a reason why I should have waited." I held myself still, waiting for the inevitable look of judgment to cross his face.

It never came. A head shake, followed by a smile. He pulled me against him, strong arms making me feel more safe, more wanted, than I ever had before. "My dear Callista, you had no idea. I wouldn't have expected that of you. And it certainly doesn't lessen what I feel for you."

"It doesn't?"

"Of course not." He bent and pressed his lips against the top of my head, and once again, delicious warmth seemed to flow through every limb. "To be perfectly honest, it makes me somewhat relieved."

I shifted slightly, just so I could look up into his face. "Relieved?"

"Yes." He released me so he could take my hands in his and hold them tightly. "At least now I can be assured that one of us knows what they're doing."

CHAPTER SEVEN

MAYBE THERE SHOULD HAVE BEEN SOME AWKWARDNESS between us after that, but, strangely, there wasn't. Raphael took me by the hand and showed me around the ship, letting me see the room where the strange drives that could hurl the vessel from planet to planet in such a short amount of time were housed. To my eyes, they didn't look like anything much, only a series of semi-translucent dark pipes with what appeared to be glowing embers floating within, but I knew if Paul Oliver had been there, he would have been beside himself. Well, when he wasn't peppering Raphael with questions as to how everything worked.

But I didn't have the same scientific mind, so I was fine with merely seeing what was there, and allowing myself to be astonished by the simple, elegant beauty of the ship. Everything seemed to have been designed for the comfort of its crew—even if that crew happened to be only one person.

He took me to another lounge, smaller than the one where we'd had our talk, but with the same enormous screens that allowed such an intense view of the Earth, hanging there in the star-studded darkness. We sat down on one of the couches, next to each other this time, and I leaned against him, my head on his shoulder. Strange how natural such a position could feel.

His hand found mine, fingers threading through one another as we sat there in the softly lit chamber. Part of the planet was in shadow, the lights from the cities there like tiny flickering embers against deep, deep black. It looked so small and fragile, as if I could reach out and cover the entire disk with my hand. And yet everything I'd ever known was contained in that blue-green crescent.

The words were out of my mouth before I even realized I intended to bring up the subject. "Do you think they'll ever stop?"

Raphael didn't ask who I meant by "they." "I'm not sure."

I swiveled to look over at him. "I was hoping for something a little more definite than that."

A shake of his head. His profile was to me, and I wanted to reach out and trace the fine lines of his brow and nose and chin. But I didn't, and instead held myself still, hoping he would know I needed more from him than the non-answer he'd given me.

After a noticeable hesitation, he said, "It is complicated, because the Reptilians, for all the difficulty they have given us and the galaxy as a whole, are still allowed to be part of the Assembly."

"They are?" I asked, shocked that the people Raphael worked for would include such a hostile race as part of their organization. "That doesn't make any sense."

"From the outside, I suppose it would not. But the Assembly is open to any sentient race that has achieved faster-than-light travel. I suppose the nearest analogue would be your United Nations. The member states are not all the best of friends, from what we have been able to discern."

There was an understatement. Yes, relations had been slowly improving over the last decade or so—and the joint Mars mission was a reflection of those improved relations—but there were still member states that caused far more problems than they solved. And yet they were still allowed to be part of the organization.

I nodded, and Raphael went on, "It is not the Assembly's place or our inclination to interfere in the business of member races, since such interventions are rarely successful, but occasionally we have been forced to it, simply because the Reptilians' depredations became too extreme to be overlooked. Afterward, they would retreat to their sector, as they always do, and we would allow them to isolate themselves and recover as necessary."

"Why would the Assembly do that?" I asked. "It seems like the Reptilians are just going to keep doing what they're doing if they have a base to operate from."

"Because we strongly believe that all the sentient races of the galaxy—and there are many, the vast majority of whom have never troubled themselves with Earth—should have their own sanctuary, their own place where no one else dare interfere."

I frowned. "But Mars isn't their place!"

"Is it Earth's?"

Well, he had me there. I would have thought we had more claim, since Mars was in our solar system, but maybe the Assembly didn't see it that way. "Okay, but when they're doing such awful things—"

His fingers tightened on mine. "Then it becomes far more difficult, yes. And what they keep attempting to do here…." The words died away, and I saw him lift his shoulders. "That is far worse, because they are trying to harness a force that should not be theirs, one that should only exist for the people of the Earth. If, of course, they ever learn to use it properly."

"What is it, really?" I asked with some curiosity. "That is, of course I've heard my whole life about Sedona's energies, and I've experienced them for myself, felt how strong they are, but the one thing no one's really explained to me is why those energies are there, of all places, and why they're different from any other planetary energy fields that might exist."

"You're hoping for answers," he said. "In most cases, I would be able to provide them. But in this instance, I really can't say for sure. Our scientists have been trying to unravel this particular puzzle for thousands of years. For whatever reason, the energy fields in the Sedona area are so strong that even those untrained in their use can still tap into them somewhat. For someone like your mother, or Persephone Oliver, who has gifts that most ordinary humans don't possess, those energies can become a potent weapon—but only if used in self-defense. That quality is the one thing about them the Reptilians have never been able to accept."

I shifted so I was facing toward Raphael then, although our fingers remained entwined. I could feel his tighten on mine slightly as our eyes met. So difficult to prevent myself from leaning forward and kissing him again, although I knew we needed to make sure the air between us was completely clear. "And is that why they keep trying? Because if they could somehow use it as a weapon—"

"Then they would utterly destroy the world as you know it," he said quietly. "I cannot say the human race would be annihilated, because the Reptilians do enjoy keeping their slaves. But I very much doubt it would be an existence that anyone would wish to have."

No, probably not. I thought of Taryn then, face earnest as she tried to think of a way we could negotiate with the Reptilians. Some people would have laughed at her for being naïve. I'd never go that far, but it was clear she hadn't grasped the whole picture. "Why now?" I asked, then shook my head. "I mean, not *now* now, exactly but why didn't the Reptilians attempt to take over a long time ago, when there weren't even any people living in the area? You'd think it would be easier."

"What makes you think they did not?" His dark eyes were grave, watching me. "That is, you say there were no people living in the area, but the Yavapai and the Havasupai have been in the region for centuries. They did not dwell in Sedona proper, since they considered it sacred land, but it was because of its sacred nature that they came to its defense when the 'lizard-men,' as they called the Reptilians, attempted to establish a base there, hundreds of years ago. The tribes knew the power of the land, and used that energy for its defense, just as your mother—and Persephone Oliver, to a lesser extent—used it as well."

"So the Reptilians went off to lick their wounds..."

"...and in the intervening time, the white men moved into the area and made it their own without clearly realizing the power of the land they'd claimed as theirs."

"But if that's the case, why did the Reptilians come back?"

Raphael's face went very still. "Because they were invited."

"'Invited'?" I repeated. "By whom?"

"Your own people." He hesitated for a few seconds, then gently released my hands so he could get up from the couch and move toward the viewscreen with its image of crescent Earth. As I stared at him in shock, he went on, not looking at me, "That is to say, certain elements in your government. After contact was made in the middle part of your last century…deals were made. In exchange for gifts of technology, the Reptilians were allowed back into Sedona. They promised to stay quiet, to remain hidden, which they did for many years. They were merely waiting for the right time."

The right time—which, according to my parents, had been that solstice in December, twenty-five years ago. I really didn't want to think about the way our government, or at least certain people in it, had been all too willing to sell us out. But then, they probably hadn't thought the Reptilians would turn on them like that. No, they couldn't have been that naïve. More likely, they had considered Sedona and the energy wells there expendable. What they hadn't realized was that the Reptilians had more or less considered the entire human race expendable.

I shivered, and Raphael came back toward me at once, sinking down on the couch so he could take me in his arms. For a long moment, I let him hold me, since I needed the warmth and reassurance of his touch. All right, even a day earlier, if someone had asked, I probably would have said Raphael was the least reassuring person in the universe. Now I knew better.

"I know it's difficult to hear," he murmured, then ran a comforting hand down my hair. "But I wanted you to have some perspective on what we were fighting. They do not give up. They suffer their defeats, but they are willing to wait and try again."

"So what can stop them?" As much as it frightened me to ask the question, I had to know. Surely there had to be an answer, something besides this ongoing pattern of fight and retreat.

But Raphael was only silent for a long moment. Then he said sadly, "I don't know."

We sat quietly for some time afterward, just holding each other. I wondered if he would try to advance things further than that, but it seemed he was willing to go slowly. Maybe since he'd already waited a few thousand years for me to show up, he didn't really want to rush into things.

Which, strangely, didn't disappoint me as much as I thought it might have. Our conversation had put something of a damper on the passion that had flamed between us. Oh, I could still feel myself react to him, but in a more muted way, not with quite that same raging fire in my veins. Just as well, probably. I couldn't go around like that all the time; I'd never be able to concentrate.

He did kiss me again, slowly, with a sort of wonder, hands tangling in my hair as he held me close. I opened my mouth to him, savoring his taste, telling myself it was enough for now. This was all so strange and new that I needed time to come to terms with the way matters stood between us. There was still plenty of time for future intimacies.

When he let me go, he said, "I must return you home now. If I keep you away too long, your parents will begin to ask questions."

"My parents." Oh, yeah, that was going to be fun. Never mind that I was an adult and could make my own choices. I'd been balanced in a precarious state for the last year or so, attempting to become more independent, but never quite managing it. Moving into the casita had been one step, and taking on part-time jobs at Aunt Kara's UFO Depot store and the Taste of Sedona wine shop another, although even put together, those two jobs didn't pay enough for me to support myself. Not that I really needed to. When I turned twenty-one, my parents had given me a large lump of cash, with careful instructions as to how to invest it—instructions I followed to the letter, since I didn't know anything about managing a portfolio. I supposed that money could have come from my father being on the *Paranormality* TV show with Paul Oliver and my Uncle Lance all those years, but I had my doubts. Finances were never an issue for us, just as they were never an issue for my grandfather

Gabriel. The star-folk they'd both come from might have exiled them here on Earth, but at least they'd done so in a way that ensured the exiles would never lack for creature comforts.

Raphael was silent for a moment. Brows pulling into a slight frown, he asked, "This is going to be a problem?"

"They're going to freak out," I said frankly.

"You Earth people do have an unusual turn of phrase." His frown smoothed itself slightly as something seemed to occur to him. "But in your world, you are certainly considered to be an adult with full autonomy. How much difficulty can they cause?"

"You don't know my parents." Raphael shot me an ironic glance at that remark, so I added, "All right, you know them slightly. But you don't know them *as* my parents. When they find out that the former Otto the Soul Crusher has designs on their daughter, they're going to go ballistic."

From the baffled look in his eyes, I got the impression he'd only followed about fifty percent of my comment. "'The Soul Crusher'?" he repeated.

"Never mind," I said. "We all know that you're not exactly on their list of favorite people, okay? Maybe after the Mars rescue, they've softened slightly, but I doubt that's enough to make them think it's okay for the two of us to be together."

He seemed to absorb that observation, then gave the slightest lift of his shoulders. "Can they stop you?"

"No," I replied. "But they can probably make my life hell before they finally give in."

Raphael's little transport gizmo—energy-jumper, whatever—was so finely tuned that after giving me a final kiss and promising me he would be in contact very soon, he was able to send me straight from his ship into the driver's seat of my SUV. I sat there for a moment, blinking at the wall directly in front of the Beemer's hood and trying to adjust to the abrupt change in scenery. His kiss seemed to linger on my lips. I pressed my fingers to my mouth, not wanting to lose a single second of that amazing sensation.

But it faded, as those things always did, and a few seconds later, I resolutely pushed the button to fire up the ignition. A fine, cold rain had begun to fall, and I was glad that I hadn't had to walk from the creek to my car. Had Raphael known, or was he merely trying to be discreet about the manner in which I reappeared in Sedona?

I took my time going home—which wasn't saying much, since the house was only five minutes away from the shopping center where Raphael and I had met. A glance at the clock on the SUV's dashboard told me I'd been gone a little more than two hours. Not really all that long to have your entire world turned upside down, I supposed.

Since I hadn't been on Raphael's ship for too

ungodly an amount of time, I found myself hoping that my parents might still be at Kara's house. After all, two hours was barely enough for that group to get up a good head of steam, most days. But when I pulled into the garage, I had to swallow my disappointment, since my parents' steel-gray Mercedes was already sitting there, its surface faintly beaded with the same fine, misty rain I'd just driven through. They must have gotten home only a few minutes earlier.

I told myself to stay calm, then fished my lip gloss out of my purse so I could reapply it. A quick inspection in the rearview mirror told me I looked more or less normal. Yes, maybe my color was a little high, since usually I was fairly pale, like my mother, but the flush in my cheeks could easily be attributed to walking in the rain to get back to my car. After all, they thought I'd been shopping for the past two hours.

Once I felt reasonably together, I got out of the car and headed for the door that led into the house. When I opened it, I heard voices coming from the kitchen. Damn. That meant I had absolutely no chance of avoiding the gauntlet.

Head high, I strode into the kitchen, praying neither of my parents would notice anything strange. They were leaning up over the counter, my mother's new silvery tablet computer propped in front of them.

"We had Thai two nights ago," my father said, his

tone not quite pleading, and despite everything, I had to smother a grin. My mother was the takeout queen of Sedona. Clearly, all the domestic genes in my family had gone straight to Kara. Or maybe she'd inherited her skills in the kitchen from her biological father. Lord knows my maternal grandmother was not the domestic type. Or so I'd heard. I'd never had the privilege of meeting the woman.

"But this new place just opened up," my mother protested, then turned as she heard me enter. "Oh, there you are. I had no idea you planned to do quite that much shopping."

"I guess the time just got away from me." I moved quickly to one of the cupboards under the pretext of fetching myself a glass so I could get some water from the door in the fridge.

"Find anything?" my father asked.

Damn. Of course, I hadn't really been shopping, so I didn't have anything to show for those two hours I'd been gone. I could say I hadn't found anything I liked, but that was really out of character. If I went shopping, I always came back with *something*.

"Um…." I swung my purse off my shoulder with my free hand so I could set it on the kitchen table, and then heard a faint crackle inside, as if from a paper bag. What the…? "Just a little something," I said.

His eyebrows lifted. "Is it a secret?"

"No, of course not," I told him. "We're way past

Christmas." Praying I wasn't making a colossal mistake, I reached into my purse and pulled out a small red bag. Inside that bag was a rectangular object.

A jewelry box.

"So you did get it after all?" my mother asked, apparently deciding the take-out debate could wait, since it was only a little after two in the afternoon.

Please, I thought, and opened the box.

Inside was the amethyst necklace I'd been coveting for over a month. It lay coiled in the box, the cut-stone beads that made up the "chain" shimmering in the kitchen light, the central pendant with its deeper purple stone and accent pale blue topazes sparkling up into my surprised eyes.

I had no idea how he'd done it, but I sent a mental thank-you winging upward to where Raphael's ship circled in silent orbit, undetectable by any human technology.

"Um, yes," I said. "I decided I couldn't think of anything else I wanted more, so I sort of blew the whole wad on the necklace." When I had a chance, I'd have to ask Raphael exactly how that particular piece of jewelry had ended up in my purse. I prayed that he hadn't just spirited it away without paying for it somehow. The necklace was worth a decent chunk of change, and I didn't want to think of some poor shopkeeper being deprived of the income.

"It's gorgeous," my mother said, but there was the faintest hint of disapproval in her voice, as if she wasn't sure I should have been quite that extravagant. But even if I had spent all my Christmas money on it, rather than having Raphael get it for me, that was my choice, wasn't it? She didn't have any business telling me what I should or shouldn't spend my money on.

I realized I was getting a little worked up…probably because the choice I was thinking of really didn't have much to do with the necklace at all. I hated lying to my parents, but right then, I didn't know what else to do.

"So," I said, after I'd closed up the box and put it back in my purse, "I would have thought you all would still be up at Aunt Kara's, hashing over the Mars mission."

My father, who up until that point had appeared faintly amused by the exchange between my mother and me, suddenly looked quite sober. "Well, Logan was tired, and Grace wanted to take him home. So they left, and everything kind of deflated after that. There really wasn't that much left to discuss, anyway. The astronauts are on their way home, and Raphael made sure they won't remember anything of what happened, so that's the end of that chapter."

I thought of everything Raphael had told me while I was on his ship and wasn't so sure. Yes, we'd snatched their prize away from the Reptilians, but they were the proverbial bad penny. They always seemed to turn up sooner or later, and I didn't know if we'd continue to prevail against them. Sooner or later, our luck would have to run out.

In the next instant, I realized that allowing myself to think of Raphael had been a very bad idea, because my mother's eyes narrowed.

"What aren't you telling us, Callista?"

Panic lanced through me, and I immediately shook my head. "I don't know what you're talking about, Mom."

My father looked similarly puzzled. "Kirsten?"

"I got a flash of something just then." Her eyes, bluer than mine, might as well have been laser beams boring into my brain. "It felt like guilt."

Damn. Now, I still hadn't been able to prove conclusively that my parents possessed the ability to read my thoughts the way Taryn Oliver could, but even garden-variety human parents had a sort of sixth sense when it came to telling whether their kids were trying to hide something. With my parents—especially my mother—that sixth sense seemed to have developed to a preternatural level.

"Why should that surprise you?" I asked, knowing I sounded a little too snotty. But maybe that was a good thing. If she thought I was only indulging in some post-adolescent brattiness, she might not try to probe too deeply into what I'd really been thinking. "I mean, weren't you just trying to guilt me about spending that much money on a necklace?"

"I wasn't doing anything of the sort." She sent a look at my father, as if she expected him to step in.

But he only raised an eyebrow at her, which seemed to be his signal that he was all too happy to sit this one out. Looking exasperated, she turned back toward me. "We gave you money for Christmas, and we'd never tell you how to spend it. I don't think the look I saw on your face had anything to do with that." She paused then, and I got the distinct impression that she was replaying the scene in her mind in an attempt to pinpoint the exact second when my expression changed. "It was right after I mentioned Raphael."

"So?" I picked up the glass of water I'd poured and drank some. "I was just thinking that it was going to take me a while to get used to calling him by that name."

"I don't see why you'd need to get 'used' to it at all," she returned, her gaze still way too focused on me. "His mission is accomplished. I'm sure he's halfway back to—well, wherever he came from." As she made the comment, she sent a questioning look at my father.

I wasn't really sure what that glance was for. My mother knew just as well as I did that all of the human-appearing aliens—commonly referred to in UFO circles as Nordic aliens, or just Nords, even though not all of them were blond or blue-eyed— came from the Pleiades cluster. But maybe that wasn't where Raphael's bosses, the "Assembly," whatever that was, had their base of operations.

"Possibly," he said, his tone neutral. "Although I

think it more likely that he's going to stay in the area for a while, keep an eye on things. Just in case."

Of course, Raphael was staying around. Maybe he had orders from the Assembly to make sure the Reptilians didn't try any more funny stuff, but he also had a very strong reason to be hanging out in our solar system for as long as possible.

That reason being me.

But damn it, there I was, thinking about him again. I drank some more water and did my very best to look only mildly curious. Too bad I really wasn't fooling anyone.

"There it was again," my mother said.

It wasn't really good etiquette to call your mother crazy—especially when she was right. About the best I could do was try to get myself out of there.

"Um…Taryn texted me while I was driving home. I'd better go see what she wanted." Horrible excuse, but it was about the best thing I could think of right then.

"It can wait." If my mother's eyes had looked like laser beams before, now they might as well have been diamond drills. "You get the strangest look on your face every time we mention Raphael."

"No, I don't," I protested. "I don't know what you're talking about."

Now my father appeared to come to attention. His gaze flicked from my mother to me, and I watched as the line between his brows deepened. "She's right. You know you always would have made a terrible poker player, Callista. What's going on here?"

"I—" Damn it, I should have sneaked out the side door of the garage and gone straight to the casita. Never mind that such behavior would have also attracted attention, since I always came in through the house first so I could get a drink of water or something. Anyway, that kind of transparent avoidance wouldn't have delayed the inevitable for very long. And, as Raphael himself had pointed out, I was an autonomous adult. I didn't need my parents' approval in this.

But God, I sure would have liked to have it. We'd always been close, brought together by the secrets all three of us had to keep from the world. I wouldn't say that we never had our differences, but they were few and far between, and never lasted very long.

My father's gaze was fixed on my face. "Were you really shopping that entire time?" he asked, his tone gentler than I'd expected.

I made myself take a breath, then said, "No."

"Where were you?" My mother, her voice quite a bit sharper than my father's.

"On Raphael's ship."

The look of consternation they exchanged after that revelation might have been comical, under different circumstances. Right then, though, I wished I could just slink off and avoid the inevitable follow-up question.

"Why?" my father asked. I could hear the faintest

hint of resignation in the question, however, as if he already knew the answer.

"Because we…." I swallowed, then made myself go on, "Because we both realized during the rescue mission that we were…." Damn, I didn't even know how to adequately phrase the feeling we shared. "Soul mates" would sound so cheesy if I said it aloud. Ditto for "attracted to one another." Failing any alternative that made sense, I said, "We're like you. I mean, connected like you are."

My mother leapt immediately into denials. "That's not possible."

"Why not?" I retorted. "It happened for you and Dad, so why is it so impossible for me and Raphael?"

"Because he's—he's—" She broke off then, looking both frightened and annoyed.

"A total asshole?" I offered.

She shot me a very sour look. "I wasn't going to say that."

"Maybe not, but you were still thinking it pretty loudly."

My father stepped away from where he'd been leaning up against the counter, then came over and laid a reassuring hand on my arm. "I don't think either of us meant to offend you, Callista. It's only that this is a little unexpected."

I did my best to push down my own highly flammable mixture of worry and irritation before I said something I knew I would regret. Of course, this had to be hard on them. But I also knew I had to act like an adult here, or I'd never get them to accept the situation. "Wasn't it unexpected when you met Mom?"

"Well, I—" He hesitated before lifting his hand from my arm. "Somewhat, yes."

"But you both came to terms with it, didn't you?"

Right then, my mother looked like she could use a stiff drink. Visibly fighting for calm, she said, "Sweetheart, that was very different."

I forgot about trying to act like an adult. "How was it different?" I demanded. "He's an alien, you're part alien. Raphael's an alien, I'm part alien. And you were only about six months older than I am now when the two of you met. So I'd really like someone to explain this huge, flaming difference, because I'm not seeing it."

The two of them looked at one another. I knew they had to be communicating in that silent way of theirs, which only made me that much angrier. If they were going to say things about me, then they could say them to my face.

When my mother spoke, she sounded a little more composed, although still clearly not happy about the news I'd just sprung on them. "I know it's different with—with the race that your father and Raphael are from. Their rules are different from our rules. But Callista, you just met Raphael. How much do you know about him? How can you possibly have anything in common?"

"How much did you and Dad have in common,

really? And how long did it take before you kissed each other?"

"Wait, are you saying—" My mother shook her head. "God, I really don't want to know."

"Actually," my father said mildly, "I met your mother almost six months before anything happened between us."

"False equivalencies," I retorted. "You met her briefly when you were here on a case, and then you went away for months, so of course there was a big gap before things started to heat up. I don't think that really counts."

Once again, my parents exchanged one of those weary glances.

"You were the one who suggested she go pre-law," my father said.

True enough, although once I graduated, I'd decided I wasn't that interested in being a lawyer after all. Something had kept me stuck in Sedona. Fate, making sure I'd be here when Raphael returned?

My mother's shoulders lifted in a helpless shrug. "I don't even know what to say anymore."

"How about 'I'm happy for you'?" I asked.

Neither of my parents responded. Disappointment was sour as bile in my mouth. All right, I hadn't expected them to jump up and down with joy or anything, considering their history with Raphael, but I'd thought they'd at least try to understand. As

I'd attempted to point out, our situations really weren't all that different.

Except that neither of them could stand Raphael.

Problem was, I didn't think I would get a lot of sympathy regarding the current state of affairs from anyone I knew. Grace, maybe, but she was probably too caught up in worrying that Logan really was okay to have time for my problems.

Then I realized I did have one sympathetic ear to bend. And it was probably better for me to get out of the house for a while, anyway.

"I'm out of here," I said, then grabbed my purse from where I'd dropped it on the kitchen table.

"Callista—" my mother said, her voice pleading.

But I ignored her as I stormed out.

CHAPTER EIGHT

"Really?" Taryn Oliver said, her green eyes wide with surprise. "*Raphael?*"

"Oh, God, not you, too," I moaned. I almost buried my head in my hands but decided I probably shouldn't be so theatrical in such a public place.

The two of us were sitting in the Red Planet Diner, partly because it was a complete tourist trap that most Sedona natives tended to avoid, and partly because they did have killer shakes and sundaes, and right then drowning in chocolate seemed like a better idea than drowning in wine. Although that might be my next step.

"Sorry," Taryn said swiftly. She swirled her spoon through the mixture of partially melted ice cream and hot fudge in the bowl before her. "I didn't mean it like that. It's just…."

I slurped up some chocolate shake through my

straw and waited for the inevitable condemnations. Because of course, Taryn could find it in her heart to wish for better communications with the Reptilians but would still tell me Raphael was one big raging asshole.

Out of the blue, she shook her head. "That's not what I was going to say at all."

I shot her a startled look, and she said quickly, a worried light entering her eyes, "Sorry. I really didn't mean to pry. But you're sort of broadcasting all over the place. Sometimes it's hard to shut it out."

"I'm sorry." The response was automatic, but I really was sorry that my brain had been bombarding her with angst.

"It's okay." She spooned some hot fudge sundae into her mouth and appeared to savor it as she weighed what to say next. "I mean, my parents don't talk a lot about what happened back then, but the times they have, they didn't make it sound as if Otto —I mean, Raphael—was that nice a person."

"That's one way to put it." As a palate cleanser, I drank some water, then returned to my shake, scooping up some of the whipped cream on top with a long-handled spoon. "And before all this happened, I would have agreed with you. But he's really not like that."

"What *is* he like?" Her tone was frankly curious.

Good question. Raphael clearly didn't have too much trouble being curt with people, and I could tell he didn't suffer fools lightly…but at the same time,

I'd seen the doubt and worry in his eyes when we'd spoken, and I knew he wasn't quite as detached as he wanted people to think. And the tender way he'd touched my face, the heat in his kisses…all right, I wasn't quite ready to confess everything to Taryn, despite our being good friends, but I did think Raphael was in need of a few more allies.

"A lot nicer than anyone around here wants to give him credit for," I told her. "I mean, yeah, he can be abrupt. But I think a lot of that stems from worry."

"About?"

I waved vaguely heavenward. "Everything that's going on right now." Since we were in a public place, there was a limit to how much we could really discuss the situation. No one around us—mostly families with kids, since the diner was that kind of place—seemed to be paying any attention to what Taryn and I were saying, but we'd all been raised to be careful what we talked about when we were out in the world. All our truly important discussions took place at home, but my house was out of the question at the moment, for obvious reasons, and I really didn't want Taryn's psychic mother eavesdropping on our conversation, either. At another time of the year, I probably would have asked Taryn to meet me out on one of Sedona's numerous hiking trails or something similarly outdoorsy and away from other people, since at least that way we could have some privacy. Unfortunately, that solution didn't work so well when temperatures were in the low forties and the sky looked like it might start snowing, or at least sleeting, at any moment.

"So he doesn't think what you all did at the Mars base was the end of it?"

I shrugged and took another sip of my milkshake. "He's not sure. But he does know certain people can't be trusted any farther than you can throw them—and these dudes are pretty big, if you know what I mean."

Being Taryn, of course she did. She gave me a troubled nod and fished a chunk of mostly solid hot fudge out of her sundae, then spooned it into her mouth. I could tell she was thinking over everything I'd told her, poking at it, trying to figure out the best way to reply without giving anything away.

When she spoke, though, her words startled me. "I think I'm jealous."

I goggled at her. "What?"

She let out a little sigh and pushed her hair back over her shoulders so it wouldn't get too close to the sundae on the table in front of her. Like her mother, Taryn had gorgeously curly long hair, although it wasn't quite as dark as Persephone's. "Well, Grace found Logan, and now you and Raphael…."

"It's not exactly peaches and cream, you know."

A laugh, and she shook her head, although whether at me or at herself, I wasn't quite sure. "Obviously, or you wouldn't have asked me to help you drown your sorrows in chocolate. But still… never mind. I'm just being stupid." Her expression sobered, though, and she went quiet, as if she was turning something over in her mind, something she wasn't sure she wanted to talk about right then.

"You're not stupid," I said. Actually, it felt good to turn the conversation toward her instead of my own "woe is me" dialogue. Wondering what it was that had her so preoccupied, I added, "But what happened with you and Noah? I thought that was kind of a thing."

Her gaze slipped away from mine, and she pushed another nugget of calcified hot fudge around in her bowl, although it didn't look as if she had any intention of eating it. "It was, for a while. But then we took sort of a wrong turn." She shrugged. "It's all right. We hadn't been going out that long anyway."

A few months, though, which was longer than I'd managed in any of my own relationships. I wondered what had gone wrong with the two of them. Noah Lerner seemed like a nice enough guy, although even when they'd first started dating, I could tell he was no match for Taryn in the brains department. Still, he was easygoing and funny, someone I thought would be good for my friend, who often took the world a little too seriously. But then, I supposed it was hard to do anything else when you had the ability to read other people's minds.

"Anyway," she went on, her tone falsely brisk, "I suppose I just need to be patient. I'm sure a handsome alien will fall into my lap any day now."

I gave her a sour look at that remark. "Well, if

we're going in order of precedent, it's probably Kelsey who should be next. She *is* almost six months older than you are."

"And totally crushing on my brother," Taryn replied, then finally scooped up the lump of fudge she'd been pushing around and ate it. "She wouldn't give a handsome alien the time of day."

I couldn't really argue with her assessment. "Does he know?"

"Michael?" Another shrug. "I think so. But he's a lot more opaque to me than most people, so I don't really know for sure. Not that I'd ever pry. Anyway, he's so focused on his doctorate that I'm pretty sure he isn't paying a lot of attention to anything else."

"Except Mars landings."

"Well, obviously, because that's all part of the same obsession, isn't it? I swear, he and my father have been out every clear night with that new telescope Dad bought, pointing up at the stars and arguing about something or other. My mother's sure they're going to catch pneumonia one of these days."

Her tone was wry, even though I could tell she was very proud of them. Taryn might not have been quite as obsessed with the heavens as her brother or her father, but she knew enough to keep up. She'd been talking about going to Northern Arizona University the next year, although to get a degree in psychology, not astronomy, since she'd about exhausted the resources at our local community college. Anyway, I figured that anyone as psychic as

Taryn could probably do pretty well as a shrink. That's what her mother had been, more or less, although from the way my mother described it, I got the feeling that Persephone had done family counseling instead of one-on-one therapy before she abandoned her practice to become a full-time psychic.

"I'll ask Raphael if he has a brother," I joked.

Something about Taryn's eyes went blurred, dreamy. We'd been friends long enough that I knew what such a shift meant. She was seeing something, although whether her vision was of an event that would take place sometime in the future or merely what might be happening across town, I didn't know for sure. Either way, it was still a little disconcerting to watch, even though I'd seen it happen before.

"What is it?"

A blink, and then she was back with me. "Oh, nothing important. I think Grace is going to ask for an indefinite leave of absence from work."

Although I could understand why, I hoped Taryn's vision was wrong, or at least wasn't showing her the whole picture. Grace had worked so hard to get her job with the National Weather Service up in Flagstaff. I'd hate to see her have to give it up. Even for Logan. Was she worried that she wouldn't be able to explain him to her friends and colleagues, once she was away from the safety net she had here in Sedona?

"That's too bad. I hope she reconsiders."

"Me, too."

I could tell Taryn didn't want to talk about it, so instead I steered the conversation to safer topics, like whether we were still going to run away to Phoenix for a week in February to avoid the inevitable crowds the Sedona film festival always seemed to bring. She went along with my obvious diversion, but I could tell from the speculative looks she was giving me that she didn't think I would actually be going anywhere with her next month. Not with this whole Raphael thing going on.

As to that, I didn't know what to say. I couldn't argue that he and I shared a connection I still didn't completely understand, but what did that really mean? Did he intend to whisk me away in his spaceship and show me the galaxy? Somehow, he didn't seem the type to settle down to a quiet existence here on Earth.

Taryn and I were both uncharacteristically silent by the time the bill came around. I grabbed it, and she shook her head.

"You don't have to treat me all the time," she protested. "I'm starting to feel like a poor relation."

"Hey, I asked you to meet me here so I could cry on your shoulder," I replied. "No way am I making you pay."

She still didn't look convinced, but to my relief, she didn't protest. It was true that I tended to pay most of the times we grabbed a snack or went out for drinks, although she wasn't much of a drinker. Her family did okay, although they didn't have an apparently bottomless alien-funded bank account the way my father did. But I didn't want her to feel bad about my having more money, especially since that was no one's fault.

After that, we walked out to the parking lot together. Since the diner was crowded and the lot almost full, we hadn't been able to park anywhere near each other.

Taryn gave me a little wave as she headed off to the spot where she'd left her car. "I'm not sure I helped any, but if you need to talk some more—"

"You did help," I said. "A lot." And that was only the truth. No, we hadn't really solved anything—that was for me and my parents and Raphael to work out —but it had still felt good to talk to a friend, to have her try to understand what I was going through. Just having someone around who didn't think Raphael was the devil was a step in the right direction.

She flashed me a smile, then shoved her hands in her pockets and headed off toward the hand-me-down Honda crossover vehicle she drove. Something in her air seemed distracted, though, and I wondered then if she'd been telling me the whole truth when I asked her about what she'd seen in her vision. Taryn was no liar, but she did have a tendency to hold things back.

Well, maybe we'd get a chance to talk later. Right then, I was trying to figure out what the hell to do next. My phone had buzzed a few times while Taryn and I were commiserating over ice cream, but I'd ignored it, guessing those messages were from my parents. I knew I'd have to face them eventually. Right then, though, I was feeling spectacularly not in the mood for that kind of a confrontation.

A movie seemed like the safest best. The theater was just down the street, and I could pick something at random and sit there in the dark for a few hours while I decided what to do next. I hadn't heard anything from Raphael, but I wasn't too surprised by his radio silence. It wasn't as if he could just materialize in the middle of a crowded diner and sit down next to me.

I parked at the theater, then went up to the box office and bought a ticket. The movie with the most convenient showing was some 3-D action flick, but I figured that watching things get blown up for a couple of hours might be a good way for me to forget my problems for a while.

Since I didn't want my eardrums to get too rattled, I sat down near the back. Because of the holiday, the theater was already halfway full and promised to reach capacity, if the way people kept filing in with their soft drinks and bags of popcorn and nachos was any indication.

Someone sat down next to me, and I let out a little resigned sigh. It was probably too much to ask that I have the buffer zone of a few empty seats on either side, given how crowded the place was.

Then I felt a delicious tingle as the man who'd sat down laid his hand on top of mine. "Callista."

His voice seemed to cut through the chatter that surrounded us. I shifted so I could look into his eyes. "How did you find me?"

"I always know where you are...now."

Maybe he'd meant for those words to be reassuring, but a little shiver worked its way down my spine, and it wasn't the thrilling kind. "What, did you put a tracker on me or something?"

He chuckled. "Of course not. Now that we've recognized the bond between us, it's something that...as your people might say...goes with the territory."

I digested his reply and tried to figure out how much it bothered me. If it really bothered me at all. Some people might have thought that close a connection a bit creepy, but considering how we still had Reptilians hanging around the immediate solar vicinity, I found myself more reassured than anything else that Raphael would always be nearby.

"Why can't I sense you?" I asked.

"Because you haven't practiced."

Well, I couldn't really argue with that. Nor did I want to right then, since the theater began to darken and the usual admonishments about silencing all personal devices, no talking, no crying babies began to appear on the screen.

Raphael touched my hand. "Do you want to stay?" he whispered.

Of course, I didn't. I'd only bought the ticket in the first place because I didn't want to go home just yet. So I shook my head, and he got up out of his seat. Luckily, he was on the aisle, so I didn't have to climb over anyone as I grabbed my purse and followed him toward the exit. While I walked, I buttoned up my coat as best I could with one hand.

"Did you drive here?" I asked. Maybe that was a stupid question, but after all, my father had driven a car when he first met my mother. Then again, he'd been pretending to be a Man in Black, a government agent. Raphael wasn't exactly here undercover, unless you counted looking like an ordinary human being instead of someone who'd been born in a star system thousands of light-years away.

To be fair, he didn't look *exactly* like an ordinary human being. But he did still appear human enough, although more like someone who should have been up on the movie screen we'd just left behind. Or maybe a billboard, modeling the latest designer boxer-briefs.

Okay, that thought was way too dangerous, since it started me on some visualizations that would probably get me in trouble. Luckily, Raphael had shaken his head in response to my question and was saying, "No, of course I didn't drive. But the stalls in the restrooms here are quite handy for the times when one needs to drop in."

"Resourceful." By that point, we'd reached the space where my SUV was parked, so I asked, "What next? Are we going back to the ship?"

"Not yet." His dark eyes were far too keen, probing my features. "You spoke to your parents?"

"Yes. It didn't go so well."

"They do not approve."

"That's an understatement." It was really too cold to stand there and talk. I unlocked the car and climbed into the driver's seat, and a moment later, Raphael followed suit, fumbling a little as he fastened the apparently unfamiliar seatbelt.

"Perhaps we should go talk to them together."

I shot him a sideways glance, my finger pausing above the ignition button. "I don't think that's a very good idea."

"Why not?" He sounded genuinely curious.

"Because, as predicted, they freaked out." All right, my mother had done most of the freaking out, but still. I went on, "What makes you think they're going to behave any better if the two of us try to talk some sense into them?"

"Because, as you just said, it will be the two of us. If they see us together, it may well be that they'll realize the connection is there, and then they will leave off with their protests so we can focus on more important things."

I wasn't sure I liked the sound of that. "So you think what's happening with us isn't important?"

At once, he shook his head. "That is not what I said, Callista. What I meant is that this conflict between you and your parents is not a good use of our energies. There are much more important things to be doing than protesting the inevitable."

"So…this is inevitable?" I asked slowly. "This thing between us?"

For a long moment, he didn't say anything. Then he leaned over and took my hand in his, pressed it to his lips. I was wearing gloves, but right then, that didn't seem to matter. I could still feel the electric shock of his touch moving down my arm and flowing out into my body. Need coursed through me, and I pulled in a ragged breath.

Then he said, "What do you think?"

He was right. It was inevitable. I was falling in toward him like a planet being pulled into the irresistible force of a black hole. I couldn't fight it, couldn't pull away.

Not that I really wanted to.

"All right," I told him. My voice shook, but I didn't bother to control it. Raphael knew exactly what kind of effect he had on me.

"Let's go meet the parents."

CHAPTER NINE

I PULLED INTO THE GARAGE AND SHUT OFF THE CAR. Beside me, Raphael was silent, watching as I sat there for a few seconds, trying to pull myself together as much as I thought I could manage at the moment. Without speaking, I picked up my purse and got out, and a moment later, he climbed out of the SUV as well.

Unfortunately, I really didn't have a plan. Raphael hadn't offered much of one, either, except to say that it was in no one's best interests for us to continue to sneak around. Which, on the surface, I totally agreed with. Problem was, he'd had a couple of thousand years—more or less—to figure out how to be an adult. I'd only been giving it a try for the past several years, and a half-assed one at that. Living in my parents' casita had given me only a very spurious sense of independence.

Truth was, I'd been drifting for the past year, working at part-time jobs instead of deciding what I wanted to do with my life. Sometimes I'd envied my cousin Kelsey for her single-minded devotion to Michael Oliver, even if that devotion didn't seem to be reciprocated. At least she knew what she wanted out of life, whereas I hadn't felt connected to much of anything.

I felt connected now, though. This attraction... connection...whatever it was with Raphael, it was real. More real than anything I'd ever experienced. I couldn't lose that, not just as I was beginning to realize my life could be something more than just me being my parents' daughter.

And Raphael was right. Trying to hide our relationship from my parents was dishonest and a very poor way to handle the situation. We needed to get all this cleared up so we could focus on more important things.

He gave my free hand a brief squeeze just as I was opening the door that led from the garage to the house. Warmth flooded through me again, but this was a very different sort of heat, one which sprang from gratitude that he understood how worried I was and wanted to offer me comfort.

It wasn't the sort of gesture I would have expected from him two days ago. But had he really changed, or only my opinion of him?

The kitchen was empty when we came inside. My first thought was that my parents must have abandoned their idea of getting take-out and had gone out to dinner altogether. But then I realized that didn't make any sense—both their cars were still in the garage, and it was still way too early, not even five o'clock yet.

The mystery was solved when I heard my father call from the family room, "Callista?"

I swallowed. Raphael took me by the hand and went in the direction of my father's voice. When we entered the room, I saw that he was sitting in his favorite chair, my mother curled up on the couch, her tablet in her lap while she read a magazine. A fire crackled away in the hearth. It was a cozy scene, but when my mother's gaze fixed on Raphael's and my hands, saw the way our fingers were twined together, a shiver went through me.

My father spoke, his tone quiet. "We were worried."

"I went to the Red Planet Diner with Taryn," I replied.

"The three of you?" he asked.

"No," Raphael put in. "I met Callista afterward."

"Ah."

My mother set her tablet on the coffee table and sat up. She'd kicked off her boots and was in her stocking feet, but her blue eyes were still fierce enough as they took in my companion.

Raphael, however, seemed completely unfazed. Maybe he was; my mother could be a tough customer, but he'd probably faced down a lot worse in his time. "We thought it would be best if we came and spoke with you."

She didn't blink. "You did? And how much of that was Callista's idea?"

"Not a lot," I admitted, before Raphael could reply. "But he convinced me that it would be better if we cleared the air."

"Thank you for that," my father said. He wasn't quite frowning, but the line between his brows was more pronounced than usual. "This development has been...difficult."

"I can imagine." Raphael's tone was dry, but once again, I felt him give my hand one of those reassuring little squeezes. "Difficult for Callista and me as well, although I'm not sure if that's what you wished to hear."

"What I'd like to hear is that this has all been a huge mistake," my mother said. "I have the feeling that's not going to happen, though."

"No, it's not," I told her. "Why should it be a mistake with Raphael and me when it wasn't for you and Dad?"

She opened her mouth, and I had a feeling that once again she was going to tell me their situation had been entirely different. But then she subsided, as if she'd realized that particular argument hadn't gone over very well just a few hours earlier, and there was no reason to think it would meet a better reception now.

My father got up from his chair and went to sit

next to her on the sofa, as if trying to show her that he understood her current inner turmoil.

"Old prejudices can be difficult to overcome," Raphael said, and I winced. I knew that comment was going to go over like a lead balloon.

"Are you calling me a bigot?" my mother shot back.

"No," he replied, looking completely unruffled. "What I am saying is that your previous encounters with me were less than pleasant, and so you are letting those memories color your current attitude. There were many reasons why I behaved as I did, most of which had very little to do with my own wishes or opinions. We were in a crisis, and I had to act accordingly."

"But now everything has settled down, and so I'm supposed to forget about all that?"

"No," Raphael said. "I fear that it hasn't all settled down. Not entirely. But I would hope that you could revisit your own beliefs and experience, and realize that what happened more than twenty of your years ago has nothing to do with how I feel about Callista. Believe me, I was as shocked by my reaction to her as you most likely were upon hearing the news. Since you have spent so many years with Martin, however, I had hoped you understand how these things work."

The problem was, I knew she understood. She'd experienced the same lightning-bolt attraction herself. But it was one thing to feel that sudden race of desire for a handsome near-stranger, and quite another to realize your own daughter had just experienced that same bolt from the blue, especially when that bolt had come from one of your least favorite people in the universe.

For a long moment, she said nothing at all. My father laid a hand on her knee, although he remained silent, too, as if understanding that she was the one who had to work through this. He might not have been entirely happy about the situation, but he did know that the connection between Raphael and me was not something that had come about because he wished to spite them, or that he'd returned to Earth simply to make my mother's life difficult. Even the Pleiadian scientists and psychologists couldn't explain exactly how these attractions worked, except that they seemed to occur on a level far deeper than our conscious wishes and desires. It was almost as if our DNA recognized who our other half was meant to be.

At last, she let out a breath and covered my father's hand with her own. "I'm not going to lie," she said. "I'm still not happy about it." Then her blue eyes took on a wicked glint that I recognized as she stared up at my companion. "You may want to do a good deal of sucking up to me on Mother's Day."

He didn't pretend to be confused. Raphael might not have known all the ins and outs of modern American society, but he'd been Persephone's spirit guide for almost two decades, and probably a guide for many others even before that. He'd had enough exposure that he understood most references.

"Of course," he said politely. "Do you prefer red roses or pink?"

"Yellow, actually."

I shook my head. She was only telling the truth, but the way she'd replied had sounded so…contrary. I asked, "So are we all okay now?"

"We're okay," my mother said. "Just okay. 'All okay' might be pushing it a little."

Well, that was better than where we'd started, so I'd take it.

"Why don't you stay for dinner?" my father asked. "We finally agreed on Greek."

I shot a helpless look up at Raphael. It was a kind gesture, and maybe I should have accepted the dinner invitation, but I felt as if we'd just attained a fragile peace. Having my mother and Raphael in the same room for several hours at a time might be pushing it a little.

He smiled and said, "That is a gracious offer, Martin. But I fear I will have to decline this time. I'd already asked Callista if she would dine with me, and since things are still new between us…."

"Got it," my father said, looking resigned. He sent a brief glance toward my mother, but she didn't seem inclined to argue. If anything, she looked relieved, as if she was just as glad as I that she wouldn't have to spend an extended amount of time with Raphael. It would probably be better if they only got small doses of one another until time had smoothed out some of the wrinkles in the way we all got along together.

"Thanks, Dad." I smiled at him, then offered a more tentative one to my mother. She didn't exactly smile back, but she did nod.

Baby steps.

"Well, we should get going," I told them, looping my arm through Raphael's. "But have a good dinner. I'll miss having some of those phyllo turnovers."

"I'd save some for you," my father said, "but I know your mother would just raid the kitchen in the middle of the night and eat them anyway."

"Damn straight." Now she was smiling a little, and that seemed the safest time to get out of there, when her mood appeared to have improved marginally.

"I won't be late," I promised, and then more or less dragged Raphael out of the family room and back to the garage. As soon as the door shut behind us, I said, "So, are we really going out to dinner? Because you kind of neglected to mention that earlier."

"True," he replied. "But I always had intended to ask if you would eat with me this evening. It's only that we won't be exactly going out for dinner...more like 'up' for dinner."

In the next instant, white light flashed around us, and then we were standing once more on the bridge of his ship, Earth glowing blue-green below us.

"Thanks for the warning," I said, my tone sour.

The jump hadn't been quite as nerve-rattling this time, but I still would have preferred to know what he'd planned.

Raphael laughed—actually laughed—and bent down to kiss me. A real kiss, mouth to mouth, tongues touching, those delicious thrills running up and down my entire body. My purse slipped from my fingers and fell with a thud to the floor. When I finally came up for air, his dark eyes were smiling down at me.

"Would you like to come to the dining chamber?" he asked. "I didn't show it to you on the first tour I gave you of the ship."

"Holding out on me?"

His gaze strayed to my lips. "Let's just say that I preferred to keep a few things for later."

Damn it, he needed to stop giving me those amazing chills, the ones that made me want to shiver and melt into a puddle of warm goo at the same time. "Then lead on. I can feel that chocolate milkshake wearing off."

He took my hand and guided me down the corridor that dead-ended at the bridge. This time, however, we stopped at an elevator, more like a transparent plastic tube, and got in. I didn't see him push any buttons, but somehow it seemed to know to go up two levels, then stop.

"Why not use your jewel?" I asked once we were out of the elevator and walking down another hallway, one similar to the first, only not quite as wide. "It seems faster."

"Because we must use our bodies, or they will not serve us when we need them," he told me. "The jewel, as you call it, does come in handy during emergencies, but otherwise, it is far better for us to walk from place to place."

I couldn't argue with that. My parents had passed their amazing metabolisms on to me, so it wasn't as if I had to worry about hiking all afternoon to work off that milkshake or anything, but living in Sedona did tend to make you get up and move around. Everyone I knew seemed to take daily walks or hikes, weather permitting.

"Here we are," he said as the wall before us parted to reveal a room that made me gasp out loud in amazement.

One wall was made up completely by an enormous view-screen. Instead of Earth hanging there, though, we looked out into a sea of stars, with the Moon floating off to the upper left, bigger and brighter and clearer than I'd ever seen it before. The ceiling overhead was dark, and twinkled with more stars, while the lighting seemed to come from the floor, a soft diffuse glow that gave enough illumination so you could walk around safely but not so much that it interfered with the starry scene outside or overhead.

"You people know how to travel, don't you?"

He smiled and led me farther into the room. The

furniture here was similar to what I'd seen in the lounge, smooth and organic in its outlines, although the stone pieces that decorated this chamber were of a darker material that shimmered with embedded flecks of reflective ore in shades of silver and gold. "If circumstances require us to spend a good deal of time on these ships, then better that we make them comfortable and beautiful, don't you think?"

"No arguments here."

Following his lead, I sat down at a table positioned just close enough to the screen to get an even better view of the Moon, but not so close that it would feel as if I was falling into that endless starscape. Raphael didn't seat himself, however, but went over to a long counter on one side of the room. It didn't seem to have any controls or access points that I could see, but after he moved his hands over its surface, two tall glasses filled with a pale peach-colored liquid appeared there, along with a platter of…well, something. I assumed it must be his people's version of hors d'oeuvres, since the delicately colored and shaped items lying on the luminous glass tray were all small, even if they were pretty to look at.

Raphael came back to the table and took the chair opposite mine after setting down the glasses and platter.

"So what's all this?" I asked, hoping I sounded interested and not at all skeptical. When I was younger, I'd driven my parents a little crazy with my picky eating. I liked to think I'd matured out of that phase, but I still tended to give unfamiliar food items the side-eye.

"This," he said, picking up his glass, "is a beverage we like to consume on special occasions. Something like your champagne, I suppose, although the components are very different."

"So it's alcoholic?"

"Not exactly. Alcohol contributes to all sorts of health problems, and there is no reason for us to consume it when there are so many better alternatives out there."

No alcohol. Okay. I supposed it was probably silly of me to think that an alien civilization as advanced as the one Raphael had come from would indulge in tossing back a few cans of beer on a Saturday afternoon while watching TV. Then again, my father had been known to do pretty much that very thing.

"You're disappointed," Raphael said, and at once I shook my head.

"No, of course not. Sometimes it just…takes me a while to get used to things."

A slow smile touched his mouth, and again I felt one of those stirrings of desire. Would these crazy reactions slow down once we'd—

All right, that was an eventuality I probably shouldn't allow myself to dwell on.

But he was watching me, clearly waiting for me to pick up my own glass, so I did. And really, the color of the not-champagne was very pretty. The drink did have teeny tiny bubbles swirling around in it, so I guessed the comparison was apt enough.

"I hope you can get used to this," Raphael said, then glanced at the starry room around us before his gaze returned to me. "All of this."

Considering that I didn't think I'd ever been in such a beautiful place, I figured it wouldn't take too much effort to get very used to it. And the company who shared it with me. "I'm pretty sure that can be arranged," I told him, just before I lifted the glass to my lips and took a sip.

Mingled sweet and tart, and fizz, and...after that words failed me, because that drink seemed to get into my blood the way Raphael's kisses did, tingling and warm and making me feel far more alive than I ever had before. Somehow I remembered to swallow, and then I blinked as I tried to get a grip on myself.

"I thought you told me it wasn't alcoholic," I said, my tone probably more accusing than it should have been.

But his eyes only flickered with amusement. "True. But I believe I also mentioned that it was a better alternative."

That was for sure. The mild euphoria I was currently experiencing didn't feel like the buzz I'd get from having a drink—especially not after only one sip. "Are you sure my metabolism can handle it? I only had a tiny amount, and I'm already feeling it."

"Of course you are. The effect is not cumulative, as it would be with Earth-based alcohol. If you continue to drink it, you will continue to feel more or less the same." One eyebrow went up, and he added, "Do not forget that far more of your metabolism is Pleiadian than human."

"Is that what you call yourselves?" I asked. "It's what I've always said, because that's how my father referred to his people, but—"

"No, that is what your people call us," Raphael said. "Our language is difficult for those who haven't been raised speaking it, which is why it is easier for me to use your own people's terms for these things."

"So your name isn't Raphael?" I wasn't sure why that possibility should be so troubling. After all, almost anything was better than "Otto."

"It is the closest approximation in your language for my name. And," he added, apparently noting some shift in my expression, "a name that I feel is mine. So you should not let a small question of semantics worry you, Callista."

"I won't," I said, although I didn't know if I was exactly telling the truth. Still, it seemed better to direct the conversation toward a safer topic. "So what's all this on the platter?"

"A little introduction to the meal. Like an appetizer, I suppose, although our own term is closer to the French phrase *amuse-bouche*."

Since I'd taken French in high school, I at least knew what he was talking about—the "mouth-amuser" that preceded a meal. "That sounds like fun."

"I hope you will think so."

Nothing for it, I supposed. And really, the drink he'd served was amazing enough that I figured the food must be equally good.

I reached for the appetizer closest to me. It was pale cream in color, and looked like some kind of soft cheese sitting on top of a very thin layer of bread or something similar. Before I could lose my nerve, I popped it in my mouth.

Just as the drink had tasted like many things at once, so did that little morsel. Savory, with the slightest hint of heat, and then a spicy warmth at the end that reminded me in a way of cinnamon, although it wasn't quite the same. After I swallowed it, I said, "That was amazing."

"I'm glad you liked it. I tried to put together items that wouldn't be too shocking to your palate."

Who would have expected the former Otto to be so thoughtful? "Thank you for doing that. I'm sure it will all be wonderful."

And it was. Everything I tasted was unusual and yet familiar at the same time, delicious and comforting and exciting all at once.

Sort of like Raphael, I supposed.

After we finished the platter of appetizers, our *amuse-bouches,* he took the tray away and then came back with several plates of food. Nothing was exactly recognizable, although I got the impression I was eating fruit and cheese and some kind of bread, although the bread was sweeter than I expected, a good foil to the fizzy tartness of the drinks he'd served.

"You don't eat meat, do you?" I asked after a few bites.

"No. My people abandoned that practice generations ago."

I wondered if he knew that my father was known to enjoy a good cheeseburger. Probably, so I didn't bother to bring it up. Maybe it was to be expected that an exile would fall off the wagon, so to speak. Anyway, judging by some of the things Raphael had said, I'd gotten the impression that the Pleiadians' food choices were based on health reasons, and not because their religion or other beliefs dictated that they couldn't consume certain items.

While I was something of a carnivore myself, everything Raphael had provided was so good that I didn't think I'd mind going without meat for an extended period of time. Which led to the next question I wanted to ask, but wasn't sure I had the courage to broach.

Where was all this headed? Had Raphael brought me here as a way to slowly break me in, so to speak, to get me used to his world, his ship, even the food and drink his people consumed? Did being with him mean that he intended me to leave my family and friends behind?

Maybe it was a little early to be asking those questions—or even thinking them—but they'd have to come up at some point. My parents' example was enough to tell me that these sorts of liaisons were forever. That thought in and of itself was frightening. Of course, I'd always hoped I would find the right person and settle down someday. I just never imagined that person might be one of my father's people, and that I might have to give up everything I knew to be with him.

True, Raphael could stay here on Earth, but I had a hard time believing he'd be content with limiting himself in such a way. Not after spending his entire life as a citizen of the galaxy, instead of one tiny corner of it.

"You're very quiet," he said.

"Am I? I suppose I was thinking." I lifted my glass and took another swallow of the effervescent liquid inside. It tickled my throat and sent some more of those delicious tingles through me.

"About?"

"Us, of course."

By that point, I'd put the glass back down, and he reached across the table and took my hand in his. "It is all very new and strange."

"Strange" didn't begin to describe it, as far as I was concerned. Not that I could really imagine being with anyone else, though. It seemed as soon as that special connection was awakened, the people involved really didn't have any desire to look elsewhere. But as much as I wanted Raphael, *needed* him, I also needed some answers.

Feeling the pressure of his fingers against mine

helped give me some courage, even though it was hard to concentrate, what with the ripples of heat his touch kept sending through me. "So where does this end, Raphael?"

"Wherever we want it to."

"That's not a real answer."

He didn't look annoyed by my words. Still holding my hand, he gazed across the table at me and said, "Time often speaks to me, telling me of how events might go, but once it sent me to you, it seemed to go silent. Meaning," he added, as one of my eyebrows began to lift, "that even I cannot say for sure. You could join me on this ship and explore the galaxy with me. Or I could take my own form of exile down on the world where you grew up. Either possibility is equally plausible."

"Are they? Are they really?" I wanted to believe him, but at the same time, I couldn't quite imagine Raphael assimilating into a life with my friends and family, of him slipping into some jeans and a work shirt and going shooting in the woods with the guys. Not hunting—my father would never have stood for that—but his scruples didn't prevent him from heading out with Paul and Lance every once in a while so they could indulge in some target practice with cans or bottles, or a bunch of rotten pumpkins once Halloween was over. Anyway, my father had integrated into Earth culture pretty well, but that had to be partly because he'd been pretending to be human for years before he hooked up with my mother. I didn't know if Raphael was quite so…adaptable.

He didn't let go of my fingers, but instead increased the pressure on them, as if he wanted me to be assured of how earnest he was. "Yes, both those futures are equally possible. I know that must be difficult for you to understand. But although I was called here to get the assistance of you and your family to rescue those astronauts, I also know that something deeper under-rode that urgency. It was time for me to return here, because it was time for me to find you. Do you understand?"

Strangely, I did. Time and the universe had washed him into this galactic backwater, bringing him to me when I was ready to accept the gifts he wanted to give. The gift of his heart, and his soul, although I knew I must be brave enough to embrace them fully.

For some reason, I found it hard to speak. So I nodded, and he rose from his chair and came over to me, kneeling next to where I sat so he could take both my hands in his. "It is easier to explore new territory if one does not have to do it alone."

I couldn't have agreed with him more. The best way to show him how I felt, I thought, was to reach out to him, to pull him close so we could kiss again, those kisses flavored with all the exquisite tastes we'd consumed during our meal.

I didn't know exactly how it happened, but suddenly I was standing, and his arms were around me, our bodies pressed together. It seemed as if I could feel his warmth even through the shirt and jacket he wore, sense it pouring into my body, making me want him that much more.

We were alone here. Was this why he'd brought me to his ship, so we could be together with no artificial barriers separating us?

I pulled my mouth away from his just long enough to say, "Maybe it's time I got a tour of your bedroom, too."

A quick flash of a grin, followed by the brighter glare of white light surrounding us, taking us away from the dining chamber to a smaller room. At least, I thought it was smaller. I didn't get much more than a glimpse of dark blue walls and several pieces of that beautifully sculpted furniture in various shades of silver and gray before we were sinking down onto a bed that seemed to embrace every inch of my body, more comfortable than any other bed I'd ever lain on.

After that, though, I didn't have time to think about the bed. Raphael's mouth was on mine, his weight on top of me, surrounding me. One hand moved down from my shoulder, then stopped just short of touching my breast.

I ached for him, but at the same time, I understood his hesitation. He didn't want to force me, or rush me…and, quite possibly, he wasn't completely sure what he should do next. Oh, probably he had a clinical idea of what was involved, but the reality had to be so very different.

"It's all right, Raphael," I whispered. "I want this. I want you."

Those words seemed to open the floodgates. In the next moment, his mouth was on my neck, his breath warm against my skin, and I shivered as his hand cupped my breast. Even through my sweater and my bra, his touch seared me, made me ache to share all of my body with him.

And I would. I reached up and began pulling at his jacket, shifting it off his shoulders. For the briefest second, he looked down at me, eyes made even darker with desire. "Let me make that easier for you," he said, his normally smooth voice rough with passion.

In the next instant, the jacket was gone. As was his shirt—and my sweater and jeans. In fact, *everything* was gone except my bra and panties, and the underwear he had on, which looked just as normal and earthly as his suit had. I gasped, although I couldn't say for sure whether my reaction was from shock or finally getting to see what his clothes had concealed. Of course, I'd been able to tell that he was tall and broad-shouldered and well built, but that wasn't the same as being able to drink in the fine muscles of his chest and stomach, a lot more defined than I'd imagined.

"Holy crap," I blurted.

"Is that a good thing?"

"A very good thing." But since actions spoke louder than words, I figured the best thing to do was to show him how good I really thought he was. I trailed my fingers down his chest and over the hard, flat stomach muscles, down to something that was even harder, but not exactly what you'd call flat. In fact, it was quite a bit bigger than I'd been expecting.

Somehow, I managed to keep myself from saying "holy crap" again. No, I brushed my hand over the bulge in his underwear, savoring the feel of it—and enjoying the way he moaned. There was an undercurrent of surprise to the sounds he made, as if he truly hadn't ever experienced anything like this before.

It did feel a little strange to be the wise and worldly one, considering I really didn't think I was all that experienced. But I knew what we both wanted, and so I didn't see any need to hold back. Not now.

Before I could lose my nerve, I took hold of the waistband of his underwear and pulled it down, then tried not to gasp. He was big, and completely human-looking—and obviously ready for me. I ran my fingers down his shaft, letting out a little sigh of my own at the sensation of that silky skin beneath my fingertips. Another moan escaped his lips, and I wrapped my hand around him, gently moving up and down. Right then, I didn't want to be too forceful, because I didn't want to run the risk of having him spend before we even got started.

No, I wanted this to last a long time.

It seemed he had the same idea, because only a

moment or so passed before he placed his hand on mine, lifting it away from him so he could press his body up against mine. Once again, his lips brushed my throat, and I shivered. A second later, I could feel his fingers at the back of my bra, undoing the clasp so he could lift the garment from my body.

A whisper of a moan escaped me. I couldn't manage anything more than that, because immediately afterward he bent his head to my breasts, burying his face in the valley between them as he inhaled deeply, breathing in my scent. And then his mouth was on me, licking, suckling, and I couldn't hold it in anymore, had to cry out as I felt his tongue slip over my flesh.

But there was so much more than that, because immediately afterward his hand slipped lower, moving between my legs, fingers pushing their way under the lacy fabric of my underwear, sliding into me.

For someone who'd never done this before, he sure seemed to know what he was doing. I shut my eyes and let the waves of pleasure run all through me, building far more quickly than they ever had before. Usually, it would take a long time for me to climax, but in that moment, I knew I would hit the edge far more quickly than I ever had before.

Which I did, clinging to him as the orgasm slammed through me. I had to hold on to him, because right then it seemed as if he was the only solid thing in my universe. I broke apart, and he put me back together.

Not-quite sobs heaved their way out of my chest. Raphael cradled me in his arms and whispered, "My dear, are you all right?"

Since I didn't know if I was capable of coherent speech right then, I only nodded. In silence, he held me until the last of the shivers had passed through me. Damn. And that reaction was only from him stroking me. What would happen when we actually joined?

Part of me didn't want to know. This was beginning to feel like far too much. It had to be the connection between us, a bond that—clearly—I hadn't fully understood. In the past, sex had been a mostly take-it-or-leave-it proposition for me, which was why I hadn't been with too many people. But it was all different with Raphael.

"I'm fine," I said at last. "It was just—" I stopped there, because I couldn't seem to find the words to articulate what I'd experienced without sounding—at least to myself—like a complete idiot. So I told him the only thing that made sense right then. "Raphael, make love to me."

His lips found mine, hungry. I could imagine they would be, after spending a lifetime made up of many lifetimes deprived of this sort of intimacy. I could feel him press against me, hard, ready. And then he was inside, moving slowly at first, finding his rhythm. God, the perfection of that touch, the way we fit together—I'd never imagined anything like it. Our bodies locked as one, speeding up, while my legs wrapped around his hips and I drove him in that much deeper.

I could tell from the intensity of his movements that he probably wouldn't be able to hold on for too long. In that moment, I didn't care. It was enough that we'd experienced this together, that I was the one who'd finally given him a chance to know ecstasy.

His entire body convulsed, and I held on to him, my own climax following just a few seconds later. Quieter, since he'd already made me come a few minutes before, but no less intense for all that. I kept my arms wrapped around him until the last shudders had worked their way through his frame, and then I placed my mouth against the hollow of his throat, tasting the faint saltiness of the perspiration there.

He'd never felt as real to me as he did in that moment.

A long silence, and then he said,

"I love you, Callista."

CHAPTER TEN

I'D BEEN THINKING THE SAME THREE WORDS, BUT I wasn't sure whether to say such a thing aloud. Not so soon, not when we'd only known each other for such a short amount of time. But Raphael had been brave enough to say it, and I wasn't about to hurt him by letting my own fear and my own limitations get in the way. I knew my heart, even if my brain might be telling me that this was all crazy.

"I love you, too," I whispered.

He ran a hand over my tumbled hair, then slid the backs of his fingers against the side of my cheek. I breathed out, softly, thrilled by even that small, tender touch, so different from the tumult of the love-making we'd just shared.

A silence fell, but a good one. We both seemed content in that moment to lie next to one another, to let the delicious afterglow wrap itself around us.

Every rise and fall of his chest beneath my cheek reassured me that he was there, apparently happy to just be with me. I couldn't even begin to imagine what that must have felt like to him, after so many years with no physical intimacy at all. It had been overwhelming enough for me, and I'd known something of what to expect, although in comparison, my previous encounters couldn't even come close, like flying an ultralight instead of the latest hypersonic jet.

But reality intruded enough for me to realize that I should probably get cleaned up a bit. "The bathroom?"

He shifted so he could look down at me and smile faintly. "Through that door in the wall opposite."

I kissed him, then slipped off the bed and went to the door he'd indicated. A few things in the restroom looked basically familiar, like the large glass-walled shower enclosure and the glass basin on the counter of smooth-planed stone. However, I couldn't find anything remotely resembling a toilet, although there was some sort of control panel on a wall that was otherwise empty. I placed my palm on the panel, since I didn't really know what else to do, and an oval receptacle extruded itself from the wall.

Okay, mystery solved. I took care of business, then went to the basin and splashed some cool water on my face. As I shut off the water, a drawer in the cabinet below opened silently, revealing neatly folded rectangles of fluffy pale blue cloths that must have been the alien equivalent of towels. I used one to pat my face dry, doing my best not to complete the ruin of my makeup that had begun with my roll in the sheets with Raphael.

In that moment, the reality of what I'd done seemed to finally hit home. I'd gotten my annual contraceptive shot a few days before my last birthday, so I knew I didn't need to worry about any of those sorts of complications arising from my intimacy with Raphael.

No, my current shaken state was due to something entirely different. Whatever else happened, my world would never be the same again.

I held on to the edge of the counter and stared into the mirror of polished metal, or whatever it was. My mascara had blurred a little, and my long pale hair, which I'd set in careful waves that morning, was a mess, but otherwise, I didn't think I looked all that different. Certainly not like someone who'd just had mind-blowing sex with her destined soul mate, but maybe that was all for the best. I'd have to go home sometime, and better to do that without the telltales written all over my face.

I returned to the bedroom. The lighting seemed a little brighter now, bright enough that I was able to see my panties lying on the smooth, gleaming floor. Blood rushed to my cheeks as I bent to pick them up, all too aware of Raphael's eyes on me as I did so.

Slipping back under the covers next to him seemed the safest thing to do. All right, not safe, exactly—I had a feeling as to what might happen between us in the next few minutes—but wandering around naked in front of him was a little too brazen for me. By that point, he had to know what I looked like, more or less, but still....

His arms went around me, and he pulled me toward him. I could tell right away that he hadn't bothered to put his own underwear back on. "Better?" he asked.

"Yes," I replied, snuggling up to his shoulder. "This definitely doesn't feel like a spaceship...more like a resort or spa or something."

"I haven't been in one of your resorts. But since we do spend a good deal of time traveling between the stars, we might as well be comfortable while doing it."

His comment sounded logical enough to me. In a way, it was sort of a relief to realize that a civilization with the technological savvy to build a ship like this still believed in providing some creature comforts along the way, that it didn't have to be all nuts and bolts and function over form.

"Do many of you do that?" I asked. "Travel between the stars, I mean."

"Those who are called to it. There are some who only visit a few systems and then return home, happy to be in familiar surroundings, while others would prefer to spend their entire lives on worlds not their own. Neither path is better than the other. It's important for everyone to find their own way."

"So you always wanted to go out into the universe?"

Something in his expression darkened then. "Not exactly. More that such a life chose me, rather than the other way around. And truly, once I realized that the universe intended me to spend this existence alone, it seemed better for me to do my work far away from the life I knew. It can be…difficult…to see everyone else happy around you, and realize you will never be able to experience that kind of happiness for yourself."

My heart ached for him after that revelation, even though everything appeared to have turned out all right after all. He certainly wasn't alone now.

"I'm sorry," I murmured.

"Don't be." He shifted on the bed so he could look me full in the face. "For now I know the universe was only making sure that I could be with you at the right time."

"You have a lot of faith in the universe."

"I've seen the way it works. Your own people might call it fate, or God. We don't think in such terms, but we live long enough to see the way the pattern grows, its harmony and power, even if these things aren't always apparent at first glance."

"What about the Reptilians?" I asked. "They don't seem too interested in peace and harmony, as far as I can tell."

"No." He was silent for a moment—so long, in fact, that I began to wonder if he intended to say anything else. When he spoke again, his voice sounded heavy, worried. It definitely wasn't the tone of a man who'd just been relieved of several thousand years' worth of biological backpressure. "They aren't interested in the natural order of things, and think us weak for letting the universe speak to us, rather than exerting our will upon it."

"I'm surprised you're not at war all the time."

Raphael's mouth tightened upon hearing that remark. "War profits no one, and is a senseless waste of lives and energy. War is the refuge of those who refuse to negotiate." He paused then, his hand reaching out to take mine. Although he sounded grim enough, I couldn't help experiencing a thrill at his touch, my body telling me that it would be more than happy to leave this talk behind so we could attend to more important matters.

But I also had a feeling that Raphael wanted to talk these things through, so I didn't interrupt him. The afterglow would last long enough. I said, "If they're that militant, I'm surprised they didn't bring the fight to you, whether you wanted it or not. I still can't quite understand how you allow them in your Assembly."

He touched my hair, a long, pale strand falling between his fingers. "You have a saying—'keep your friends close, but your enemies closer.' And while the Reptilians do seem to be a focus for everything that is dark in the universe, they are far outnumbered by those who do not believe as they do. My people

—*your* people," he added, smiling a little now, "are only one race in the greater galaxy. Some are very like us, some are not, but what we have in common is the belief that we do not have the right to impose our will on others. I have no doubt that there are some who would say our hands-off policy does some damage, for we don't interfere in what the Reptilians do in their sector, on the worlds they control, and so can't help but allow harm to come to those who live on those worlds."

"You interfered here," I pointed out.

"Yes, but only after we came to the conclusion that staying away would do far more harm than good." Although the temperature in the room seemed comfortable enough to me, even with only a sheet pulled up to cover my bare torso, I thought I saw the faintest of shivers move over him. "Your people are at a crossroads now. You have made a great deal of progress since the last time I was here, are so very close to reaching the point where you are ready to become citizens of the galaxy. But that cannot happen if the Reptilians interfere and do whatever they can to stir up fear and discord among the people of Earth."

Hearing that revelation, I wanted to shiver, too. The Mars mission had been the culmination of years and years of research, endless finagling behind the scenes, and more setbacks than a regular civilian like me knew anything about. But it was also the first time the world's powers had worked together on something that was greater than any single one of them. Yes, the United States and China and Russia had contributed the most to the effort, along with several private space agencies, but the commander was Spanish, and Marta Levin, the geologist, German or Austrian. I couldn't remember for sure.

Anyway, I had no doubt that the Reptilians would have enjoyed throwing a spanner into the works to see what kind of fallout would result. "So did they plan the whole thing?"

"No," Raphael said at once. "It was an unfortunate coincidence that the expedition landed so close to the place where they'd set up their base. Or perhaps not a huge coincidence, since the terrain there allows for a safe landing site, as well as enough level ground to make building a large-scale compound relatively easy."

"If it was that big, you'd think our instruments would have picked it up."

"And do you think our adversaries don't have their own ways of concealing their presence? Yes, the Reptilians are not quite as advanced in some things as our own people, but they certainly possess the technology to ensure that no one on Earth would have any way of detecting their activities on Mars." He stopped there, then reached out to me with one arm. Grateful for the chance to get close to him again, I scooted over so he could pull the covers over us both. Once we were snuggled against each other, he continued, "No, I fear that was a crime of opportunity, but an opportunity they were all too willing to exploit. They could have their human specimens and also incite an incident that would be sure to cause tension among the very nations that had worked together to make the mission happen in the first place."

I wanted to say that sounded like a real dick move, but something about being with Raphael made me want to curb those sorts of remarks. A civilizing influence, so to speak. "And so you were sent to enlist our help, because in this case, *not* interfering would have been a lot worse than the alternative."

"Precisely."

The weight of his arm around me made me feel safe, but right then, I wondered how safe anyone could be when a race like the Reptilians could go around doing more or less exactly what they wanted. No, that wasn't exactly true. I was able to read between the lines and tell that the Pleiadians stepped in from time to time. It wasn't exactly the Wild West in our galaxy. Even so, I hated to think that the Reptilians were out there, plotting, trying to come up with a way to create as much discord as possible. And if they could get their clawed hands on Sedona's energy fields as a nice side bonus....

I decided I really didn't want to think about that right now. Raphael had already assured me that they now knew they'd been put on notice and wouldn't try anything again. Not in the near future, anyway. I had no doubt that they'd be back to their regular tricks after they thought they had everyone fooled.

"What about us?"

In the room's dim lighting, Raphael's eyes looked nearly black, although I knew they were really a warm chocolate brown. When he spoke, he sounded almost amused. "Are you asking if I think the Reptilians are going to interfere in our relationship?"

"No, of course not," I replied, a little annoyed. But only a very little. It was hard to get too irritated with someone who held you like that, whose every touch seemed to be another reinforcement of how much he cared about you. "What I meant was…this isn't going to be a problem for your superiors, is it? I mean, my father ended up exiled—"

At once, Raphael pulled me even closer. The sheet slipped, and the hard muscles of his chest touched my breasts. I gasped, and he kissed me, mouths coming together so we could explore one another all over again. An endless moment spun me around as I grew dizzy with his nearness, his taste, the enticing scent of his skin.

But then he let go and said, "My love, your father was not exiled because of his relationship with your mother. Our people consider the soul bond to be a sacred thing, and, once it is established, no one would ever attempt to separate the two people involved. This is why your father did not fight very hard when it became clear to him that you and I had also formed such a bond. No, he was exiled because he was strictly forbidden to do anything except teach your mother how to use the powers that had lain dormant within her, and yet he ignored those orders and came to her aid during the night of the solstice when the Reptilians had planned their attack. In hindsight, we all realized that it was probably better for him to have done so, but the judgment to exile him had already been handed down."

"Is that another reason why this time it was okay to interfere?" I asked. "Because your superiors have realized they aren't quite as infallible as they thought they were?"

"I won't presume to guess at their thought processes. But...perhaps."

It sure sounded that way to me. However, I could tell Raphael really didn't want to delve into that subject, and I decided to let it go. The person who should really be angry with them for making that kind of flawed decision was my father. Not that he talked about it much. Every once in a while, though, I would catch him standing outside and staring up at the night sky, an unreadable expression on his face. He loved living on Earth, loved my mother and me even more, and yet I could still tell he wished things might have turned out differently, that he could have shared his world with us, rather than be trapped here forever in ours. And since he'd seemed resigned to his fate, and certainly happy enough with our life in Sedona, it didn't appear to me that he held any kind of grudge, especially not after so many years.

My mother was a different matter. I knew she was still angry over the way he'd been treated. But again, that wasn't her fight. And I couldn't say that I was too disappointed over growing up on Earth, surrounded by my family and friends, rather than off on some world I'd never even heard of.

"Does my father have any family?" I asked abruptly. "He would never talk about it, but—"

For some reason, Raphael looked almost sad. "Some distant relations, yes. No siblings—we most often have only one child. Occasionally two, but never any more than that."

I supposed that helped to explain why my parents had been content to stop after I was born. Then again, the controlled chaos of my Aunt Kara's household could have had something to with it as well. I loved my cousins, but before Grace moved out and all four of Kara's children were under one roof, it had seemed kind of overwhelming to an only child like me.

"His parents?" I almost hated to ask the question, but I wanted to know. Yes, I had Gabriel, my mother's father, but my father never talked about his own parents. When I was younger, I'd tried to ask my mother what she knew, but she'd always shut me down. Now I wondered if she'd done so because she didn't know anything, either.

Raphael's arms tightened around me. "They were scientists. Their last expedition was to a world at the edge of our territory. It should have been safe."

"But...."

"But the Reptilians disputed our people's claim, said the world in question should have been under their control. They slaughtered the research team."

The breath tightened in my throat. No wonder my father had never spoken of his parents. "And there weren't any reprisals?"

"The matter was brought up in the Assembly. The Reptilians were found to be guilty, and were compelled to make reparations. Unfortunately, those reparations could not bring back the dead." Raphael's lips touched the top of my head, gently, as if seeking to give me what reassurance he could. When he spoke, I could feel his warm breath against my hair. "So you see now why your father asked to be assigned to your world, to assume the role of what the people there refer to as a Man in Black. He could not retaliate openly, but he could work to make sure he was able to thwart his enemies in more subtle ways."

Unfortunately, I could see it all too well. And I thought that Raphael's latest revelation also helped explain why my father had been willing to risk everything to come to my mother's aid. Yes, of course he loved her—but beneath that lay a darker motivation.

Revenge.

So much for my hope that I might be reunited with more family members if I managed to venture out into the greater galaxy. At first, leaving the bounds of Earth for interstellar adventure had sounded like an exciting prospect, but now I wasn't quite so sure. Even with as powerful as the Pleiadians seemed to be, I got the impression that they couldn't control everything. I didn't know if I was willing to take the risk.

"I know these things must be difficult to hear," Raphael went on. "But you needed to know the truth."

He was right. I knew my father had his reasons for keeping these things to himself, but they were his reasons, not mine. Now I had a better idea of what we were up against. I'd known the Reptilians were evil, but until this very moment, until the revelation that they'd murdered my grandparents, I hadn't realized how evil they truly were. Because of them, my father's family had been shattered. No wonder he'd wanted to make sure his new family was sheltered and safe in Sedona. It must have taken a great deal of courage for him to allow me to come along on the Mars rescue mission, knowing the type of adversary we faced.

"Thank you," I said quietly.

Raphael's fingers played with my loose hair. With his touch came another of those almost overwhelming waves of desire, my need for him surging through every vein. It took less effort than I'd thought to push aside everything he'd just disclosed and allow myself to fall under his spell once again. Our lips met, and I ran my hands down his body, feeling how ready he was for me. Just as I was for him—his fingers sank into me, stroking gently but insistently.

I moaned, my own fingers closing around him, and he gasped. Something about that shocked inhalation only spurred me on, and in the next instant I was pushing him down against the bedclothes so I could lower myself onto him, feeling him penetrate even deeper than the first time we'd made love.

His hands closed on my breasts, stroking me, and I had to bite my lip to keep myself from crying out at his touch. Maybe he wouldn't have cared, but this was all still very new to him, and I didn't want to intimidate him.

Not that he probably would have minded. His eyes were wide, staring up into mine, and the love and desire I saw there was enough to push me over the edge. I did moan then, the sounds tearing themselves from my throat as his hands dropped to mine and held on, squeezing tightly as he convulsed with his own climax.

It wasn't until his harsh breathing had calmed somewhat that I carefully slid off him, then pressed my lips to his cheek. "You know, you're picking up this whole intimacy thing pretty well," I murmured.

"I have a good instructor."

He looked so beautiful and perfect, eyes half-lidded, forehead lightly sheened with perspiration. I wanted to stare at him forever...but I also realized that hours and hours must have passed since I came here, and I'd promised my parents that I wouldn't be out too late. It did seem silly to have to run home like a teenager who didn't want to violate her curfew. We'd have to come up with some sort of solution to my strange not-quite-independent state, because I hated feeling like I should be guilty because of the time I'd spent with Raphael. In the meantime, though, I thought it was probably best to be circumspect. Yes, my parents had backed off a little, apparently trying to resign themselves to the inevitable, but I didn't see the point in making things any harder than they already were.

So I told him that I probably needed to get home, and although a look of disappointment passed over his face, he didn't protest, only said, "Yes, it would be best to avoid an incident."

My clothes, which he'd made so neatly disappear at the beginning of our first round of lovemaking, turned out to be hanging in the wardrobe on one side of the room. I got into them in silence while he did the same. A flicker of surprise went through me as I realized he was getting back into the suit he'd worn earlier, rather than the white robes that I'd thought were his usual garb.

"Going all corporate on me?" I teased, but he didn't smile, and instead looked thoughtful.

"No. These garments are surprisingly comfortable. So I thought it was logical enough to put them back on."

I went over to him and placed a kiss on his cheek

as he was about to finish buttoning up his shirt. "Well, I don't know about logical, but I do think you look sexy."

His eyebrow went up. "That was not my intention."

"I know. That's the whole point. Nothing sexier than a guy who doesn't think he's sexy."

He still appeared more puzzled than anything else, but he didn't seem inclined to argue with me. I was just slipping my boots back on when a soft chime sounded in the chamber.

"Expecting company?" I asked.

"No, the chime was a notification that I have a new communiqué from my superiors."

I wasn't sure I liked the sound of that. This was the first time he'd mentioned any kind of communication with the people running the show, although I assumed he must send reports back at regular intervals. I just hoped those reports didn't include anything about me, other than my involvement with the Mars rescue mission.

But I only replied with a noncommittal "oh." He went over to the wall and laid his hand against it, giving me a chance to admire his long, strong fingers and the elegant shapes they made against the dark surface. In the next moment, a screen appeared there, almost looking as if it was somehow floating inside the deep blue burnished metal.

And what appeared there—Raphael had said it was a communiqué, but the flowing shapes and colors didn't look like any alphabet I'd ever seen. I thought then of the arch-shaped lights in the ship's corridors, with their flowing patterns of color. When I'd first seen them, I'd thought they were only some kind of decoration, but now I wondered if those lights were now some type of sign or other form of communication.

As his eyes scanned over the ever-changing hues and forms on the screen in front of him, Raphael's expression gradually grew more and more grim. Even though I had no idea what he was reading, I couldn't ignore the anxiety that began ratcheting up inside me. Yes, he'd said that his superiors wouldn't interfere with our growing relationship, but what if he'd only been blowing the proverbial sunshine up my skirt?

"What is it?" I asked. Better to know the worst, although having to face bad news after an evening of lovemaking felt like stepping out into an icy rain shower after enjoying a warm bath.

He came over and took my hands in both of his, surrounding them with the soothing heat of his flesh. "Apparently, a claim has been filed against you for killing one of the Reptilians on the Mars base."

"I—*what?*" The words were English, but they didn't seem to be making any sense. "I *killed* someone?" Heart beginning to pound, I tried to remember exactly what had happened when we broke into the bio-lab at the Reptilians' base. All right, I had blasted a bunch of them, but I thought I'd seen them moving afterward. As far as I could tell, they'd only been knocked out cold.

Not dead.

"According to this, yes." His fingers tightened on mine, and he said quietly, "You can't blame yourself. They would have killed Logan, and possibly me as well, if you hadn't stopped them the way you did."

Maybe feeling that way made me a terrible person, but right then, I couldn't get too choked up about accidentally whacking a Reptilian. Nice people they were not. I was more worried about this so-called "claim."

"Can they do that?" I asked. "I mean, I thought your people had as little as possible to do with the Reptilians."

"That is true, but sometimes they are impossible to ignore. Now, though, because they've seen a way to make things complicated for us, they've filed a claim."

"So what does that mean? Is it like suing someone?"

Raphael appeared to consider my question for a moment, then inclined his head slightly. "I would suppose that is the closest analogue to the laws of your world. Because this claim has been filed against you, you must appear in person to contest it."

Probably because I didn't really want to accept the implications behind them, those words took a few seconds to fully sink into my brain. "What…you mean I have to go and defend myself to the Assembly?"

He let go of my hands, then reached over to push a lock of hair away from my face. Something in the tenderness of that gesture made sharp tears spring to my eyes. He couldn't stop this thing, but he also wanted me to know that he would be with me the entire time.

"You'll be assigned counsel to defend you," he said. "But yes, you will have to go before the representatives of the Assembled Worlds and give them your side of the story."

Although it had tasted wonderful at the time, all the strange food I'd eaten earlier that evening began to churn in my stomach. "There's no way to get out of it?" I asked, desperation clear in my voice. "After all, Earth isn't even a member of these Assembled Worlds. How can they have any jurisdiction?"

An approving light filled his dark eyes, but his tone was heavy enough as he replied, "I fear that doesn't matter. Your father is a citizen of the Assembled Worlds, despite his exile, as is your grandfather. As the members of the Assembly see it, your heritage is far more Pleiadian than it is of Earth, and therefore you are subject to their laws."

Even though up until a few minutes earlier, I hadn't even known they existed.

"So when does this all happen?" Even though I was more a fan of getting unpleasant things over with as quickly as possible, I secretly hoped the evil day would be far off in the future. After all, even in an out-of-the-way place like Yavapai County, Arizona, you usually had to wait months to get a court date. I couldn't begin to imagine how impacted the justice system of these Assembled Worlds—however many of them there actually were —must be.

"In thirty-six of your hours," Raphael said.

Oh, shit.

CHAPTER ELEVEN

THIRTY-SIX HOURS WAS NOT A LOT OF TIME WHEN IT came to covering vast interstellar distances, even in a ship as amazing as Raphael's. We had to leave right away.

"But I don't have anything with me!" I protested. "No changes of clothes, no toothpaste...no deodorant, for God's sake!"

"I can provide all of that," he said, clearly not all that worried by my lack of hair serum to fight the frizzies. "It will be fine. I will be with you the entire time."

Thwarted on that front, I tried another angle of protest. "And what am I supposed to tell my parents?" Jesus, talk about flipping out. Having them discover that I'd been intimate with Raphael was a drop in the bucket compared to having to inform them that I was about to travel halfway across the galaxy to face some sort of tribunal.

"The truth, of course." He extended a hand, and suddenly my purse was dangling from his fingers, even though I distinctly recalled leaving it in the dining room. "Although I would suggest that sending a text might be less complicated than an actual phone call."

Not bothering to ask how he'd managed to conjure my purse from one side of his ship to the other, I took my bag from him and dug out my phone. "Um, I'm pretty sure that AT&T doesn't exactly reach this far."

"No need to worry about that. I'll make sure the message gets to them."

Of course he would. I wanted to ask if there was anything he couldn't manage; so far it seemed as if the answer was no. However, I wholeheartedly agreed with his assessment that it would be better to send a text. Yes, avoiding an actual conversation was the coward's way out, but I was okay with being a coward right then if it meant not having to argue with my parents about the situation.

So I unlocked my phone, ignored the blinking "No Service" message in the upper right-hand corner of the display, and started typing on the screen. Normally, I dictated all my texts so the process wasn't so time-consuming, but I wasn't sure I really wanted to have Raphael overhear what I had to say. Maybe I was being unnecessarily cautious. After all, there was a very good chance he'd still be able to read the message as he helped it zoom across thousands of miles of low-orbit space, all of which were woefully lacking in any cellular towers, the last time I checked.

Short and sweet would probably work best here. My fingers moved over the screen as I desperately attempted to come up with a message that would give my parents the gist of what was going on without turning them into nervous wrecks. Somehow, I had the feeling I'd fail in that objective no matter what I said.

Mom, Dad, I've run into a teeny speed bump. I guess when I zapped those Reptilians at their base, I didn't know my own strength, and one of them didn't make it. Now the Assembly needs me to give my version of what happened, since the Reptilians aren't happy. Raphael is going to take me and make sure everything goes smoothly. But obviously I won't be home tonight. I guess with travel times added in, this will probably take a few days. Tell Aunt Kara she'll need to get someone to cover for me at the UFO Depot. I'll contact you again when I can. ~Love, Callista.

Oh, yeah, that was going to go over real well.

Right then, I was just glad that I'd asked for some time off at the wine-tasting room until after New Year's. The tasting room's owners weren't expecting me back for a week. I hoped this would all be resolved by then, one way or another.

As for my parents, well, I hadn't wanted to lie to them, and they needed to know what was going on. I supposed my father could fill in a lot of the blanks for my mother, since he had to be more or less familiar with the procedure involved. As to the penalties....

"So what happens if they find me guilty?" I asked as I handed the phone over to Raphael. He didn't even look down at the screen, only placed his hand over it, as if he could transmit my message that way. For all I knew, that was exactly what he had planned.

"I doubt they will." His voice was so calm, he sounded as if he was discussing the weather forecast.

That wasn't what I'd asked, though. "But if they do?"

"I will be there to provide an eyewitness account. It was clearly an act of self-defense, or at least defense of others in your party. While we abhor violence—which is why the mindset of the Reptilians is especially foreign to us—we do recognize that sometimes it is necessary to defend oneself. You truly have nothing to worry about."

His words should have reassured me. But I could still feel my stomach twisting itself into a nervous knot, and I wasn't sure I liked the way Raphael had responded. It was probably just my nerves talking, but right then he'd sounded a lot more like Otto, the overly clinical asshole, than Raphael, the impassioned lover, the man who swore I was the match of his soul. And he still hadn't answered my question.

Something of my worry must have shown in my face, because he set the phone down on the table next to us, then pulled me into his arms. He stroked my hair. His next words sounded in my mind, using the mental communication that those who were soul-bonded could share. *My love, you will be fine. I promise you this. I was there. And the Assembly trusts my judgment.*

All of a sudden, the nervous knot in my midsection loosened, and I let myself fall under the spell of his touch, his voice. I had to trust him. After all, he knew this Assembly, knew what they would expect to hear. I couldn't let myself fall into despair.

If I did, the Reptilians would win.

True to his word, Raphael did have everything I needed. All the toiletries a girl could want, even the hair serum, and, more importantly, a change of clothes. Well, as many changes as I might require, since it seemed that the ship could manufacture pretty much anything I asked for, although Raphael did gently suggest that I adopt Pleiadian styles for my court appearance.

I wouldn't argue with his advice, since I doubted that jeans, a sweater, and a leather jacket comprised the best ensemble to appear before that august assembly. Much better to show up wearing a dress just as flowy as Raphael's robes, but which hugged my body exactly where it should. The fabric didn't feel exactly like cotton or silk or anything else, but it was the same cloudy blue-gray as my eyes, shot through with silver threads, and I felt like a princess in it.

Somehow, though, I managed to resist the urge to twirl. "You're sure it's not too much?"

The heat in Raphael's eyes told me that he didn't think it was over the top. "No, it's lovely, as are you. The Assembly will appreciate that you have chosen to appear before them in a manner that reflects your heritage, even if you were raised on Earth."

Yes, there might be that one-quarter of my blood which was Swenson, purely terrestrial, but far more of me had its origins in the system we traveled to now, and where I would have to face judgment. I'd tried my best to ignore that fact for most of my life, since I'd never thought I would have anything other than an earthly existence, but I needed to remember now that I was nearly as much a citizen of the galaxy as any of the people I'd be facing.

And Raphael loved me. That mattered more than any of the rest of it.

I'd slept in his arms the night before as the ship brought us closer and closer to our destination. No reply from my parents—not that I'd been expecting one. I was sure Raphael wouldn't allow a message from them to get through, for the simple reason that I needed to focus on presenting my arguments to the Assembly instead of wasting my energy on back-and-forth debates with my parents in text format.

Being around Raphael did help to calm me.

Knowing he was there and had no intention of letting me face this ordeal alone quelled the panic in the back of my mind. Well, mostly. After all, even having to show up in court to argue a traffic ticket could be stressful, and this situation was several orders of magnitude beyond that. However, getting my wardrobe sorted out helped to distract me, as did the long shower I took. Something about letting the water flow over me, just this side of too hot, so it felt like a massage, kept me from being entirely too wretched. Raphael had explained that the ship's synthesizing units could create as much water as we needed, so I didn't have to worry about rationing it.

I supposed I hadn't been too far off the mark when I compared his ship to a resort and spa. All I needed was someone to do my nails and hand me a glass of nicely chilled white wine, and I should be set. With all its amenities, however, those two luxuries were something the ship didn't have.

Traveling this way was strange, though. I supposed I'd been expecting the streaky star lines of hyperspace the way they were depicted in the Star Wars movies, or maybe odd, psychedelic colors and shapes as the drive dropped us out of realspace altogether. What I saw outside the view-screens, however, was even stranger than that. The stars looked normal, but they kept shifting their positions almost every second, as if the ship was performing thousands of micro-jumps as it brought us closer and closer to the star cluster Raphael's people called home. I couldn't feel any movement—the ship was as solid and silent as a house—but I knew we must be moving at unimaginable speeds to be able to reach a destination more than four hundred light-years away in less than twenty-four hours.

As far as I was concerned, I would have been happier if the journey had taken just a little while longer. Yes, I was more a "get it over with" kind of person, but even I had my limits.

"What's it like?" I asked as I fussed with my hair one last time. Raphael had informed me that we would be reaching orbit in approximately twenty minutes, which had sent me into a frenzy of last-minute primping. He'd looked on, his expression half amused and half befuddled, although he hadn't told me to step away from the mirror. We might not have been together for very long, but already he seemed to realize that this kind of fussing was my coping mechanism for too much stress.

He looked much as he had the first time I'd ever laid eyes on him, his carefully tailored suit replaced by those flowing white robes with their strange opalescent cast. The ensemble did make him look almost impossibly handsome and otherworldly, but I thought I liked the suit better. Those robes hide way too much of the shape of his body. "The Assembly?" he responded.

"Well, that, but also…your world. Just everything."

"I fear that 'just everything' is a bit too much to

pack into a single conversation. You'll see for your-self soon enough."

I supposed I would, but a little bit of mental preparation never hurt anyone. Holding back a sigh, I set down the brush I was holding and went out into the bedroom. The bed was now pristine and smooth, revealing no sign of the activities it had hosted the night before, although I hadn't seen Raphael make it. More Pleiadian magic, I supposed.

Right then, I did feel just the slightest tremor of the ship beneath my feet. I sent a questioning glance toward Raphael, and he nodded. "We're there. Come, you should see it from this vantage point before we go down."

He held out his hand, and I took it. Our garments made soft, whispery sounds against the polished floor as he led me to the lounge, whose view-screens were even larger than those on the bridge. And what a view they revealed.

I was certainly no astronomer, but even I knew that the Pleiades were part of a star cluster, its indi-vidual suns all bright enough that they were visible to the naked eye on Earth. Now the ship orbited a planet that circled one of those suns, the light pouring over its surface hot and intensely blue-white, very different from the warm yellow radiation of my own solar system's sun.

And the planet below—it was blue in tinge as well, obviously as blessed with oceans as the Earth, although I could make out the shapes of unfamiliar continents as well. It had at least three small moons that I could see, but they weren't the only objects revolving around the unfamiliar world. The space above it also glittered with constructs that were clearly manmade, delicate spires and discs and elongated rectangles.

"Are those all space stations?" I asked.

"Yes. We have many visitors here, some of whom are not adapted to the conditions on the planet's surface. Those stations were put there for their use."

I thought about that explanation for a few seconds. "Aliens, you mean."

He smiled, but then he shook his head. "We would prefer not to use that term, for are we not all alien to one another? But yes, as I told you, the Assembled Worlds encompass many races, some of whom are like us, and some of whom…are not."

"Like the Reptilians."

"Actually, the Reptilians are not so very different from those of us who belong to the human-appearing races. At least they are humanoid—two arms, two legs, two eyes, and so forth."

My unease only increased after that revelation. Yes, Raphael had told me there would be more than just the Pleiadians in attendance at my hearing, but for some reason, I'd thought the other aliens would still be humanoid. If he was counting the Reptilians as more like us humans than not…. I swallowed. This could be interesting. I had to pray that I wouldn't act too startled by the appearance of these new aliens. The last thing I wanted was to, well, alienate anyone.

Ready, my love?

I managed not to startle at the sound of Raphael's voice in my head. We'd shared only a little of that nonvocal communication the night before, just so I could begin to get used to it, but I was far from adept. Still, I understood why he was speaking to me in such a way now. It would be useful for the two of us to communicate with each other without anyone else being able to hear us.

Truthfully, I wasn't ready at all, but I knew I couldn't delay. That would only make me look guilty, as if I was trying to avoid punishment rather than being eager to have a chance to clear the air.

Ready, I told him. I hesitated, then asked, *How in the world am I going to understand anything of what's going on? It's not like they're going to be speaking English, right?*

No, they will be speaking the common language the worlds of the Assembly use to communicate with one another. But there's no need to worry. As long as you keep hold of my hand, you'll be able to hear and understand everything just as I understand it. We do have translators, but they're not as accurate as this method.

His reply relieved me somewhat. Not only that I wouldn't be standing around and listening to a babel of languages I couldn't comprehend, but also that I'd be able to hold his hand throughout the entire ordeal.

All of a sudden, the upcoming trial didn't seem quite as frightening.

Of course, the thought of heading down to an alien planet was scary enough all on its own. Clearly, I didn't need to worry about the atmosphere or the gravity or any of those things, just because my ancestors had come from this world, but there would still be plenty to see and absorb.

And plenty of chances to make yourself look like an idiot, I thought. *So it's probably best if you keep your mouth shut as much as possible.*

Raphael came to me and took my hand in his. He must have felt my tension right through my fingertips, because he said gently, "It will be fine." And then he reached down to touch the jewel hanging from the belt at his hip, and the ship disappeared around us.

CHAPTER TWELVE

BY THAT POINT, I WAS ALMOST USED TO THE FLASH OF
white light and the abrupt change in scenery that it
heralded. What I couldn't have possibly been
prepared for was the world we emerged in this time.

We stood in the open air, in a large outdoor space
with two stately rows of white columns that marched
their way toward a tall building topped by multiple
domes, all done in some sort of metallic finish that
echoed the same pale, blue-white hue of the sunlight
streaming around us. On either side of the columns
were narrow ribbons of still, blue-green water,
framing a walkway that led directly to the tall doors
in the front of the building. The air was soft against
my skin, not cool, not warm, but some ideal balance
that probably would have put it around seventy-two
degrees Fahrenheit. And it smelled good, too, of
something clean and aromatic. Not flowers; the scent

reminded me more of the junipers back in Sedona, and of the spicy scent they would give off when the sun warmed them.

All around us were—well, people who looked like regular humans, albeit humans who seemed to be in the peak of physical perfection. And those whose appearance was close enough to human, except with coloring you'd never see appear naturally—dark blue hair, or hair red as a fire engine, someone else whose skin was a gorgeous shimmering copper color. But then there were those who could still be classified as humanoid but didn't look anything like humans, as if their ancestors might have been cats, or bears, or mammals I couldn't even identify, while I caught glimpses of others who appeared to only be a shimmer in the air, or a glowing blob of protoplasm that floated a few feet off the ground.

I tried not to stare. In a way, I didn't really want to, because my first glance at these surroundings hadn't revealed any Reptilians in the immediate vicinity, and that was just fine by me.

This way.

Raphael guided me toward the building with all the gleaming domes and over to its tall doors, three stories high, made of the same shimmering pale blue metal as the building's domes. No one seemed to pay us any particular attention, and I uttered a silent thank-you to the universe for the apparent indifference of the people around us. This was difficult enough without having to walk a gauntlet of staring onlookers all the way up to the front doors of that imposing building.

Is this the Assembly? I asked Raphael.

It is the place they use, he replied. *The actual Assembly is the group of people who oversee our corner of the galaxy.*

I supposed that made sense. *How many of them are there?*

Five hundred.

Five hundred? I repeated, aghast. For some reason, I'd been expecting something like a Supreme Court setup, with a manageable number of around nine or ten people at the most. This was going to be like stating my case in front of the United Nations.

I swallowed, and Raphael brushed his thumb over the back of my hand. *It will be all right. Most of them will only listen. The Secretary will ask most of the questions.*

Even more like the United Nations. I couldn't exactly be relieved, not when I was expected to speak my piece in front of such a throng, but I did feel slightly better that I wouldn't have to be fielding questions from hundreds of people, none of whom I would have been able to understand on my own. I had to remember to hold on to Raphael's hand, no matter what happened. Thank God he was there with me. I couldn't imagine having to go through this on my own.

We entered the building. I couldn't see any

guards, although I did have a feeling of being watched. No doubt they had some kind of highly sophisticated surveillance system in place here, one that tracked our every move.

The corridor we walked through was also three stories tall to match the doors, filled with light and air, the stone or whatever the building was constructed from carved into gentle fluted patterns that crossed overhead, rather like the branches of a tree. It was a beautiful place, but I couldn't allow myself to enjoy it.

The same bewildering variety of humanoids and aliens filled the corridor. One or two of them seemed to recognize Raphael, and inclined their heads or waved a tentacle, but they didn't speak, and he remained silent as well. Maybe they could tell we were here on official business.

At the far end of the hallway was another set of doors, although these ones were only about fifteen feet high. They swung open as we approached, although no one seemed to be operating them. I thought then of the fluid metal "doors" on Raphael's ship, and how they came and went as they were needed. A different kind of technology seemed to be at work here, because the architecture, while unfamiliar, was still not that far off from something I might have seen back on Earth. Maybe it was far, far older than the ship that had brought us to the Pleiades cluster.

Raphael and I went through the doors, our fingers

still twined tightly around one another. This space was cavernous—and cacophonous, because it sounded as if all the beings assembled there were talking all at once. Even with Raphael supposedly helping me understand what was being said, I couldn't make out any of it. All of those in the Assembly were seated in ascending rows of chairs in a semicircular layout, not unlike some movie theaters I'd been in, although each of the Assemblypeople also had a small desk in front of them, presumably so they could lay out any devices they needed to take notes or possibly record the proceedings.

As Raphael and I entered, the crowd quieted. Now I could feel the impact of five hundred sets of eyes—at least half of them not anything close to human—focused directly on me, and I had to force myself to keep walking at my companion's side, rather than give in to my sudden urge to bolt back in the direction from which we'd come.

He led me to a table of pale blue stone-like material. Three chairs had been placed directly behind it. Well, that looked familiar enough. I'd seen plenty of similar setups on crime dramas…only this time, I was the accused. But Raphael couldn't be my lawyer, because he'd said I would be assigned my own counsel.

A door I hadn't noticed previously opened off to one side, and a tall female alien entered the room. She was clearly one of the humanoid but not exactly like us races—she had to be almost seven feet tall, and her hair was a shocking cobalt blue. With her high, sharp cheekbones and full mouth, though, she was also impressively beautiful.

"I am Anda Bilar," she said. "I have been assigned as your counsel. You are Callista Marie Jones, correct?"

I nodded, my mouth dry. Right then, I was just glad that Raphael had been right; as long as I held on to his hand, I seemed to be able to understand whatever was said to me.

"Do not worry," Anda told me. "I have reviewed the facts of your case. This will be no problem."

I wished I could be as calm about the situation as Anda seemed to be. But I made myself nod, praying that my expression appeared even half as serene as hers.

"As I have already assured her," Raphael said. "But I am glad that you have the same opinion."

Her long, pretty nose wrinkled. "It is more of the same. Our Reptilian friends do enjoy their petty troublemaking."

I slanted Raphael a look at that remark. Not that I'd really expected to find a lot of fans and supporters of the Reptilians here, based on what he'd already told me, but I was a little surprised to hear my counsel being quite so blunt about her apparent bias.

Raphael gave the faintest lift of his shoulders but didn't say anything, either aloud or inside my head. Just as well, probably, because in the next moment I heard a murmur go through the crowd behind me, just as another door, this one opposite the one Anda had used to enter the chamber, opened and a tall man entered.

And he did look just like a regular human. Well, a perfect human, the same as Raphael and my grandfather Gabriel and the other Pleiadians I'd seen so far. Like Gabriel, this man appeared to be older, with a faint brush of gray at his temples, but still handsome, his back perfectly straight as he went to the podium of carved and fluted stone that stood at the front of the chamber.

"Gentlebeings," he said, in a deep, rich voice. "I crave your attention."

At once, the last of the murmurs in the room died down. I didn't know if I could have heard the proverbial pin drop, but I knew I could hear my heart beating. In fact, it had started thumping so noisily in my chest that I was surprised it hadn't echoed off the back walls of the Assembly chamber.

The Secretary—at least, I assumed that was who the stately man must be, even though he hadn't identified himself—glanced over at me. His eyes were a piercing green. "Honored Callista, you may stand."

Caught off guard, I stumbled slightly as I got to my feet, since the tip of my shoe got trapped in the voluminous folds of the dress I wore. Somehow, I managed to steady myself, though, and kept an iron grip on Raphael's hand, even though he made no move to stand when I did. Apparently, only the accused wasn't allowed to sit during the proceedings.

Still, the Secretary's eyes were kind enough, and he even sent me the slightest of smiles, as if to reassure me. Or maybe he was just trying to prepare me for what was to come next.

The same door Anda had used to enter the chamber opened again, and the Reptilian delegation came through it.

Back at the Mars base, the lighting had been dim and the situation so confused and chaotic, I hadn't gotten a good look at them. Not that I'd really wanted to, anyway. Now, though, with the bright diffuse light that seemed to be filtering right through the domed roof of the Assembly chamber—even though I would have sworn it was solid metal—I could see the Reptilians all too clearly. My entire body stiffened, and the breath caught in my throat.

There were five of them. All tall; they'd give my counselor Anda a run for her money in the height department. Well, four of them were that tall, anyway. I realized the fifth member of their party looked human, or nearly so, and while he was probably close to Raphael's height, he definitely wasn't scraping near seven feet. The strange man's hair was dark, and he didn't appear to be more than a couple of years older than I was. However, a second glance told me there was definitely something off about him, since his skin had a faint greenish tint, and when the light from overhead caught his eyes, they seemed to be the same dark ruby shade as the eyes of the rest of his companions.

A hybrid? That didn't seem right to me, since Logan was a hybrid and Grace had a hybrid father, and they both appeared completely human. But I supposed it was possible that there were hybrids and then there were hybrids, and they didn't necessarily all have to look alike.

The Reptilians, on the other hand, didn't resemble anything except overgrown bipedal lizards. All right, not exactly—their faces were more humanoid than that, even with their wide lipless mouths and slits for noses. One of them was a uniform coppery brown color, like the aliens I'd seen at the Mars base, and two had scales in striped patterns of muted green and black, while the last one was far lighter in tone, almost a pale gold. He seemed to be the leader, because he swept to the middle seat in the group of chairs that had been set out for the delegation and sat down before any of his compatriots took their seats.

They all wore high-collared robes in dark shades of black and brown and gunmetal gray, even the one who looked far more human than Reptilian. His gaze slid toward me for a bare second before he took his seat, but I couldn't read anything in his features. He was as expressionless as the aliens who accompanied him.

I had to set the enigma of his identity aside for the moment, though, because the Secretary had begun to speak again. Bright green eyes fixed on me, he said,

"Honored Callista, it has been brought to our attention that your actions resulted in the death of a member of the Reptilian people. What say you?"

What the hell was I supposed to say? I glanced over at Raphael. His fingers squeezed mine, just a quick, gentle pressure.

Tell the truth. It will be fine.

All right. I did have to wonder what the point had been in assigning Anda to me as a counselor, since she didn't seem ready to offer me any real advice, only sat there and gazed serenely at the Secretary. But I had Raphael, and he was the only person I needed. Strange how I could trust him so implicitly after we'd known each other for such a short time.

I cleared my throat. "Honored Secretary, if one of the Reptilians lost his life, I am truly sorry for that. The act was not premeditated in any way. We were attempting to rescue members of an expedition who had been taken hostage by the Reptilians at their Mars base, and when one of the hostile forces there tried to retaliate, I had no choice but to defend the members of my party."

The Reptilian delegation bent their heads together and began whispering in that same sibilant, frightening language I'd first heard in the bio-lab at their base. Even though I'd continued to hold Raphael's hand, I couldn't make head or tail of what they were saying, which must have meant that he didn't speak their language, either.

Then the one I'd assumed was their leader

pushed his seat back and got to his feet. I wasn't short by any stretch of the imagination, but he still made me feel like a dwarf, even though he stood at least three yards away. When he spoke, I could understand him, although his speech still had a strange, sibilant quality, one that seemed to drill right through my eardrums and send shivers all down my back.

"This human and her party were trespassing. They had no right to be where they were. My people were well within the bounds of the law to ensure that they were neutralized before they could do any harm."

"We were only trespassing because you kidnapped our astronauts!" I shot back. Yes, the Reptilian leader scared the hell out of me, but I wasn't about to stand there and let him completely misrepresent the situation.

Raphael leaned over and whispered something to Anda. A nod, and then she was standing as well, chin held high—no doubt using her height to all our advantage. It was difficult to look at anything other than her, with her striking cobalt hair and flowing silvery-gray robes.

"The rescue mission that the honored Lir Shalan mentions was approved by the Assembly," Anda said. "Because of that, it cannot be considered tres-passing."

I was a little startled that she would admit such a thing openly in court. It couldn't do much to improve relations between the Assembly and the Reptilians, which already seemed pretty frosty to me.

The Reptilian—Lir Shalan—didn't seem too pleased by her revelation, either. "Interfering in the business of a sovereign government again?"

"Only because we had no other choice," the Secretary said. From the distinct chill in his voice and the slight narrowing of his eyes, I got the impression he wasn't overly affected by the Reptilian leader's wounded tone. "Our actions were supported by a majority of the Assembly. You know very well, honored Representative, that we do not make such decisions lightly, and only when we have no other choice. If we had wished to conceal our involvement from you, then we would have instructed our agent"—he inclined his head slightly toward Raphael—"to make sure that you could not detect his identity. At any rate, if you wish to lodge a complaint regarding that particular matter, of course you are within your legal rights to do so. For the moment, however, we will leave aside any questions of trespassing and focus solely on what occurred within the laboratory of your base some seventy-two standard units ago. Do you understand?"

It looked as if Lir Shalan understood all too well...and wasn't happy about it. His voice took on a distinct rasp as he said, "Yes, honored Secretary. In that vein, however, I would ask your agent to explain why he brought along several untrained humans on such a venture. Such foolishness almost guaranteed that there would be a mishap."

I could feel Raphael's fingers grip my hand more tightly at the word "foolishness," but he glanced at the Secretary and got a nod of affirmation before standing so he could speak.

"The honored Lir Shalan is welcome to his opinion, but I would point out that both Callista Jones and her mother possess Pleiadian blood, and so had unique gifts they could bring to assist with the rescue mission. The decision to bring them along was not made lightly."

That response earned Raphael a scowl from Lir Shalan—or at least I assumed that's what the creasing of the Reptilian's brow ridges meant. I'd never had to try deciphering an alien's facial expressions before. "I object to the term 'rescue mission.' The interlopers were being held for routine questioning, nothing more. They would have been set free in due time. Unfortunately, the Assembly's agents deemed it necessary to assault my people, injuring several and killing one."

"'Routine questioning'?" I burst out. Raphael squeezed my hand, clearly attempting to keep me from saying anything else, but I couldn't take any more of the Reptilian's lies. "If that's the case, what were the two female prisoners doing in your bio-lab, half-undressed?"

From behind me, I could hear a babble of voices break out, the members of the Assembly apparently pouncing on what I'd just said. Anda Bilar shook her head. Her features also weren't terribly easy to read, but I got the impression that she wasn't too thrilled with me right then.

"Order!" the Secretary called out. The hubbub behind me lowered to a dull roar, even as Lir Shalan shot me a venomous look, red sparks all but shooting out from his ruby-colored eyes. I noticed for the first time the vertical slits of his pupils, the complete lack of lashes or brows or any kind of hair at all.

I shivered, but at the same time, I made myself glare back at him. Too bad that I wasn't supposed to say such things in open court. I knew what I'd seen. All right, maybe the "half-undressed" part was a bit of an exaggeration. But it didn't take a great leap of the imagination to figure out why those two women's jumpsuits had been unzipped and their shoes removed.

"Do you have any evidence to back up your claim?" the Secretary asked, sounding ragged. He probably hadn't been expecting that particular bomb-shell…or had he?

"No," I admitted. "That is, Raphael was there and saw the same things I saw. But unless you can subpoena the security recordings from the Reptilian base, I'm not sure whether the evidence exists."

The Secretary's brows drew together at the word "subpoena," and I had a feeling it had come out in the original Latin, meaning there wasn't an analogue for it in the Pleiadian language, or whatever it was that we were currently speaking. I still didn't know how this all worked. To me it felt as if I was speaking English, but clearly that wasn't the case, because otherwise, no one would have been able to understand what I was saying.

"If no evidence other than hearsay exists, then we will have to leave your allegation aside for now." The Secretary didn't sound very happy to make that ruling, but I understood it, even if I didn't like it very much. "Back to the question of the wounded men and the one who lost his life. What was your intention in striking out at them?"

"'Intention'?" I repeated. God, everything had happened so fast. The one alien had shot Logan, and I didn't think. I only reacted, taking the energy coiled up within me and flinging it at our attackers. I certainly hadn't meant to kill anyone, just incapacitate them so we could get away. Speaking slowly, I said, "Self-defense only. Really. One of the Reptilians wounded Logan, and—"

"Who is this Logan?"

"A member of our party." I hesitated and glanced down at Raphael. He gave the slightest shake of his head, as if letting me know that it was better for me not to say too much on the subject of Logan's identity. "He's—um, he's engaged to marry one of my cousins. I suppose I was doubly upset because of that, and so I wasn't really thinking about what I was doing. I just wanted to get him out of there so we could take him to the medical bay on Raphael's ship."

"Understandable." The Secretary transferred his gaze from me to Lir Shalan. "So far, I have heard nothing to indicate this is anything more than a simple case of self-defense. What say you, honored Lir Shalan?"

The Reptilian representative bared his teeth, which were far more pointed than a human's. There seemed to be a lot more of them, too. I was surprised that the Secretary didn't recoil, and then I realized that baring of teeth might be the Reptilian equivalent of a smile. "Our forces were within their rights to be shooting at this so-called Logan. He is a traitor and a deserter."

Raphael's fingers clamped down on mine so hard that I couldn't refrain from wincing. However, I managed to resist the impulse to pull my hand from his, since I knew doing so would only prevent me from understanding what came next. I could understand why he'd done so. This was the first we'd heard that the Reptilians even knew who Logan was.

Then again, why wouldn't they? If he'd been able to detect their presence, it made sense that they'd be able to figure out he wasn't a regular human. Which meant...what? That they'd allowed us into the biolab as a sort of elaborate trap?

Possibly. I could see them not wanting to let a couple of female newcomers slip through their fingers.

Apparently unruffled, the Secretary asked, "On what do you base that claim?"

"We know our own. He is a failed experiment, nothing more. Indeed, I would hesitate to say that he was worthy of defending at all. Would you support the wounding and murder of sentient beings for the sake of your food synthesizer or the computer that guides a ship through otherspace? Logan is not a person, but a construct, and therefore this *human*"— again, Lir Shalan shot me a baleful, ruby-hued glare —"had no right to take a life in his defense."

On the other side of Raphael, Anda was frowning. Apparently, she hadn't seen this particular wrinkle coming. But it couldn't matter that much, could it? All we'd have to do was make the Secretary and the rest of the Assembly understand that Logan wasn't a construct at all, but a living, breathing man who was certainly worthy of defending.

I began to open my mouth say as much, but Anda cut in before I could even begin. "Honored Secretary, I would ask for a brief recess so I might discuss this matter with my defendant."

"No recess," Lir Shalan rasped. "There is nothing to discuss. This 'Logan'—a name someone must have given him, for he only had a numeric designation—is one of our hybrids. He is our property, and therefore has no rights."

Judging by the frown that creased the Secretary's otherwise fine brow, I guessed he didn't exactly agree. What was the Assembly's position on hybrids, anyway? The Reptilian leader clearly didn't think they were worthy of any special consideration, but surely a government as apparently enlightened as the Assembly might have a different position on the matter. Or was this another area where they chose not to interfere?

For some reason, I couldn't help glancing past Lir Shalan's bulky form to the strange young man who sat with the rest of the Reptilians. He also was frowning slightly, but more as if he was trying to wrestle with some complex mental puzzle than because he was upset by something. In profile, the reddish hue of his eyes was nearly undetectable, although nothing could hide the green tint to his skin. If he really was another type of hybrid, shouldn't he be perturbed by the intimation that he wasn't truly a person at all? And if that was what the Reptilians thought of their creations, what was a hybrid doing here with them in the first place?

Then the Secretary looked back over at me, and something in the depths of those green, green eyes made me go cold all over, although his fine features remained impassive. "In light of this new evidence, it seems I have no choice but to rule that excessive force was used. Because of that finding, the Reptilians are entitled to whatever reasonable reparations they might request."

Reparations? What was he talking about? Some sort of cash settlement? I didn't have a lot to give, but they were welcome to it. But what would the Reptilians want with U.S. currency anyway? It wasn't as if I was sitting on a pile of gold or other precious metals.

My thoughts swirled around one another as Raphael held on to my hand so tightly that I wasn't sure I could have pulled it away even if I'd wanted to.

Stay calm, my love, he told me.

I am, I responded. *Can't we appeal or something?*

There is no authority higher than the Secretary, I'm afraid.

While I was digesting that reply, Lir Shalan had stepped forward so he stood in front of the table where the rest of his companions were seated. For the briefest second, he glanced over at me, and something in the garnet glitter of his eyes sent a stabbing shiver of ice down my spine.

"Our request for reparations is simple," he said. "While we cannot replace the one we lost, or adequately compensate for the pain the others have suffered, we will take the one thing we believe will help to balance the scales.

"We will take the female, Callista Jones."

CHAPTER THIRTEEN

THE CHAMBER ERUPTED ONCE AGAIN. IN A PANIC, I whirled toward the Secretary, pulling my hand from Raphael's grip. All at once, the commotion around me took on an extra level of insanity, because what had formerly been at least semi-coherent exclamations and conversations became a cacophony of otherworldly squeaks and trumpets and shrill sounds I couldn't begin to describe. Even the human voices frightened me, since their words were equally incomprehensible.

Face white, Raphael grabbed for my hand again and rose to his feet. "That is impossible. Callista and I are soul-bonded."

"Are you?" The Secretary looked as if he wanted to scrub his hands through his hair and was refraining from doing so simply because it would have been very unprofessional. "Congratulations.

And I am sorry, honored Lir Shalan," he went on, directing his words to the Reptilian leader, "but the Assembly does not traffic in flesh, human, Pleiadian, or otherwise. I would have denied your request even if the honored Callista Jones had not already been bonded, but now it is doubly impossible, I'm afraid. You will have to think of another alternative."

Lir Shalan looked like he wanted to spit fire. Maybe he could; I didn't know much about Reptilian anatomy and didn't want to. "There is nothing else that we want."

"Take some time to think about it," Anda offered, brilliant aquamarine eyes guileless, and the Reptilian leader only glared back at her, a low hissing sound emanating from somewhere in the back of his throat. Caught in their crossfire, I wished that Raphael would touch the jewel he wore and energy-jump us right back up to the ship.

But of course he wouldn't—if that jewel even worked in here. For all I knew, they had devices that prevented the jewels from functioning while inside the Assembly chamber. Otherwise, you could just beam yourself right out of there whenever the going got tough.

"I think that is an excellent idea," the Secretary said. He looked over at Anda. "If you would take your defendant and her companion outside for a bit—"

Talk about your good ideas. I thought that

sounded like a great one. The more distance I could put between me and Lir Shalan, the better.

"Of course, honored Secretary," she replied, then glanced down at us. "If you would come with me—"

I wasn't about to argue. Raphael and I both followed her out of the chamber. As I went, though, I could feel the muscles in the center of my back clenching, as if the Reptilian leader was trying to bore a hole in my spine with his eyes while I was walking away.

Once we were outside, in a private little courtyard area that seemed specifically designed for people escaping the Assembly to cool their heels when necessary, I let out a relieved breath. "What do you think they're going to ask for instead of me?"

"I don't know," Anda replied. "I have never encountered a situation like this one before."

"Nor I," Raphael said. His attention seemed to be fixed on the chamber we'd just left, and his dark eyes were narrow, angry. "They asked for such a thing, when they already knew the Secretary would never allow it."

"So why did they ask?" I already felt enough out of my depth, but now I was trying to understand the motivations of the Reptilians, and that was a crazy-making prospect if I'd ever heard of one. "Just to be assholes?"

Anda's fine blue brows drew together, and I guessed that "asshole" wasn't something easily translatable into Pleiadian.

"I doubt it's that simple," Raphael said. His mouth was tight, but even so, I really wished Anda wasn't there so he could take me in his arms and hold me and kiss me and tell me everything was going to be fine. "More as if...they asked for something they knew to be impossible in order to put themselves in a place of moral superiority."

"There's a good one," I remarked, tone bitter. "Reptilians and moral superiority aren't exactly two things I generally think of in the same sentence. Or even paragraph."

"Needless to say, I believe that is their game. What they hope to gain from it, I am not sure yet." He looked up at Anda. I wondered if that felt strange to him, a man who was usually tall enough to hold his own against anyone else in the immediate vicinity. "Do you have any insights, Counselor?"

She turned her hands so the palms faced up toward the sky. I wondered if that was her race's way of shrugging. "Not at the moment. The motivations of the Reptilians are, unfortunately, often inscrutable. I doubt they mourned their lost comrade too much, but rather were glad of the opportunity he gave them to gain some leverage. But, as you said, they had to have known that the Secretary would deny their request."

I couldn't even feel too relieved by my reprieve, since it seemed obvious that the whole thing had been carefully manipulated. But why? If they really didn't want me, then what *did* they want?

An odd little musical note sounded from the bracelet Anda wore on her left wrist, and she looked down to touch the blue jewel embedded in it. "They are calling us back in."

Damn. I would have liked to stay out in the fresh air for a while longer. Big as it was, something about the Assembly chamber felt oppressive, claustrophobic, to me. Possibly it gave off that impression because of the weight of watching eyes within it.

Or maybe it was just having to be in such close proximity to the Reptilian delegation.

When we reentered the room, however, I was surprised to see that the chairs the Reptilians had occupied were empty. Anda looked startled, too; she took her position behind the table that had been designated for our use and said, "Honored Secretary? Where have the complainants gone?"

"Back to their ship," he said heavily. "They claimed they could not think of adequate reparations at the moment, and so they wished to return to their sector, since it was clear that Reptilian life was of no great concern to this Assembly. I informed them that they had up to one standard year to offer a more acceptable form of reparations, and they left."

"Then is the defendant free to go?"

"It would seem so." The Secretary didn't quite sigh, but he did give a very small shake of his head, as if at a loss. "Under more normal circumstances, honored Callista Jones, I would ask that you remain in this sector, since your home world is not part of the Assembly. However, because you are soul-bonded to Raphael, you may return to your own part of the galaxy—if he provides surety that you will return here if and when you are summoned again."

"I do provide that surety," Raphael said at once. His voice rang out strong and firm, and I felt a little better, hearing him promise that he would be there to bring me back if necessary. I'd been dreading the possibility of having to remain on this world—beautiful as it might be—until the Reptilians figured out what they did want from me.

"You may go, then." The Secretary's gaze flickered over to Anda. When he spoke again, his tone was dry. "You may want to advise them on the necessity of a retainer."

"Of course, honored Secretary." Smiling slightly as she looked down at Raphael and me, she added, "Please follow me."

Once again, she led us from the chamber, only this time out the doors that led into the building's main hallway, and then on until we'd emerged in the open air of the colonnade. I drew in a deep breath of that air, letting it fill my lungs. That felt better.

Raphael glanced around, but none of the people who came and went down the walkway seemed to be paying us any attention. When he spoke, though, he seemed to be making an effort to keep his voice low. "What do you think are the chances of our having to return here?"

Another of those gestures with Anda's palms

turned skyward. "I wish I could tell you. The Reptilians are not generally those who would walk away from something they felt were owed. At the same time, they may feel that they will be in a better bargaining position the next time they need something from the Assembly if they at least pretend to be magnanimous." She looked over at me and smiled, her teeth so white that they, too, appeared to be tinted faintly blue. "I know it is not an enjoyable prospect to have such a thing hanging over your head, but I must advise you to return home and go about your life as well as you can. In the best case, you will never hear from me again, but if the occasion arises...."

"I know we can count on your help," I said. "Thank you, Anda." I extended a hand to her, and after a brief hesitation, she took it.

"Curious custom," was her only observation, and then she took her leave of us and hurried off. Because of her height and shocking blue hair, she couldn't exactly disappear into the crowd, but she walked swiftly enough that she was soon gone from eyeshot.

Raphael and I looked at each other. Roughly a million emotions swirled through me right then—relief, worry, doubt, confusion. Anger that no one had really stood up for Logan and his rights as a person, no matter what his origins might be. Disappointment that, for all its advanced technology and millennia of history, the Assembly seemed just as flawed as my own world's United Nations. Fear that

I could be dragged back here at any time, that I might be separated from my world, my family, from Raphael.

But above all that, need. I wanted him so badly to take me back to his ship.

And he seemed to understand that need, because he took my hand in his and ran the index finger of his other hand over the surface of the jewel that hung from his belt. White light flashed once again, and in the next instant, we were standing in the ship's lounge.

"I thought you might want a drink after that," he said.

What I'd actually been imagining was him taking me back to his bed and erasing all memory of that encounter with the Reptilians, but some of the fizzy drink he'd given me earlier might not be a bad idea, either. So I nodded and watched as he fetched two glasses for us, then filled both of them with the soft peach-colored liquid.

I took my glass from him and sipped. At once, I felt about ten pounds lighter, all those wonderful bubbles flowing through my bloodstream and doing wonders for my mood.

"What do you call this stuff, anyway?"

"*Rahliss.*"

"That's pretty."

He smiled. "I fear it is nowhere near as lovely as you."

Warm blood rushed to my cheeks. I'd never been

all that good with compliments, mostly because I didn't think they were all that deserved. More than one person had called me beautiful, but what did that even mean? Mostly that I was lucky enough to have very good-looking parents, parents who'd passed their otherworldly genes on to me.

Raphael was watching me closely. "Perhaps we should sit."

That sounded like a very good idea. It wasn't until I'd lowered myself to one of the couches that I realized how wobbly my knees actually were. Too much to absorb, I supposed, starting with walking on the surface of a whole new world and ending with the realization that, while I might have been granted a reprieve, I wasn't exactly home free yet.

I sipped some more of the *rahliss*. More lovely bubbles, washing away the memory of the way Lir Shalan had glared at me. As Raphael came and sat next to me, I asked, "Who do you think that one man was?"

"Which man?"

"The one with the Reptilians. The one who looked almost human, but not quite. Was he a hybrid?"

Raphael frowned. "His presence puzzled me as well. If he is a hybrid, he is unlike any I have ever seen or heard of. The Reptilians' goal with their hybrids was always to make individuals who could pass among humans undetected. The man in question certainly could not do that. But the Reptilians are always experimenting, and it is possible that, after their last defeat, they decided to take their genetic manipulations in another direction."

I supposed his explanation made sense, although I couldn't quite figure out why Lir Shalan and his cohorts would bring their latest science experiment along to a public hearing. Then again, I was having a hard time understanding just about anything they did or said, so I could probably file this mystery away along with all the others.

"Are we headed home now?" I'd almost inquired as to what he thought the Reptilians were doing, but he'd already admitted that he didn't have a clue. At the moment, I wanted to pretend really hard that they didn't exist.

"We are going back to Earth, yes."

His reply reminded me that Earth might be my home, but it certainly wasn't his. "Was that your home world?" I asked.

"No. I was born in another of the systems that make up the cluster, but I have spent a great deal of time on Penalta, since it is the seat of government for the Assembled Worlds."

For some reason, realizing that Penalta wasn't Raphael's home saddened me. Even though we shared an intimacy beyond anything I'd ever experienced before, I still knew so little about him. He hadn't mentioned anything of his own family. Were they gone, too? How long did Pleiadians actually live, anyway? Hundreds of times longer than Earth humans, obviously, but there was still a big difference between being exceptionally long-lived and outright immortal.

"I can see all the questions in your eyes," he said, then moved closer to me so he could drop an arm around my shoulders and pull me in toward him. I leaned my head against his chest, so glad to feel his warmth surround me, to hear his heart beating beneath my cheek.

"Was I being that obvious?"

"Perhaps. But it is only fair, I suppose. After all, I know a great deal about you."

I hadn't even thought about it that way, but then I realized he—and the people he worked for—must have a fairly hefty dossier on me and my family. That notion made me feel uneasy, but I gave a not very convincing laugh and said, "Really? All right… what's my favorite color?"

"Purple," he replied, completely deadpan. I honestly didn't know if he was trying to tease me or just relating the facts he had in his possession.

All right, purple was actually my favorite color, but…. "Okay, then," I said. "What about your family? Do you have any brothers or sisters?"

"No. As I mentioned before, our families are usually small. It is necessary, because of our long lives. Even so, we have spread to all the worlds of the cluster, and to systems beyond that."

"Terraforming?" I asked, and a faint look of surprise passed over his features. Smiling, I added, "I do actually listen to my father and Paul and Michael

Oliver when they start going off about this stuff. Well, sometimes, anyway."

"Yes, that is what we do. Obviously, we have a different word for it, and we are very careful about the worlds we select, so there is no chance of altering a planet that has the potential to develop life on its own." He paused for a moment, and I felt his lips brush against my hair. A warmth that had nothing to do with the *rahliss* began to spread through me. "Which brings me to my own parents. They are scientists, members of the one of the advance teams that survey worlds and assess their viability for transformation."

While I was very glad to hear that his parents were alive and well—Raphael's story of what had happened to my paternal grandparents still haunted me—I did find it a little strange to think of him as being part of a family, of having any connections at all. He seemed so very alone.

Well, not entirely, of course. Not anymore. He had me now.

"Do you see them often?"

"No. Their work, as you might have guessed, keeps them occupied and far away from my own areas of activity. Also, the dynamics of family are very different for us. Of course, it is every parent's wish that his or her offspring is healthy and happy and successful, but because we live such long lives, we begin to…drift, for lack of a better word…after a time. We do not share in each other's lives on a regular basis the way you do on Earth."

"Oh." That didn't sound very friendly to me, but I had to admit I might be just a bit biased. My mother and my Aunt Kara had definitely over-compensated when it came to the whole family togetherness thing, most likely because they were still dealing with the emotional fallout of having their own mother walk out on them when they were little girls. And the Olivers just got wrapped into the big extended family because of everything they'd gone through with my mother and aunt, even though Persephone's parents were still alive, as was Paul's mother, although his father had passed away before he even met Persephone. Anyway, even though I was an only child, I didn't feel like one at least half the time simply because I spent so much time around my cousins. An existence where I wouldn't see either of my parents for years or even decades didn't exactly compute.

Raphael spoke again. "This troubles you."

It wasn't a question. "Yes, I guess it does." I shifted, moving so I could look up at him instead of lying there with my head on his chest. "Don't you miss them?"

His eyes wouldn't exactly meet mine. "Perhaps I did at first. But as the years went on, and I became immersed in my work, it did not seem to matter as much. And it's not as if we have no contact at all.

From time to time, my mother will send a communiqué, just to make sure that I'm still doing well."

"That sounds cozy," I said dryly. "You should get in contact with them soon, though. Maybe they'd like to hear there's finally a chance they'll be grandparents."

"Indeed?" he replied. The remote expression left his face then, and he even smiled. "Wouldn't you say you might be, as your people put it, jumping the gun?"

"What, you don't want kids right away?" I asked, but I made sure he could hear the teasing note in my voice. "Don't worry, Raphael—I'm not in any hurry. But wouldn't you like to have a family of your own someday?"

"A family," he repeated. A flicker of sadness came and went in his dark eyes. "I had long ago put away the hope of ever having a child of my own. I suppose I will have to revisit that concept, now that it is no longer such an impossibility."

Although I understood its source, I still hated to see such sorrow in his expression. So I pressed my lips against his and felt his mouth open to mine, tasted the sweet-tart flavor of the *rahliss* on his tongue. His arms tightened around me as he deepened the kiss, and even through my voluminous skirts and the heavy robes he wore, I could feel his arousal.

"Should we take this to the bedroom?" I whispered.

His breath was a soft, warm huff against my cheek as he chuckled. "I see no reason to move."

And then he was shifting so I was buried beneath him, and his fingers were finding the hidden fasteners of my gown, so that in the next second his hands were sliding over my bare skin, awakening such need that I realized I didn't care where we were, as long as I could have this with him. As our bodies connected once again and I drew him deep inside me, I knew that this bond could never be broken, no matter what machinations the Reptilians might attempt, no matter what my friends or family might think.

Raphael might not be the only thing I needed, but in that moment, I couldn't think what else I might require to make my life complete.

CHAPTER FOURTEEN

AT SOME POINT, WE DID FINALLY MAKE IT TO THE bedroom, although by then I was ready to merely sleep in his arms, nothing more. I'd never slept with anyone—really "slept"—before Raphael, and I was a little surprised by how much I enjoyed being there with him, of waking up to see his heavy dark hair rumpled and the taut lines of worry smoothed away by sleep. No five o'clock shadow, though; back on Earth, when he'd been attempting to pass himself off as one of us, I had detected a faint hint of stubble by the end of the day, but that clearly wasn't Raphael's natural state.

When I opened my eyes, I remembered we would be back on Earth sometime later this day. My stomach clenched. You'd think facing down my parents would be a piece of cake after the ordeal I'd suffered in the Assembly chamber, but my physical reactions seemed to indicate otherwise.

"It will be all right," Raphael said, then sat up next to me and ran a comforting hand down my back.

If it had been anyone else, I might have asked how he knew what I was feeling, but with him it was different. We were soul-bonded. I seemed to be an open book to him, although I had a little more trouble detecting his emotions. Why, I wasn't sure, but then, he did have a lot more experience when it came to using this strange sixth sense that all Pleiadians seemed to possess.

"Easy for you to say," I replied morosely. "They weren't exactly thrilled about us being together at all, and then to disappear like that for days so we could go deal with the Reptilians? I can already imagine the guilt."

His brows drew together, and he lifted his hand from my back. "They should not treat you like a misbehaving child."

"Well, you and I know that, but we might have a difficult time convincing them. You've been out of the house for thousands of years, Raphael, but I still get treated to the 'while you're under my roof' speech on a regular basis."

At first, it seemed as if this remark puzzled him, but then he gave a faint nod. "They believe that you should adhere to their rules as long as you still share a home with them."

"Exactly. I probably should have stayed up in Flagstaff after college the way Grace did, but I was already tired of the whole roommates thing. Living in my parents' guest house sounded a lot better to me, although I'm beginning to regret that decision."

He moved closer so he could lift my hair away from my neck and kiss the sensitive skin there. The touch of his mouth to my flesh sent thrilling little shivers all over me. "There is no reason for them to have this power over you. Come live with me."

That suggestion made me go rigid with shock. I pulled away and stared up at Raphael, not sure I'd heard him correctly. "You want me to move in with you?"

"Yes." One side of his mouth quirked, as if he was amused by my consternation. "We share the soul bond, Callista. This means we are meant to be together forever. In light of such a connection, your terrestrial notions of what is acceptable simply do not apply."

When he put it that way, I could see what he meant. We'd only been intimate for a few days, but even that short span was more than enough time for me to know I could never be with anyone else, no matter what my parents' views on the matter might be. So it really wasn't so strange that Raphael would want to make sure I was with him all the time.

"Where?" I asked. "On this ship?"

"It has been my home for many years, but we

could live somewhere else, if you prefer. An apartment on Penalta, perhaps?"

The little I'd seen of it seemed to indicate that it was a beautiful world, but how could I ever fit in there? I knew nothing of their culture, didn't speak the language. True, I'd have centuries to learn how to fit in, but the prospect still intimidated me.

Apparently noting my hesitation, he said, "Or would you prefer that I took your father's path and remained with you on Earth?"

My eyes widened. "You would do that? Leave everything to be there with me?"

He found my hand where it was burrowed under the bedclothes and took it in his. "My love, I suppose I could represent such a choice to you as a great show of self-sacrifice, but the truth of it is...." Pausing, he let out a small gust of breath, then went on, "There is not so very much that I would be giving up. Some comforts of the technologies I know, but not even as much as you might think. I would be making a voluntary choice to be on Earth with you, not forced into exile there because of my actions as your father was."

"And it wouldn't be a problem?" I really had no idea what the consequences of such a decision might be. Clearly, Raphael had been in service to the Assembly and its government for many, many years. Was it the sort of service he could even leave voluntarily without invoking some kind of penalty? I asked as much, and he shook his head.

"No. I am not some conscript who cannot call his destiny his own. I have always had the option to leave, should circumstances require me to do so, but up until now I have had no reason to make a change in my vocation." He reached out and touched my hair where it fell over my shoulder, his fingers running down the length of it. "I would have to give up this ship, however. Even with all its safeguards against detection, there is always the remote chance that it still might be discovered, and that would create problems."

Logically, I understood what he was saying. At the same time, though, I couldn't help experiencing a little pang of disappointment. I would much rather remain on Earth, of course…but it would have been awfully fun to have access to that ship whenever we wanted.

"So you would be exiling yourself, even if you don't want to call it that."

His arms went around me then and he pulled me to him, my cheek against the firm, taut skin of his chest. "No, my love, it is *not* exile. Not really. Should the need arise, I could always call for someone to come and fetch us."

"In case we want to vacation on Penalta?"

I could feel his body shake slightly as he chuckled. "Yes, in case of that, or if my parents want to meet you, once they hear the news. Anything at all."

Would his parents even ask to see me? Raphael had made it sound as if they barely had any contact with him at all. I had to admit that the prospect was a little daunting. Yes, the Secretary of the Assembly had been very charming, and seemed pleased that Raphael and I were soul-bonded...but he wasn't any kind of relative. He didn't have any reason to look down at the provincial girl from the backwater planet, a world so behind the times that it wasn't even a member of the Assembly yet. Whereas Raphael's parents certainly would be expecting some kind of paragon. Who else could finally connect with their son after so many years of his being alone?

"Stop that," he said, and I looked up to see him watching me, a stern expression on his perfect features.

"Stop what?"

"What you're doing to yourself right now. Do not think any less of yourself because you come from Earth, or because you are young as the universe counts such things. You are perfect, unique, the match to my soul." His hands went to my face then, gently touching each cheek as if he thought such perfection required a frame. "They will love you because I love you."

"Then they're a lot more evolved than my parents."

He shook his head. "Martin and Kirsten want what is best for you. Nothing less. I cannot fault them for that. I now regret some of the exchanges I had with them, for our shared past colors the present. But since I do not possess the ability to change the past, the most I can do now is show them how much I do care for you and want to do the right thing by you."

"Even if it means living on Earth."

"Yes, even that."

His words had such a ring of sincerity to them that I really couldn't find it in me to argue with him any further. I'd thought about asking him how we would live, where we would get the funds, but that had clearly never been a problem for Gabriel or my father, so I guessed Raphael would be given the same golden handshake.

In which case….

I couldn't prevent a grin from spreading across my face, even though I knew I still had to confront my parents, even though the Reptilians could decide at any moment that they wanted the contents of my bank account or my shoe collection, or whatever.

"What is it?" Raphael asked, looking vaguely alarmed by my sudden expression of glee.

"Well, I know we'll have to sort some things out first. But then" — I reached over and squeezed his hand—"then we'll get to go house hunting."

———

Since Raphael had energy-jumped us out of the garage at my parents' house, that was where he brought us back to Earth. It did feel sort of anticlimactic to be standing in the faintly damp-smelling space after everything I'd been through over the past few days.

Both my parents' vehicles were there, which meant I wouldn't be able to sneak inside and then act all casual whenever they did come home. I had no idea what time it was, except that I couldn't see any daylight seeping in around the edges of the garage door. All right, maybe that was better. If it was the middle of the night, we just might be able to slip out the side door of the garage and into the casita I called home.

"It is slightly past eight o'clock in the evening," Raphael said, and I started. He sent me an apologetic glance, adding, "You were thinking rather loudly."

I decided I'd better let it go. "All right, then I suppose we'll just have to go in. We could go straight to the casita, but they'd still see the lights come on, since it's right across the courtyard from the family room."

"You need to stop hiding, Callista." His voice sounded gentle enough, but underneath I detected a note of steel.

He was right, anyway. I did need to stop hiding, or acting as if what Raphael and I shared was somehow wrong.

A deep breath, and then another. *Be strong.* Besides, it wasn't as if my parents were the boogeyman or something. We'd always been close. They only wanted the best for me. I'd just have to figure out how to make them understand that Raphael *was* the best.

His fingers wrapped themselves around mine, and I nodded. Then I reached out and turned the doorknob.

Good thing they didn't generally lock the door that led from the garage into the house. Raphael and I entered the kitchen, and I began to head toward the family room, where I thought I heard voices. My parents must be watching one of their favorite shows, or possibly a movie.

But then I realized those voices belonged to not just my mother and father, but my Aunt Kara and Uncle Lance as well. Wonderful.

I shot a panicked look up at Raphael, but he only shook his head and murmured, "This changes nothing."

Well, maybe for him it didn't. If my aunt and uncle were over here, it meant that my parents probably had wanted to discuss me with them in a safe setting where they wouldn't have to worry about Kelsey or Melissa eavesdropping. Kevin couldn't have cared less, but my other two cousins were always desperately afraid they were going to miss out on something important. And while I loved Kara and Lance, I sort of doubted they would be too sympathetic to my cause, Kara because I knew she'd agree with my mother that I was too young to be making any kinds of momentous decisions about my personal life, and Lance because he was probably tired of seeing the women in his family hooking up with aliens.

But I'd come this far, and I certainly didn't want Raphael to think I was a coward. I'd cleaned myself up properly on his ship and gotten back into my regular clothes, so I knew at least outwardly I wouldn't show any signs of what he and I had been up to for the past few days on his ship. Somehow, I knew my parents would guess, though. My mother had definitely known when I'd lost my virginity, although the only thing she'd said was, "Is there anything you'd like to talk about, Callista?" When I'd shaken my head, she'd just lifted her shoulders and gone on drinking her coffee. The sad truth was, there hadn't really been anything I'd wanted to talk about. The experience hadn't been that great, and I'd gotten my shot when I turned eighteen—plus I made sure he used a condom—and so the whole incident was something I would have preferred to ignore.

Well, if she started asking awkward questions, I'd fire back by inquiring how much time she'd actually spent with my father before they jumped in the sack together. That might deflect the situation. Maybe.

Raphael and I entered the family room, where Aunt Kara and Uncle Lance were sitting on the couch, and my parents were in the chairs that flanked it to either side. My father was saying, "Yes, but now it's been almost three days—"

Clearly, he'd been talking about my disappearance, but he stopped mid-sentence when he caught sight of Raphael and me. My mother actually gasped, and Aunt Kara set down the wine glass she'd been holding with an audible *clink*. Only Lance didn't seem to react, although I noticed the way his eyes narrowed as he took in Raphael, who'd changed back into his suit.

"Um, hi, everyone," I said. Completely stupid, but it was the first thing to come to mind.

"You're all right!" my mother exclaimed.

"I'm fine," I told her. "We're fine."

"What happened?" That was Lance. He always did have a way of cutting to the chase.

There was a question. I decided it was probably better to start with the Reptilians and then circle back to Raphael and me—if I even had to go there at all. With any luck, my tale of getting dragged before the Assembly would be enough to occupy them so they wouldn't ask any more personal questions.

So I related what had gone on in the Assembly chamber on Penalta, or at least tried to. I hadn't gotten very far before my mother interrupted me. "You mean the Reptilians were actually there in the courtroom with you?"

"It's not really a courtroom," my father pointed out. "She was questioned in front of the Assembly because her actions resulted in the death of a citizen of an Assembly world, while she herself was not such a citizen. That makes it a diplomatic concern, not a criminal one."

"Exactly," Raphael put in. "But in the end, nothing much came of it."

"Nothing much?" Lance said, looking skeptical.

"Well...." I hesitated. The last thing I wanted to say was how even the Secretary, who'd seemed more or less sympathetic, had ruled on the side of the Reptilians when it came to Logan's humanity. I doubted that sort of decision would go over very well with my aunt and uncle, considering their daughter was now shacked up with that supposed non-human. "I guess I'm more or less guilty, but since they couldn't agree on reparations, the Reptilians took their toys and went home."

"Guilty of what?" my mother demanded. "All you were doing was defending the people you were with!"

"True," Raphael said. "Unfortunately, some finer points of convention were involved, and so we had to abide by the Secretary's ruling."

"But they still let you come home?" Kara asked, looking confused. I didn't blame her; I was still feeling a bit befuddled by the whole thing myself.

"Yes," I replied. "That is, I'm still on the hook for reparations, I guess, but since the Reptilians don't seem to want my shoe collection, I think I'm safe." *For now,* I added mentally. I wasn't about to say that out loud, though. The situation was tense enough already.

I couldn't tell if my deliberately flip attitude was

fooling anyone. Probably not. But I didn't have much more to offer beyond what I'd already told them.

My father's jaw set itself in grim lines. "The Reptilians never give anything up voluntarily. Ever."

Anda, my counsel, had said more or less the same thing, and the two of them should know, far better than the rest of us did.

Raphael said, "They did in this case because the Secretary would not grant them the one thing they asked for."

"And what was that?" From the way my father's eyes narrowed, it seemed he already had a pretty good idea as to the content of that request.

"Me," I said in a very small voice.

Both my mother and my aunt burst out, "What?" while Lance shook his head in disgust. And my father didn't seem to react at all, only sat there with that same taut look to his jaw.

Ignoring their consternation, Raphael said, "Of course, the Secretary told them such a request was impossible. They did leave soon afterward."

Silence fell. The really horrible thing was that no one asked why a bunch of lizard-descended aliens might want me, even when on the surface we seemed so biologically incompatible. They all knew. My mother's face was almost as white as the T-shirt she wore under her V-necked sweater.

"Anyway," I went on, "it was basically no harm, no foul, so we came back."

"Yes, you did," my mother said. "Thank you for bringing her back to us, Raphael."

The dismissal in her tone was so clear that I had to keep myself from flinching. From the way his lashes swept down over his eyes before he glanced back up at her, he'd heard it, too, and was trying to resist the urge to make a cutting retort.

When he spoke, his voice was almost too calm. "You are welcome, Kirsten. As to bringing her back to you, well...perhaps Callista would like to comment on that."

No, Callista really wouldn't, especially not with Kara and Lance looking on. But I knew I had to make a stand here, even though Raphael and I hadn't made any concrete plans. Yes, I was itching to go house hunting, but I sort of doubted my parents would be exactly keen to have him stay with me in the casita until we found a place to live. I supposed the two of us could go back up to his ship. For some reason, that felt like backtracking, though. He'd committed to staying with me here, on this world, and that was where we should remain.

The words came out in a rush. "Raphael is going to stay here. With me. So...I guess we're going to find a suite or room in one of the local hotels until we can get something more permanent."

That was quite possibly the first time in my life that I'd ever seen my uncle look flummoxed. His mouth opened, as if he'd intended to say something, and then he shut it with an almost audible snap, apparently realizing that this was something he needed to stay out of. If I were his own daughter, matters would have been different, but otherwise….

Kara was twisting the eternity band on her ring finger, the diamonds sparkling as it went around and around. She, too, had the appearance of someone who desperately wanted to say something but who knew this wasn't her fight. And God bless her for that, because in the past, she hadn't always kept her nose out of our business. She'd probably thought it was her right to do so, since she was the older sister.

My mother still had that drained, pale expression on her face, while my father—well, something of the tight, angry clenching of his jaw actually loosened, although I couldn't say he looked exactly relaxed. More just…tired.

"So that's what you've decided?" he said.

We hadn't, not really. At least not the hotel part. But Raphael gave me a barely perceptible nod, and I said, "Yes. I know it might not be what you wanted to hear, but this thing between us isn't going away. So I hope you and Mom can learn to be happy for us."

"*Are* you happy?" she asked, a sort of terrible urgency in her voice.

I didn't even have to stop to think about her question. The universe had become infinitely stranger over the past couple of days, and I still didn't know what was going on with the Reptilians, but even so, there was only one answer I could possibly give. "Yes."

"Then we'll be happy for you." She got up from the couch, then came over and put her arms around me, hugging me fiercely. I caught a faint hint of the perfume she always wore, something fresh and woodsy, clean and bright, just like she was.

I had to fight back the sudden stinging in my eyes. I really didn't want to break down in front of everyone, especially when there was such a strong chance someone might misinterpret my reaction.

Then she surprised me by letting go of me and embracing Raphael in the next instant. The sudden widening of his eyes told me her reaction was about the last thing he'd been expecting, but he awkwardly returned the hug. Luckily, she didn't hold on for very long, but let go after a second or two, just as my father rose from the couch. He hugged me as well, and afterward sent Raphael an amused glance as he held out his hand.

"Welcome to the family."

Looking infinitely relieved that he wasn't about to be pulled into another uncomfortable embrace, Raphael took my father's hand and shook it. "Thank you, Martin."

Back on the couch, my aunt and uncle glanced at each other but didn't say anything. I could only imagine what they must have been thinking. Then Lance cleared his throat.

"Well, it looks as if it's all's well that ends well, so

we'll get going." He paused before adding, "I don't like this news about the Reptilians, though."

"I don't think any of us do," Kara said. "But since Callista is home safe and things seem to be quiet for now, we probably shouldn't worry about it too much yet."

"Hmph." It was all he said, although he managed to communicate worlds of disapproval in that single syllable.

But then they made their goodbyes, Kara smiling at Raphael and me, Lance giving my companion a single appraising look before the two of them headed out to the entryway, where they retrieved their coats from the hall tree there and let themselves out. They shut the front door quietly enough, but it still seemed as if the sound echoed throughout the house.

"Well, then," I said, as we all stood around awkwardly, "I guess I'd better go get some stuff put together."

"Do you even know where you're going?" my mother asked.

"Not yet," I replied. "But we'll find something."

"On New Year's. In Sedona."

Technically, the holiday had come and gone, but I could see what she meant. It was Saturday, and the exodus to leave town and head back to wherever people had come from wouldn't start in earnest until Sunday at the earliest. Even so, there had to be *something* available.

I said as much, and she gave me a dubious glance.

But I didn't want to argue. I just wanted to go pack a few things, make some calls, see what I could figure out.

My father put a hand on her arm and she took a step back, remaining silent as I asked Raphael to follow me out to the casita. Once we were inside and I'd shut the door, I couldn't help heaving an exaggerated sigh of relief.

"Thank God that's over."

He stood in the middle of the space, looking around. Yes, technically it was a guest house because it was separate from the main house and had its own bathroom, but it really wasn't that large. Room enough for my bedroom furniture and a desk under one window and not much more. At least I'd left it neat and clean, since in a space that small, just one thing out of place was enough to make it all look like a mess. Still, I couldn't help wondering what he thought of the pine furniture and the pieced-silk coverlet from India and the tea-dyed Persian rug on the floor. It was all very different from the sleek, elegant furnishings aboard his ship.

"It looks like you," he said after a moment, ignoring my previous comment.

"Um...thanks." For some reason, my cheeks warmed. Was that because of his compliment, or because he was standing only a few feet away from my bed?

Not that the bed was going to get any action. This might have been my space, but I couldn't imagine being intimate with Raphael there. No, we needed to get ourselves to a hotel room, stat.

"Anyway," I said, "I need to make some calls. I know this town is packed with tourists, but there's got to be something available somewhere. Once I have that figured out, I'll pack my things and we can go."

He nodded, still looking around at the hangings on the walls, the candleholders, the jewelry tray on the nightstand. I'd gone with tapestries and fabric hangings from India and Guatemala not just because they appealed to me, but also because the casita was sort of drafty, and having all that fabric hanging on the walls seemed to help.

Then the depressing business of calling hotel after hotel, getting more and more "no, sorry, we're all booked" replies as I went down the list I'd pulled up on my laptop, which had been sitting on my desk on its charging pad the whole time we'd been gone. I was trying the mid-priced places at first, mostly because I didn't know how long we'd have to stay, and also because I didn't know if I was the one who'd have to fund this little venture. But when I ran out of options, I started trying the higher-end hotels and resorts, who all gave me the same answer.

Until I called Enchantment. I'd actually avoided contacting them, just because I couldn't forget that it was from Enchantment that my mother had set out to confront the Reptilians all those years ago. It seemed like tempting fate to go back there now. But since I was out of options, I tried them anyway—and they'd had a cancellation on one of their junior suites.

The words "I'll take it" were out of my mouth even before I started scrabbling in my purse for my credit card. Raphael shot me a curious look, and I nodded.

Once the arrangements were handled and I'd told the front desk clerk that we'd be there within the hour, I ended the call and set the phone down on my desk. "All right, we have someplace to land."

"Good. I could tell you were beginning to become concerned."

Beginning? I wanted to shake my head but decided to let it go. "It's—it's fairly close to the abandoned Reptilian base. Is that going to be a problem?"

Raphael's eyebrows lifted at that revelation, but I could tell from the faint smile he wore that he wasn't overly concerned. "No. They have been gone from there for many years, and they know not to come back."

Well, that was the hope, anyway. I still couldn't guess what they were really plotting, but as long as they stayed far away from Sedona and Boynton Canyon, where the Enchantment Resort was located, then I wouldn't allow myself to stress about it.

I figured I had plenty of other things to worry about.

CHAPTER FIFTEEN

It was strange to go back into my parents' house with my weekender bags slung over my shoulder and make my goodbyes, but by then they seemed to have resigned themselves to my departure. My mother's eyes were a little too bright, and my father seemed too quiet, as if he was holding back the things he really wanted to say. However, they were civil enough to Raphael, who treated them with that grave charm I loved so much. I could see it beginning to have an effect on my mother; she didn't exactly fawn over him, but I could see her start to unbend, as if her bad memories of the way he had acted all those years ago were starting to be overridden by her current encounters with him. I had to hope so, anyway.

My father was friendly enough as well, although I could tell from the careful politeness of his smile that he was only being civil for my sake. I hoped his opinion of Raphael would change as they spent more time around one another, but in that particular moment, I thought it was probably better if I put some distance between them until things settled down.

It wasn't until I'd backed out of the driveway and was heading westward along Highway 89A toward the resort that I turned to Raphael and said, "You don't have any luggage."

"Don't I?" he replied.

Mystified, I allowed myself a quick glance over one shoulder and into the back seat. Sitting there were two dark blue bags that definitely hadn't been there a few minutes ago. "Do I want to know how you managed that?"

"Just a modified form of an energy jump. I thought of the things I might require to survive here on your world for an extended period, then put them in acceptable-appearing receptacles and had them sent down here to your vehicle."

"All in the space of five minutes."

"Less than that, actually." There was a glint near his waist as he slipped the jewel he always carried with him into his pocket.

"What are those things, anyway?" I asked. "Magic?"

"Magic doesn't exist. The jewel is tuned to the frequency of my thoughts, no more."

"Well, I've seen you do a lot more than just talk to

it. Or have it talk back to you."

This time, he did chuckle. "It is also connected to the ship—its drives, its food and materials synthesizers—all of those functions. So when I send a request through the device, it works with the ship to deliver the things I need."

I could almost visualize what he was talking about. Not the nuts and bolts of it, since I was pretty sure that involved science beyond even what Paul or Michael Oliver could comprehend, but enough to get the gist of how it all worked. I slowed to take the turn onto Dry Creek Road so we could head into the hills and toward the resort, then asked, "But what happens if you don't have your ship?"

The smile he'd been wearing abruptly faded. "Then I'm afraid the jewel can do very little for me. They're linked, you see."

How was I supposed to reply to that? He'd said he would stay here with me, but that meant giving up his ship. And without the ship, the jewel wouldn't be much more than a pretty bauble.

His voice sounded in my mind, soothing, warm. *I knew what I was committing to when I said I would stay here. It is not something I offered lightly, Callista. I will still have some powers of my own, after all. And if the need arises, I can have the ship returned to me.*

That explanation did reassure me somewhat. *How? Do you just...call for it?*

In a manner of speaking. That is, the jewel strengthens my thought patterns, and I can send them all the way to

*Penalta if necessary. One of my people would receive the
call and set forces in motion to ensure that I had a ship. I
cannot say my ship, for it isn't truly mine, but one of our
fleet. But there would always be one for my use if the situation
should require it.*

The idea that he could project his thoughts all
the way across all those light-years was staggering.
And yet he spoke of the process as if it wasn't that
big a deal. "All right," I said aloud. "It still bothers
me, but if you're sure you're all right with being
here…."

Both my hands were on the steering wheel, but he
reached over and laid a hand on my knee. "I can't
think of any place I would rather be. That is the truth,
Callista." He fell silent for a moment, clearly gathering
his thoughts. "You have ties here, a way of
being connected to these people and this place. I
wouldn't wish to take that from you—indeed, I am
beginning to see it is something I never had, and now
wish I might have been able to experience for
myself."

My heart ached for him. Yes, he might be from a
civilization so advanced beyond ours that I still had a
difficult time understanding much of how it even
functioned, but in that moment, I thought maybe
they'd lost something along the way. Being with the
people who knew you and understood you—and
loved you anyway—was just as important as being
able to travel among the stars.

"You will," I said as I came to a stop next to the

guard shack that stood watch at the entrance to the resort. "I'll make sure of that."

───────

After that, everything went smoothly enough. I was just paranoid enough to worry that our suite would turn out to be unavailable after all, but my worries were for naught, since we checked in without incident and then were directed to the casita where we'd be staying. For how long, I had no idea. I'd booked us for a week. After that, I supposed we'd have to see what happened.

Once we were done putting our things away—which didn't take very long, since neither one of us had brought much—we sort of stopped and stared at each other. I cleared my throat. "Well…."

"Well," he echoed, then came over and took my hands in his. At once, the nervous butterflies in my stomach subsided, although they were only replaced by a warm quiver of nervous excitement. Was this when he would lead me to the bed, make the room truly ours?

But he only lifted one hand to his mouth so he could lay a kiss on my palm. "We have come a very long way today, my love. And as much as I am going to enjoy being here with you, I think some fortification beforehand might be wise."

"'Fortification'?" I echoed. Even while I spoke, though, my stomach growled, and I clapped a hand over it as Raphael's mouth quirked. "All right, 'fortification' is probably a good idea. Especially since I don't even know how many Earth hours it's been since we last ate."

"Long enough. Did I see signs as we came in pointing to the restaurant?"

"Restaurants," I said. "They have several here on-site, which makes it easier. We won't have to go very far." I glanced at the clock on the table across the room. It was a little before nine. Late for dinner, but not so late that the resort's restaurants wouldn't still be open, especially on the Saturday night of a holiday weekend.

We got back into our coats and went outside. The sky was clear, but snow shone in the moonlight on the higher elevations of the bluffs that surrounded the resort. It hadn't been snowing when Raphael and I left Sedona a few days earlier, although it was certainly cold enough now to explain why that precipitation had turned to snow. I turned the collar of my coat up around my throat, wishing I'd dug one of my scarves out of the drawer where I'd stowed them.

But it still felt good to walk alongside Raphael, to feel his hand in mine as we followed the winding paths that led to the main building where the restaurants and outdoor bar were located. Of course, no one was sitting outside now, not on this bitterly cold January night. Water still filled the pool, though, glowing blue-green in the darkness as wisps of steam rose from its surface.

Because it was so late, the restaurant was beginning to empty out, and we got a table right away. The table sat next to the windows on the eastern side of the room, but you couldn't see anything in the vast black out there, not even the stars, because of the reflections from within the restaurant against the floor-to-ceiling glass. Something about that impalpable darkness made me think of the Reptilians, out there somewhere, watching and waiting…for what?

I shivered, and Raphael immediately reached out to touch my arm. "Will it be too chilly here by the window? There seems to be an empty table toward the center of the room—"

"No, it's fine," I said. I wasn't about to let myself get overcome by the heebie-jeebies, not when I was in a warm, safe place with the man I loved. "There aren't any drafts at all."

He nodded, but still looked troubled as he helped me out of my coat and laid it on one of the spare chairs at our table. I sat down while he took off his own coat and set it on top of mine. The hostess, who'd been waiting for us to divest ourselves of our outerwear, handed over the menus and said our server would be along shortly. I managed to smile at her, although I still felt cold.

Maybe it was only the proximity of the resort to the base the Reptilians had once called home. Their former base wasn't actually here in Boynton, despite much speculation in various chatrooms and forums on that point, but over in the Secret Canyon wilderness, several miles away. But that still felt way too close, even though I knew the facility was completely deserted now. My parents had gone with Grace to the alien base and had confirmed that nothing of the Reptilians remained. Possibly I was only feeling the psychic residue of the place they'd inhabited for so long, although in general I would have said that sort of woo-woo observation was more up Taryn's alley.

To distract myself, I opened up the wine list the hostess had laid on the table between the place settings. Some people might have advised against wine after the day I'd had, but right then I thought I could use a drink.

I looked over the edge of the leatherette folder at Raphael, who held a menu open in front of him, a slight frown pulling at his brows as he attempted to parse its contents.

"Can you—can you read English?" I murmured. After all, just because he'd spent a lot of time hanging around Earth as a spirit guide, that didn't mean he'd ever needed to actually sit down and read something.

His dark brows drew together at once, and I realized I'd misstepped. "Of course I can," he snapped, sounding more like the Otto of old than the Raphael I'd come to know. His blood sugar must have been getting precariously low.

"Sorry." Then I recalled how he'd told me that his

people didn't eat meat, and I quickly set down the wine list so I could glance over the menu and analyze it to see what he actually could eat.

"You could do the mac and cheese if you ask them to hold the ham," I suggested. "Or any of the salads would work. Or this flatbread margherita—it's a flat type of bread baked with cheese and herbs."

The frown disappeared. "That sounds as if it would be good."

"I'm sure it is. I've never had anything here I didn't like."

The waitress appeared then to take our orders, and I hesitated over the wine list. Raphael had also said he didn't drink alcohol, but I didn't know for sure if I had the willpower to become a teetotaler on his behalf. Anyway, he was here, and he could drink or not drink. That was his choice. I, on the other hand, knew I wanted a glass of merlot. At least my part-time job working at the wine-tasting room uptown had let me know which of the local vintages were the best.

I ordered the wine and some chicken enchiladas. Raphael sent me an inquiring glance while the waitress asked for my I.D. and inspected it closely before writing down my order. I lifted my shoulders. *I doubt one glass is going to put you under the table*, I told him. *But you can have water or tea or something like that. I'm afraid we don't have anything that's similar to* rahliss.

He looked up at the waitress, who was a pretty girl about my age or a little older, probably Native

American, with her long black hair and dark, almond-shaped eyes. "The margarita flatbread...and a glass of the same thing she is having."

The girl smiled and made a note of his order, although she didn't ask for his identification, and then told us she'd be out with our drinks in a little bit. After she'd gone, I said, "Living dangerously?"

"Perhaps. As you said, one glass should not have any seriously deleterious effects, not based on my body mass."

I winked at him. "Next time we can order a bottle and see what happens."

That remark earned me a pained glance, but he didn't reply, instead sipping at his water. "I've never understood the human urge to destroy so many brain cells on purpose."

"Because it feels so good while you're doing it?"

"But doesn't the aftermath feel decidedly *not* good?"

A few parties I'd attended over the past year or so came to mind, and I winced slightly. Mixing tequila and vodka was never a good idea. Actually, it was partly those experiences that had led to me drinking mostly wine these days—plus being around wine on the job. At least if you stuck with one type of alcohol, the odds of a hangover were a lot lower. "It can be kind of brutal if you drink too much. But one glass isn't going to do a lot, one way or another."

A theory that would be put to the test soon enough,

since the waitress reappeared right then with our wine. She set my glass down in front of me first, and then placed Raphael's near where his hand rested on the tabletop. Was it my imagination, or was she lingering just a little closer to him than strictly necessary?

"Your food will be out in a few minutes," she said, then headed over to check on a table against the opposite window.

Good. That way I wouldn't have to keep fighting the urge to rip out her liver.

Possessive, my love?

Clearly, he'd seen the side-eye I just shot the waitress. *Only about you, dear.*

He shook his head, but I could see the glint in his eyes. I doubted he'd ever admit it, but I got the impression he was a little pleased by my pricks of jealousy.

Well, why not? I thought then. *This is the first time he's had anyone around to get jealous.*

Which just seemed wrong for someone as amazing as Raphael. What strange twist of fate or DNA or timing had made it so he'd had to wait so many years until I came along?

I'd probably never know, but I was saved from having to brood about the situation by him lifting his glass in my direction. "To all our firsts," he said.

That sounded like a wonderful toast to me, so I raised my glass as well. "To all our firsts."

Then we both drank, but I watched him the whole

time, wanting to see his reaction to his first taste of Earth alcohol.

He blinked, then swallowed, then sat there for a moment, staring down into his glass but not speaking. I took another sip of my wine, wondering if there was something wrong with it. But no, it was a merlot from a local winery, and tasted just fine to me. Better than fine, actually, nice and fruity. Fruit forward, that is. One day, I'd get all the nomenclature down pat.

"If you don't like it, you can order something else," I said.

At once, he gave a slight shake of his head. "No, that's not it at all. I suppose I wasn't expecting it to taste good."

I couldn't help but laugh. "Why wouldn't it taste good? I'll admit there's some stuff out there that really doesn't, but I'd say most of us want to enjoy the experience of drinking it just as much as we like its effects."

"I didn't know that. It always seemed to me that people of Ear—that is, people drank for no other reason than to get drunk."

"Well, yeah, if you're a frat guy at ASU, I can understand that. But up around here in northern Arizona, wine is a big deal. People want to savor it, choose the kind that will taste best with their meals."

He appeared to absorb my words, then drank again. His eyes went heavy-lidded, and he looked so sexy in that moment that it required some effort to prevent myself from launching across the table at him, public place or no. Somehow I managed to keep it together, however—mostly because I made myself take another sip of wine.

When he spoke, his tone was filled with wonder. "It is as if I can taste the fruit and the earth and the sun, all at once. It's quite…astonishing."

I thought he was pretty astonishing, too. To be able to taste all those subtle characteristics the first time he'd ever drunk wine?

"Well, it sounds like you can always have a fall-back career as wine critic if nothing else pans out," I said, only half joking.

But he seemed to take me seriously. He lifted his glass to his lips again, and I had to make myself act as if watching him close his eyes and savor that sip in the most sensual way possible—full lips pressed together, lashes sooty crescents against his cheeks—was something I did every day. Then those lashes lifted, and he was watching me, chocolate-brown eyes almost black in the dim lighting of the restaurant. "You realize that I don't require a career at all."

I'd been waiting for a chance to ask the question, and now Raphael had given me the perfect opening. "The same way my father never seemed to have to work?"

"Precisely."

"And you would never get bored?"

He only smiled. "Boredom, my dear Callista, is a symptom of an inferior mind. The universe presents so many opportunities for enrichment that boredom should never be an option."

That did make some sense. After all, my father had never had a "real" job after he was exiled here on Earth—unless you counted his stint on *Paranormality* —and yet it seemed as if he was always occupied with something. Reading, or fiddling with the telescope my mother had bought him one Christmas, or exploring the area around Sedona with Lance and Paul when they weren't running Jeep tours, in the case of the former, or writing yet another book, in the case of the latter. And my parents were always going to concerts or gallery openings or day hikes or—well, all right, they didn't seem to get bored very easily.

"Even here on dull old Earth?" I inquired, then drank some more of my merlot.

"This world is not dull. Backward, perhaps, but not dull. It possesses astonishing natural beauty."

No one who'd grown up in Sedona the way I had could argue with that statement. In high school, everyone had always complained about how dull Sedona was, how there was nothing to do, but even then I'd thought those remarks had a lot more to do with sounding cool than because anyone actually felt that way. And even though Raphael had called Earth "backward," I couldn't get angry with him for saying so. Compared to the place he'd come from, it was backward. But he was still able to acknowledge its loveliness for all that.

The waitress came by with our food, and we left

aside the discussion about Earth's backwardness so we could dive into our meal. And oh, the things Raphael had fed me were delicious, but in my humble opinion, they couldn't compete with a smoked chicken enchilada with black beans. He seemed to be enjoying his flatbread, too, from the way he appeared to be savoring each bite in the same way he'd savored his wine, and I allowed myself a mental sigh of relief. Maybe he would be able to acclimate to life here after all.

It definitely seemed as if he was acclimating when he flagged down the waitress and asked for another round of drinks. After she'd gone, I raised an eyebrow at him and asked, "You sure about that?"

"Of course," he replied calmly. "I had finished mine, and there is still a good deal of my meal left. It's logical to order more so they even out."

"If you say so," I said, more amused than anything. After all, we didn't have that far to go to get back to our casita. At least I didn't have to worry about him driving or anything.

The waitress was all too happy to bring more, especially since it gave her an opportunity to loiter by his elbow again and ask if everything as all right.

"Wonderful," Raphael told her, while I agreed, if a bit less enthusiastically.

She smiled at him, gave me a brief nod, and headed back toward the kitchen.

A sound that might or might not have been a

growl emerged from my throat, and Raphael sent me an amused look.

"Jealous, my love?"

"No," I said coolly. "I'm just going to fling a forkful of black beans at her if she comes around and starts batting her eyelashes at you again."

"Wasted effort on her part. You are the only one for me. You know that, of course."

Something about that "of course" made my knees go a little weak, even though I was sitting down. He'd said it so matter-of-factly, as if his possible wandering shouldn't even be an item of concern. Among the Pleiadians, I supposed such things weren't. They found their soul mates, and that was it. No cheating, no lying, no running around or thinking the grass was greener on the other side. It was the way things were with my parents as well, but I'd never thought I'd be that lucky, never thought I'd meet anyone to share that sort of spiritual harmony. But Raphael had changed all that.

"Of course," I echoed, then spooned up some more chicken enchilada and washed it down with wine. Midway into my second glass, I was starting to feel a little swimmy. Not drunk, maybe not even tipsy, but elevated. Not really of this earth. Too many hours since my last meal, too many light-years between now and when I'd woken up this morning.

If the slightly unfocused state of Raphael's eyes was any indication, the wine had had its effect on him, too. He smiled at me somewhat blearily from across the table, and I wondered exactly how he felt right then. His system, untouched by alcohol for its entire existence, must have been working overtime to handle the unfamiliar toxin.

Which was why I flagged down the waitress and told her we were ready for the check. Raphael blinked at me but didn't protest. And when the check arrived, I was ready, and waved my phone over the reader built into the waitress's clipboard without even looking at the total, then pushed the button to have twenty percent added to the bill for her tip. Right then, I figured the best thing to do was get paid up and out of there before my companion was completely incapable of locomotion.

All right, maybe that was a little unfair. When the time came, he stood up more or less steadily, and even retained enough presence of mind to help me into my coat. I was just glad he hadn't argued with me about paying the bill. Yes, the Pleiadians seemed to have some secret sauce when it came to making sure their people hanging out on Earth had an inexhaustible flow of funds, but I didn't know if Raphael had even made his intentions known to them. It seemed safer to use my bank account, which I knew was reliable.

Once again, he took my hand as we walked. The night seemed even colder now, the stars glittering like chips of ice overhead. I tilted my head to look up at them, realizing that only earlier that day I'd been traveling among those very stars. Had anyone seen our approach and thought Raphael's ship a satellite or space station, rather than the interstellar vessel it actually was?

Then I reminded myself his ship possessed such good stealth technology that even the Reptilians couldn't detect it with their instruments, let alone a human being staring up into the night sky with the naked eye. Still, I found myself somewhat humbled by the thought that I'd traveled so very far away.

"You're quiet," Raphael said.

"Just thinking about all those stars," I replied. "And being up there among them with you."

He didn't answer, but pulled me close to him so he could kiss me, his mouth warm in the cold night air, his tongue sweet with wine. A fire kindled inside me, one that did a very good job of making me forget how chilly it really was, out there on the path.

A moment later he moved away slightly, whispering, "Let us go inside."

I didn't need any encouragement. Not that I ran exactly, but my steps did speed up as we headed toward our rented casita. Once we were inside, we barely made it inside the door before his arms were around me and his lips had pressed against mine again.

This was a new, forceful Raphael—fueled by merlot, I had no doubt. I didn't mind, though. It was a sweet wine-kissed haze that surrounded us as we fell onto the bed, clothes being flung this way and that. And it was an entirely different homecoming with his naked body next to mine, all heat and fire and aching need, as if we both knew we had to love one another all over again here on this world that was the only thing I'd ever known, and the place he'd somehow, despite all expectations, decided to make his.

He entered me, and I enveloped him, and we became one together.

CHAPTER SIXTEEN

IN THE DAYS THAT CAME NEXT, I REFLECTED IT WAS A good thing I'd only had casual friends in high school, and didn't stay very connected to any of them after I graduated. I had Taryn and Kelsey, of course, but they were different. They were family—all right, Taryn not by blood, but she might as well have been. We'd been raised by people who were fighting the same fight, who had the same secrets to hide. Getting close to the girls at my school had been impossible, not when I knew I could never tell them the truth about who my father was, or what kind of blood really flowed in my veins.

Anyway, Raphael would have been hard to explain to any of those high school acquaintances. Men who looked like movie stars—or gods descended from heaven—weren't exactly to be found wandering the streets of Sedona, unless they happened to be in town for the city's annual film festival. But the festival was still more than a month away, making Raphael's presence all the more improbable. As out of place as he might appear, however, he was still easier to account for than how I'd suddenly managed to move out of my parents' house and into a home that just skirted below the two-million-dollar mark.

I didn't actually set out to get something quite so ostentatious. When someone like Raphael gives you a velvety smile and says, "Choose whatever you'd like," as you're perusing the local real estate listings, though…well, let's just say it's hard to exercise much self-control in that kind of situation. And if the house of your heart turns out to be a Tuscan-style mansion perched on a hillside with almost 360-degree views of the red rocks and a reflecting pool on the patio… all right, call me weak-willed. I wanted it. And I wanted to share it with Raphael.

Even in Sedona, which had more than its fair share of the rich and famous who owned vacation homes there, buying a house at the price point with cash was bound to raise some eyebrows. So I was really glad that my high school friends had more or less fallen by the wayside, although fate or evil coincidence had decreed that Leisha Pendleton, my nemesis who'd thought I was trying to steal her boyfriend from her, was working in the real estate office that handled the transaction. I thought her eyes were going to pop out of her head when I walked into the place with Raphael, and those eyes only got bigger when we came back a few days later with a cashier's check that had a whole lot of zeroes on it.

But because she was the office assistant, and not our real estate agent, Leisha knew enough to keep her mouth shut, although I could tell she was just dying to ask where the heck I'd found Raphael and how someone who wasn't even scraping thirty years old could pay cash for a house like that. If she'd asked, I would have been really tempted to tell her he was the hottest thing in Bollywood right then, since he did have that sort of look, but I kept my mouth shut. Best not to stir things up any more than they already had been.

The house was sold furnished. Normally, I would never have bought a house that way, except that the self-help mogul who'd owned it before us—his meditation techniques had been recently debunked, leading him to a quick divestiture of all his assets—had pretty much the same taste I did, and so I didn't see much that needed changing. Or maybe it was his interior designer whose style was similar to mine. In the end, it didn't matter one way or another, except that now I wouldn't have to bore Raphael with dragging him around to furniture stores to find the things I needed.

I didn't want to question why the universe had smoothed the way so much for us. Frankly, I didn't want to think about anything except the life we had begun to build together. Because if I thought too much, then I'd start to wonder whether this might all end, if the Reptilians might descend at any moment and snatch all our good fortune away. Better to sail through my days as if I didn't have that particular sword of Damocles hanging over my head.

Once all the paperwork had been signed and the keys handed over to us, we drove to the house. Raphael surprised me by saying he didn't want to go in via the door that led from the garage to the interior, but through the front door.

"Why?" I asked. Another storm had begun to move in, and although snow wasn't falling yet, the wind had picked up and clouds blocked the sun. Even in my down-filled coat, I could feel the bite of that icy breeze.

"Isn't it a custom of yours? To carry the wife over the threshold?"

"Raphael, we aren't married," I pointed out gently. Nor had there been any discussion on the subject. To be honest, marriage hadn't seemed that important. We were committed to one another, and besides, I couldn't think of anything more permanent than having our names together on the title for a house.

He placed his finger under my chin and tilted my face upward so he could kiss me. Just a soft press of lips to lips, but it was enough. I actually marveled at how much he liked to kiss—and how good he was at it. Making up for lost time?

"My love, we might as well be. And we should be

sometime soon, if only to satisfy the conventions of your people. In the meantime, however, I would like to carry you over the threshold."

What girl could argue with such a request? I smiled at him and said, "You're right, Raphael. I'd be honored."

In the next instant, his arms were reaching under me, and then he'd lifted me off the ground, eliciting a startled laugh. Thinking ahead, he had the house key in his hand, even though the front door lock also opened with a combination. Only a little bit of fumbling, and then we were crossing over the afore-mentioned threshold and into the foyer, with its travertine floors and the wrought iron and alabaster chandelier overhead.

"There," Raphael said, setting me down so he could close the front door. I supposed he could have kicked it shut, but that would have seemed disre-spectful. "Now everything is official."

"It was official when we signed the paperwork," I pointed out.

"Perhaps. But it still did not feel real to me until now."

I could understand that feeling. Actually, I wasn't sure if the whole situation still felt all that real. Things had moved so very fast, but wasn't that what you were supposed to do when everything seemed exactly right?

"Well, we're here," I said. "And it is starting to sink in. So let's explore our demesne, shall we?"

We'd already walked over the house several times, but now it was different, because the place was ours. The movers had already collected my belongings from the casita at my parents' house and brought them here, and Raphael really didn't have much of anything except the few items of clothing and other sundries he'd accumulated during the short time he'd been here in Sedona.

The house felt new to us as we went from room to room, understanding fully that this was the home we would now share. Not forever, of course. Sometime in the future, twenty-five or so years from now, people would start to notice how we shared a perpetual youth that couldn't be solely attributed to the wonders of plastic surgery and other appearance-enhancing treatments, and we'd have to move on. In the meantime, though, we would have plenty to occupy us.

Starting with the bottle of Cristal that our real estate agent had left for us in the refrigerator. Some people might consider such a gesture generous, but really, compared to the commission from a house in that price range, it wasn't all that much.

Nevertheless, I couldn't help experiencing a little spurt of excitement as I retrieved the bottle from the refrigerator and set it down on the kitchen counter. "Now we just have to hope there are some champagne flutes in these cupboards," I told Raphael as I started opening doors one by one.

"'Flutes'?" he repeated, looking puzzled. His

mastery of the language was, well, masterful, but sometimes the finer points escaped him, especially when they involved objects he would never have had any reason to use in the past.

"Glasses," I explained. "Tall, thin—never mind." The items in question were sitting on a shelf in the third cupboard I checked, and I brought them down and placed them on the counter.

"You require special glasses just to drink champagne?"

"Concentrates the bubbles or something. I'm not an expert." Of course I'd had champagne on special occasions, but no one would ever accuse me of being a connoisseur. Which meant the Cristal was probably going to be wasted on me, but I wasn't about to let that particular lack stop me from sharing the bottle with Raphael.

He'd picked up the bottle and was inspecting the foil on top. "Interesting."

"Have you ever opened one of those things?" Not that I was an expert, either. On the other hand, at least I'd watched other people do it on numerous occasions.

"Of course not. But it seems like a simple enough procedure." As he spoke, he removed the foil and set it on the counter, then ran his fingers over the little wire cage, as if attempting to determine its pressure points.

"Um, Raphael, that's a really expensive bottle of champagne—"

"Don't worry." He lifted the wire frame off the cork and placed it next to the discarded foil. "I think I have determined the best way to manage this."

I decided to keep my mouth shut. If he fudged the whole thing, made it so he sprayed Cristal over the whole kitchen, then I'd just make him go out and buy me another bottle. Assuming you could even get Cristal in Sedona, a particular point I'd never had to contemplate before that moment.

His fingers, long and strong, worked at the cork. Despite my trepidation, I couldn't help admiring those hands and the smooth light brown skin that covered them, or remembering the way those hands moved over my body with a skill that still astonished me.

Maybe that wasn't such a good idea, because all I'd accomplished was to get myself hot and bothered. I pulled in a breath and tried to think of something else, like the house-warming party I'd threatened Raphael with. Okay, that was better. It was a lot harder to be aroused when you were trying to figure out which day would work best, and what kind of food to serve, and whether to invite anyone outside your immediate circle—

Pop! The cork went flying out of the bottle and bounced off one edge of the coved ceiling, but it didn't seem to do any actual damage. By some miracle, only graceful drifting fog swirled up out of the bottle, and not the geyser I'd feared. I hurried over to the flutes and held them out to Raphael so he could fill them up. He did so with care, waiting for the bubbles to subside before he continued to pour. For someone who didn't know anything about champagne, he seemed to have a pretty good handle on its care and feeding.

Then he put down the bottle and took one of the flutes from me. "This is where we drink to something, correct?"

"Yes," I replied. "We just have to decide on what it should be."

"Oh, I know exactly what we should drink to." His eyes met mine and held. Here in the brightly lit kitchen, I could see the swirls of warm brown and dark copper and even slate gray that combined in his irises, like muted but beautiful stained glass. He lifted his champagne flute, and I did so as well.

Smiling, he said, "To the future."

We did have a housewarming party, but I decided discretion would serve me best, and so it was a small crowd—Persephone, Paul, Michael, and Taryn; Kara and Lance and my cousins, including Grace and Logan; my parents.

Apparently, Logan had talked Grace down from resigning her position with the National Weather Service up in Flagstaff. He certainly looked in good health and spirits as he entered the house. I would have had a hard time believing he'd been so badly wounded in our raid on the Reptilian base if I hadn't seen the whole thing unfold before my eyes.

"Logan didn't want me to quit," Grace told me as she sipped her chardonnay and glanced around the living room with a mixture of astonishment and envy. "He kept telling me he was fine, and you know, he really is. Those healing pods on Raphael's ship must be pretty amazing."

"It's not his ship anymore," I said, even as I wished we could have come up with some way to hang on to it.

Grace's blue eyes widened. "What do you mean?"

I didn't exactly sigh, but the breath that escaped my lips was a little bit more than just a simple exhalation. "When he decided to stay here with me, that meant he was no longer an agent of the Assembly. It's really the Assembly's ship. So he sent it back."

"So he's stuck here, just like your father and grandfather?"

Well, that was one way of looking at it. "Not exactly. I mean, he can't come and go as he pleases, but he's not totally stuck, either. If something comes up, he can contact his people, and they'll send a ship for him."

"Convenient." She took another sip of her wine, eyes tracking across the room to where my father and grandfather were discussing something with Paul Oliver. What, I couldn't tell from this distance, but from the way Paul gestured upward on more than one occasion, I guessed it had to be something sky-

or star-related. Possibly our astronauts, still heading for home at speeds that would have been unthinkable even twenty years ago but which felt like crawling to me, now that I'd experienced the faster-than-light jumps Raphael's former ship could manage. Grace went on, "Do you think they'll ever relent? About your father and grandfather, that is."

"I don't know." I'd wondered the same thing myself on more than one occasion over the past few days. After all, the Assembly had authorized the Mars raid. A small bit of interference, true, and not quite the same as helping to wipe out an entire Reptilian base—or getting an Earth woman pregnant with the child who'd have the ability to take such action—but still, it seemed to me as if the Assembly and its leaders might be softening slightly. What harm could it do, really, to allow my father and Gabriel to have some interaction with the world where they'd been born, even if Earth was now their home? "I hope so. My father did get his powers back, so that's a start."

Grace was silent for a moment. Then I noticed the way her gaze flicked toward Raphael, who was talking to Persephone, of all people. I would have loved to know what they were discussing. Was he apologizing for bailing out on her as her spirit guide? Whatever they were talking about, it didn't seem to be too controversial, since she was nodding, while he wore that grave, subtle smile I loved so much.

"So...." For as forthright as a person as she

tended to be, Grace looked downright uncomfortable. Her eyes didn't quite meet mine. "You and Ott
—I mean, Raphael. I'm still trying to wrap my head
around that one."

"You and everyone else." What could I do except
shrug? Deep down, I'd hoped Grace would understand, since she'd felt a similar pull toward Logan.
Not the same as the soul-bond of the Pleiadians,
more like attracting like, but still, she knew what it
was like to feel an overwhelming attraction that came
out of basically nowhere. "But at least my parents
have backed off a little."

She grinned, a flash of white teeth accented by a
little dimple, the one I'd always envied, at the corner
of her mouth. "Well, he is hot-damn gorgeous, especially for a guardian angel. Or whatever he was
supposed to be."

"Spirit guide," I said. "A little bit different."

Her only reply was another smile and a slight lift
of her glass before she took another sip of chardonnay. Then she headed off toward Logan, who
appeared to be deep in conversation with Lance and
Kara. Talk about mending fences. They certainly
appeared to have accepted him into their family. I
didn't really know what Grace's long-term plans
were for her hybrid lover, but I wondered if he
would end up getting folded into the family business
the way her younger brother Kevin had been. It did
seem as if my Uncle Lance was always looking for
new drivers for his Jeep tour company. And Logan,

who'd been trained as a soldier, probably wouldn't have too much of a problem taking orders from Lance. Within reason, that is.

For some reason, the thought made me a little melancholy. Not on Logan's behalf; I guessed that he and Grace would be able to make things work, no matter what they ended up doing. No, it was more that I didn't know exactly what I planned to do, except be the lady of leisure Raphael had described to me earlier. That sort of lifestyle had worked out well enough for my parents, but was that really what I wanted to do with my own life?

I didn't know. For the moment, all I could do was brush the slight twinge of discontent aside, and go back to my guests.

Time flowed. It appeared that single twinge was the only one I'd be troubled with, because I did seem to be kept busy with all sorts of minutiae. I resigned my position at the wine-tasting room, and also backed off on my hours at the UFO Depot. It really wasn't that big a deal; January was a dead time for retail anyway and they didn't need me, although I could tell my aunt wasn't terribly thrilled with me over my defection.

Raphael and I relaxed into one another, getting used to our rhythms, learning how to share a life together. New territory for both of us, since he'd never been with anyone else, and the few relationships I'd had were so fleeting and inconsequential that I'd barely gotten to the fourth or fifth date stage, let alone contemplated actually living with someone.

Logan did start working for Lance a few days a week, and the couple moved into a bigger apartment in Flagstaff. I had no doubt that Lance probably had the funds to help them buy a condo or something, except that wasn't how my uncle operated. He was a firm believer in earning things for yourself, which meant he might loan them the money for a down payment in a few years...and would expect to be paid back at some point. Some people might have thought he treated Grace that way because she wasn't his blood, but I knew he'd expect exactly the same thing from any of his biological children.

And Michael went back to Flagstaff as well to immerse himself in his doctoral program, sending my cousin Kelsey into another fit of the blues. Both Taryn and I attempted to gently suggest that she should try dating someone—anyone—to get her mind off Michael, but she wouldn't even entertain the idea.

"No way," she said flatly when we all met for drinks at the local martini bar, although Taryn had opted for a glass of white wine instead of a martini. "It's easy for you to give advice, Callista—you already have the love of your life. But I'm not going to settle just because Michael is busy with his degree."

Taryn and I exchanged a weary glance. I'd had to bite my lip to keep from pointing out that Taryn certainly didn't have the love of her life—or anyone at all, for that matter. But saying such a thing right then felt borderline cruel to me. It wasn't that Taryn ever bemoaned her single state. No, she was pretty quiet on the topic, although I knew she hadn't found anyone to replace Noah, her last boyfriend, as far as I could tell. Her single state made me think all the guys our age in Sedona and its environs must have rocks for brains, because Taryn was smart and beautiful and fairly low-maintenance, all things considered. But she was also a powerful psychic, and I had a feeling that singular quality was a pretty tall hurdle for some men to jump.

I also wanted to tell Kelsey that she'd never had a single word of encouragement from Michael, so it was a little silly to be pinning all her hopes on him. Of course he was friendly and polite to her, same as he was with me or Grace. Well, things were still a little awkward with Grace, because apparently they'd had the mother of all first date disasters a few years back. But Michael didn't treat Kelsey any differently than he did the rest of the girls in our extended "family," so I had no idea where she'd gotten the notion lodged in her head that they'd have their own happily ever after once he was done with school and off being a world-famous astronomer, or whatever it was he planned to do with that degree.

Since I knew Kelsey would be all over me if I tried

to say anything along those lines, I just swirled my pear martini a few times and took a sip. Once again, Taryn had the same faraway look on her face that I'd noticed more and more lately. Several times during the past few weeks, I'd made a comment about her head being in the clouds, and she'd just smiled and said something about planning her transfer to NAU. Maybe that was the true reason for her distraction, but my sixth sense kept jangling away in the background despite her explanations.

Things had been all quiet on the Reptilian front, but the relative peace hadn't calmed my nerves any. Actually, I could feel myself getting more and more tense, certain the other shoe was going to drop even though I had absolutely no idea how or where. The tension wasn't quite enough to prevent me from enjoying my time with Raphael, but it did keep things from being completely idyllic. I was jumpy and nervous, having to ask him to repeat himself a good deal of the time, simply because I was thinking about what might happen next, rather than what was happening in the moment. Luckily, he seemed to understand the reason why I was so distracted, and didn't chide me for it.

Focusing on Kelsey's problems helped to take my mind off the situation, although I had to wonder if some of her current angst came from the realization that Valentine's Day was coming up and she'd be spending it alone...again. Her fault, though. Personally, I admired Taryn's more exotic looks because they were so different from my own, but I knew that my cousin's blonde girl-next-door appearance was more the type to attract the locals. Lord knows she had turned down her fair share of dates in the past and would continue to do so until she got over this Michael crush.

There was a joke. She'd been mooning over him for three years now with no end in sight.

The waiter came up and asked if we wanted another round. I was about to shake my head no, but Kelsey recklessly ordered another dirty martini, so I shrugged and asked for another pear-tini. Since Taryn had barely touched her pinot grigio, she smiled and said she was fine.

He went off toward the bar, although I noticed the quick glance he sent over his shoulder at Kelsey as he walked away. Girlfriend really needed to wake up, because our waiter was pretty damn cute...for a regular Earth guy.

Then I heard a murmur of voices coming from the bar, and someone saying, "Turn it up! Turn it up!"

Mystified, I swiveled in my seat toward the muted commotion. On the wall above the bar was a group of projected heads-up displays showing the usual—several different sporting events, although pickings were pretty slim in early February, now that football season was over; some kind of infomercial; a news broadcast. It was this last that had everyone's attention. And as I listened, I began to understand why.

"...transmissions abruptly cut off approximately thirty minutes ago. Since that time, mission control reports absolutely no contact with *Venture*. Teams are working now to determine whether this is a simple equipment malfunction or whether *Venture* has encountered something far more serious. The ill-fated mission took off from Cape Canaveral seven months ago and has a crew of four men and two women. It is too early to tell...."

I turned toward Kelsey and Taryn, both of whom were staring back at me, white-faced. Taryn especially looked scared half to death, green eyes again fixed on some point that only she apparently could see.

"Is it them?" I demanded. "*Is it?*"

"I—I don't know."

I'd always known her to be a truthful person, but right then, I could tell she was lying. Why, I had no idea, but I didn't have time for that kind of crap.

"Don't bullshit me, Taryn."

Her glance strayed to the screen, where some talking head was now expounding on apparently every single one of the ten thousand things that could have gone wrong with the mission and how it was far too soon to start panicking. Or words to that effect, anyway.

Meanwhile, Kelsey was looking back and forth between us, not quite baffled. That is, I think she *wanted* to be baffled, to pretend that she didn't know what we were talking about, who "they" were. I always got the feeling she would have much preferred to have been born into a nice, normal family that didn't have part-alien half-sisters and cousins and whatnot, but instead she got our current collection of craziness.

Taryn picked up her glass of wine and drained what remained of it—more than half the glass. I stared at her, startled despite my worry. She was not the type to chug her drinks.

"It is them," she whispered. "But that's all I know."

For a second, it seemed as if I couldn't move. Then I was digging in my purse for my car keys. I had no idea if Raphael had heard anything yet about what seemed to be going on somewhere in the black spaces between Mars and Earth, but right then all I could think about was being with him, of having him hold me and tell me this latest development wasn't as bad as it sounded.

Even if it was a lie.

CHAPTER SEVENTEEN

Although he had complained that it was a clumsy form of communication, Raphael had allowed me to pick out a cell phone for him. Yes, we could communicate mentally, but the farther apart we were, the more difficult our subvocal discourse became, and the martini bar where I'd been with Taryn and Kelsey was on the opposite side of town from the house I shared with Raphael, and there were a couple of very large hills in between.

So I told my car to call Raphael's cell, then felt my fingers begin to tighten on the steering wheel as the phone rang and rang before it went to voicemail. The factory-standard message came over the speakers, since he'd never bothered to change it.

I resisted the urge to hang up without saying anything, even though I knew that he'd already developed a bad habit of leaving the phone sitting on the nightstand rather than carrying it with him. "Raphael, there could be some trouble brewing. I'm on my way home. I'll be there in five."

After ending the call, I drove far too fast the rest of the way to the house, pulling around some tourists who were waffling at the entrance to one of the traffic circles that joined 89A and Highway 179. I earned an angry honk for my trouble, but I barely noticed as I sped up once again, and ignored the flashing "speed limit 35" warning on my dashboard. So what if I was going nearly twenty miles an hour over that?

That level of speed wasn't possible on the road which wound up to the house, so I slowed down to around thirty and gritted my teeth as I swung around every curve. When we'd picked out the property, I'd been attracted to the way it sat far up on the side of the hill, distant enough from the highway that you could barely hear the background murmur of traffic. Now, though, I found myself cursing the very isolation I'd once thought so desirable. Would I *ever* get home?

Eventually I did, of course. I pushed the button for the garage door opener when I was still half a block away, then let out a sigh of relief when I saw the little convertible Raphael had bought for himself sitting inside the garage. He was still learning to drive, but that hadn't stopped him from getting that shiny red BMW.

Which meant he must be around somewhere. Possibly roaming around the garden, although it would be at least three weeks or so before anything but the evergreens showed any real signs of life. I reminded myself how irritated I got whenever people expected me to be reachable all the time, but I wasn't sure how much good those self-admonishments did.

"Raphael!" I called out as I came into the kitchen. "Have you seen the news?"

Silly question, really. While he did possess a keen interest in what was going on here on good old planet Earth, he never watched the television news, calling it "blather and bloviation."

No answer. Well, he could be in the bedroom we'd designated as the study, with his and hers desks and laptops to match. He did like to listen to music while he read the news online—usually the feed from the BBC—or amused himself by lurking in conspiracy theory and UFO chatrooms. I'd told him that was a bad habit to pick up, since he knew the truth of the situation while the people in those online forums obviously didn't, but he'd only given me a gorgeous but infuriating smile and said that such a pastime was far more entertaining than watching any scripted shows on television.

So be it. I hurried toward the back of the house where the study was located, only to find it empty as well. I stopped in the middle of the room, trying as best I could to push back the panic rising within me.

"Raphael!"

Nothing. We'd debated getting a dog but hadn't

reached a decision yet, mostly because Raphael was still getting used to cohabiting with me, let alone a canine, and so the house felt empty. Completely, strangely empty.

I went from room to room, wondering if Raphael was napping in the master bedroom, or fixing himself a snack in the kitchen. Nothing. Not even a note on the countertop saying that Martin had swung by to take him shooting in the woods. The gang had been trying for a while to get Raphael to join in their outdoor activities, but he'd seemed more puzzled than anything else that people would find shooting cans off the top of fence posts an enjoyable way to pass the time.

Biting my lip, I went out to the living room. Not that I expected to find him there—it was open to a good deal of the house, and so it would have been impossible for him to ignore me calling for him—but because I didn't know where else to go.

Then I saw something gleaming on top of the coffee table. Something flat and metallic, almost like a dog tag, except it was bigger than that, a little smaller than a business card. A frown pulling at my brow, I went over and picked it up. The metal was a dark, dull gray, almost the color of lead, except far lighter in weight.

Scratched into the surface of the metal was a set of characters I'd never seen before and certainly didn't recognize. They looked halfway between Cyrillic and kanji, but I knew enough to realize they were neither of those. As I stared down at them, though, they seemed to shift and sharpen, morphing into words of recognizable English.

We have him.

Everyone assembled in my living room. Generally, Aunt Kara's house was the location for such convos, but expecting me to drive after the shock I'd experienced was probably presuming a bit much. I'd had just enough presence of mind to call my mother's cell before breaking down into hysterical tears, and that was about all I could manage.

Now I sat on the couch, my mother next to me, while my father kept turning the strange piece of metal over and over in his hands. "*Menkh,*" he said.

Lance raised an eyebrow. "What?"

"The material this is made of. The Reptilians use it. Nearly indestructible at the beginning, but also brittle and short-lived. It'll shiver into dust in the next couple of hours."

"Convenient," I remarked bitterly. "No evidence." Nevertheless, I'd still taken a picture of it with my phone, although I doubted that would help much. Evidence more compelling than a piece of metal had been faked plenty of times before that. I blinked away my tears and stared up at my father. He was the best authority on anything alien-related at that point, since Raphael had been taken by the Reptilians and my grandfather Gabriel was miles away at his home in Flagstaff. "But if it's Reptilian, why could I read what it said?"

"Because it was written in the common language of the Assembly. I've never taught it to you because I didn't see the point, but some memory of it must have been passed along to you through my blood."

Right. That wasn't creepy or anything. And why could I read those words, but not understand what people were saying when I was on Penalta? I decided the conundrum wasn't worth worrying about. Instead, I sniffled, and my mother pulled another tissue from the box on the coffee table and passed it over to me.

The television was on in the background, although Paul Oliver was the only one paying it much attention. More talking heads dissecting the continuing radio silence from the Mars mission, trying to fill up hours of air time with very little real information. Kelsey and Taryn had taken up residence on a couple of the dining room chairs, while Kara and Lance sat on the couch opposite the one where I'd more or less collapsed. Both Melissa and Kevin were at work, so they'd have to get filled in later. Persephone stood at the window, staring at the last sullen dregs of the late-winter sunset as if attempting to read them like tea leaves.

For all I knew, she could. I still didn't have an exact handle on how the whole clairvoyance/clairsentience thing worked. As intimidating as it could be, Taryn's ability to read minds seemed much more straightforward, although I knew there was a lot more to her talents than simply reading minds. Like her mother, she also had the ability to see things no one else could.

"There were no other attempts to communicate?" my father asked then. His tone was kind, soothing even, but something about the way he was asking his questions made me wonder if he was hearkening back to a time before I was even born, when he'd been pretending to be a Man in Black. How many other people had he questioned in such a way?

"No," I said, blotting my eyes with the tissue. My mother had also had the presence of mind to bring a small trashcan from the guest bathroom when she fetched the box of Kleenex for me. I dropped the used tissue into the receptacle. "Nothing else. Just that." I stared balefully at the rectangular piece of metal—*menkh*—which my father had just set back down on the coffee table. "It's like an intergalactic 'fuck you.'"

Neither of my parents commented on my language, probably because they knew that would only open the door to more cursing, which tended to be my last resort when I couldn't think of what else to do. "I suppose you could call it that," my father said. "So…they took him. But why? What purpose could holding him hostage serve?"

"I don't know. In that crazy hearing on Penalta, it

sounded as if they wanted me, but the Secretary put the kibosh on that. So is this revenge?"

My father ran a hand through his hair, disarranging the expensive cut. "I doubt it. The Reptilians are a bloodthirsty race, but they're also calculating. They know how to play the long game. Revenge rarely suits their purposes, as it shows a loss of control."

"Admirable," Lance said dryly.

"I wouldn't go so far as to say that."

Persephone came back toward the spot where we were all sitting. Maybe she'd given up staring out the window because dusk had finally given way to full dark. "If they were simply out for revenge, I think they would have done something a little more... final." She stopped there, but there was no need for her to continue. We all could guess what she meant by "final."

"It's true," my mother put in. "I've had some contact with their minds, and it's...well, it's not pleasant, not by a long shot. Even that brief exposure was enough to tell me that they enjoy prolonging things, making a person suffer. And mental anguish is often the worst suffering there is." She squeezed my hand, as if to tell me that she hated saying these things, even though they might be necessary for getting to the bottom of what was going on. "Giving someone a quick death isn't their style."

If that comment was supposed to make me feel better, it wasn't doing a very good job. I gulped down some air and told myself that crying wasn't going to help anything. I needed to keep my head screwed on straight.

Taryn spoke up for the first time. "If they left a message, it sounds to me like they intended to keep the lines of communication open. Otherwise, they would have just taken Raphael and left us all to wonder what had happened to him."

I supposed she had a point, although I couldn't help feeling a little irritated that it seemed to be back to "communication" with her. "Then why haven't they contacted me? Just to keep the torture going a little longer?"

"Maybe," she said. "I wouldn't know much about that. I haven't had any contact with them the way you or your parents have."

Again, I got that strange flicker from her, as if there was something she wasn't telling me. If circumstances had been different and we'd been alone, I might have pushed and tried to get her to open up. But I had way too much to worry about right then.

"They're aliens," Lance said then, his voice harsh. "And not the good kind. Expecting any kind of logic from them is a waste of time."

Paul turned away from the television, using the remote to mute the sound, although he already had it set fairly low so as not to disturb our conversation. "I don't believe that at all. Every move they've made indicates something they've been planning for a while. It may not feel logical to us because their goals and motivations are so different from ours, but that doesn't mean they're lacking in logic. Just the opposite, in fact."

My uncle looked unconvinced. "So if you were a coldly logical alien, what would you be planning?"

A smile at Lance's question, and Paul shook his head. Unlike my father, he'd gotten a good bit of gray over the past five years or so, but it didn't look bad, just reinforced the impression he gave of a retired college professor. Which I supposed he was, even though that retirement had been pretty much forced because of his belief in UFOs and aliens.

"I don't want to speculate," he said. "I don't have enough data. It feels as if we're still missing something here. Yes, we know that the Reptilians wanted to tap into Sedona's vortexes to give them a power unlike anything you can find elsewhere, but I'm not sure if that's the whole story."

"Well, what else do we even have that they'd want?" I said, realizing as I spoke how plaintive I sounded. "Some sort of element or other resource you can only get here?" Even as I asked the question, I knew I was probably grasping at straws. If the Reptilians truly had been working behind the scenes with some of the world's leaders, then I had no doubt they would have gotten exactly what they'd wanted in exchange for handing over some of their technology secrets.

"There is none," my father replied. "Earth is certainly not the only planet of its type in the galaxy, and it doesn't possess anything that can't be found in abundance elsewhere. There is the vortex energy, but...." He shook his head. "There is something strange about their desire for that energy. Their race simply doesn't have the ability to tap into it the way anyone with Pleiadian blood can, or even the way a human might."

"Could they force a human to use it?" Taryn asked, and everyone looked at her with some surprise. I noticed a tinge of pink on her cheeks, but her voice was steady enough as she went on, "I'm just wondering because of what you'd said about your interactions with them, Kirsten."

Since she sat so close to me, I could feel my mother go rigid. "I—I guess I never really thought about it from that angle."

My father ran an abstracted hand over his chin, as if rubbing at stubble, although his chin looked smooth enough to me. In general, Pleiadians didn't seem to be all that hirsute. "It could be possible," he said, the words coming out slowly, as if he was puzzling through them as he spoke. "Their mental abilities are different in nature from ours, but they can touch another's mind if they concentrate hard enough. So I can see how they might try to use a human as a puppet to get at the energies they want to bend to their own uses."

"Which would explain why they would want to keep a few choice specimens around, even if they wanted to kill most of us off." My mother's voice was hard, brittle. I knew that the Reptilian leader from her time had shown her images of destruction… but also of slavery. A fate the human race had avoided, thanks to the people who now sat in my living room with me.

I shivered, but at the same time, a terrible impatience seized me. "That might explain what they did then, but it still doesn't explain what they're doing *now* with Raphael. He's not human. He doesn't have any particular ability when it comes to accessing the energy here. I mean, no more so than any Pleiadian. They would have done better to get me, since I'm at least a quarter human. Or Mom. Or even Persephone or Taryn."

Persephone's dark, winged brows drew together at that remark, although her voice was level enough as she said, "Callista has a good point. If it's true that they need humans to get at Sedona's energies, then there are many more viable options available." She sent a worried look toward her daughter, who sat quiet and still on one of the dining room chairs. Once again, Taryn had that "listening" look on her face, although I supposed that wasn't so strange, since that was what she'd been doing for most of the conversation.

"Maybe that's not what they want at all," Lance put in. He got up from where he'd been sitting next to my Aunt Kara on the second of the two living room couches, and headed over to the window. The light outside had turned dark and bruised, purple shot through with streaks of blood color. Mouth twisting, he reached up and grasped the curtains, then pulled them shut.

For some reason, having the world outside hidden away made me a feel a little better. I loved the views from the house, but it wasn't until Lance had closed the drapes that I realized how exposed we'd been, as if malevolent eyes were somehow able to pierce the gloom and spy on our conversation.

"Then what do they want, Lance?" Kara asked.

He paused, cool gray eyes flicking toward me before he returned his attention to his wife. In a way, that oddly dispassionate gaze seemed to strengthen me. I could always count on Lance to tell it like it was, with no coddling or hand-holding. Over the years, he'd gotten impatient with my parents on more than one occasion, since he clearly thought they spoiled me, but his disapproval didn't change his affection for me. When he gave advice or offered input—which wasn't often, since meddling in other people's business was anathema to him—I knew it was in my best interest to listen to him.

When he replied, his tone was very gentle...for him. "I'm worried that they took Raphael solely as a bargaining chip."

CHAPTER EIGHTEEN

My stomach seemed to drop roughly a thousand feet. But I managed to keep my voice calm—well, almost calm—as I stared at my uncle and demanded, "A bargaining chip for what?"

"I'm not sure. At first, I thought it might have been some sort of revenge for the member of their team you inadvertently killed during the Mars raid, but then I realized that didn't fit." He crossed his arms and settled his weight back on one foot, as if he intended to remain standing for a while. Who knows —maybe he thought better that way. "After all, they know they already have you on the hook for some kind of reparations, whenever they figure out what they want those to be. Also, Paul's remark about them being cold-blooded and logical got me thinking. If revenge is out, and Raphael's of no use to them as a conduit for Sedona's energy"—despite knowing that those energies were actually real, Lance still couldn't keep himself from grimacing slightly when he mentioned them—"then it's logical to assume that they think he's valuable because of how they can use him to make other people do what they want. Whatever that might be."

"Couldn't we make an appeal to the Assembly?" I asked. Again, I could sense the futility of such a question before I even voiced it, but I was determined to keep poking away until I came up with something useful. "I mean, he's still a citizen, even though he's chosen to stay here with me. Surely the Assembly won't just stand by—"

"Unfortunately, standing by is what the Assembly does best," my father cut in, lip curling. "It exists to ensure that relative peace exists in the galaxy, but its main policy is non-interference unless there is absolutely no choice. We were allowed to rescue the Mars astronauts because leaving them to their fate would have interfered with the progress this world has made toward its own form of peace and co-existence. But stepping in to save one man?" He stopped there, mostly because my mother had given him a single shake of her head, mouth tight with worry. For all I knew, she'd also sent him a subvocal reprimand to stop talking about Raphael as if he was some stranger rather than the man their daughter had decided to spend her life with. Looking slightly chastened, he added, "I'm only saying that this isn't the sort of thing they'll step in to handle."

Which I'd already pretty much guessed. "So what do we do now?"

"Wait," my father said. "As Taryn pointed out, they did communicate by leaving that note for you. So it's reasonable to assume they'll make contact again. In the meantime—"

"In the meantime, you're coming home with us," my mother cut in. "There's no way I'm letting you stay here alone when a bunch of Reptilians could drop by at any time to leave another note."

"That's not exactly how it works—" my father began.

"Even so," she said, her tone flat. When her voice sounded like that, we all knew it was better not to argue, my father especially.

I got to my feet. "It's all right. I'd get the screaming heebie-jeebies if I stayed here by myself anyway. Let me go throw some things together."

An uncomfortable silence fell as I left the living room and headed back to the master suite to round up what I'd need for an overnight stay. Or maybe it would be much longer than that. After all, I had no idea how long the Reptilians planned to hold Raphael. Maybe they'd never let him go, would torture him, then—

Stop it, I told myself. *If Lance is right, then Raphael is valuable to them. They won't hurt him.*

Much.

My hands were shaking as I pulled down my weekender bag from the top shelf in the closet. I clenched my fingers into fists, then released them. The trembling seemed to subside a little. Good. I had to maintain at least a semblance of calm, even if I felt as if I was flying into a thousand pieces inside. A solution hadn't presented itself yet, but if the Reptilians truly had taken Raphael as a bargaining chip, then that meant they wanted something. We'd just have to figure out what it was.

I wasn't very neat about my packing, but only threw things into the bag willy-nilly as they occurred to me. Eventually, though, I seemed to have everything I would need. And if it turned out that I had forgotten something important, I could just come back to get it, or one of my parents would fetch it for me. I was only going about a mile away, after all.

Paul was murmuring something to Persephone as I came back into the living room, but everyone else had remained quiet, apparently content to sit in silence while I got my things together. Raphael's kidnapping had blown my original reason for coming home completely out of my mind, but seeing Paul and the now silent TV made it all come rushing back.

"Is that part of it?" I asked, pointing with my free hand toward the blank screen of the television.

"Possibly." Paul exchanged a troubled glance with Persephone. A few feet away, Taryn sat quietly in her chair. It didn't look as if she'd moved at all, whereas I could tell Kelsey was starting to get impatient, one cowboy boot–clad foot tapping against the leg of the dining room chair where she was sitting. As I stared at Paul, he amended, "Probably."

"But won't that bring the Assembly down on them?" I couldn't quite quash down the tiny flicker of hope that began to rise in me. Maybe the Reptilians had just made a massive blunder.

My father's shoulders lifted almost imperceptibly. "I don't know. It depends."

"Depends on what?"

"What their intentions are."

I sent him an annoyed glance. "Well, those intentions can't possibly be anything good, right?"

"Probably not, but…." He shoved his hands in his jeans pockets, most likely because he wasn't sure what else to do with them. "We'll just have to see what happens. In the meantime, we should get you home."

That slip-up earned him one of my patented narrow-eyed glares, and he amended, "Back to our house. The Reptilians know precisely where that is, too, so if they have something to say, they can come there and say it to our faces."

I wasn't sure I liked the sound of that. Confronting a group of Reptilians in front of the Assembly, where I knew they couldn't try anything, was bad enough. But at my parents' house, with just the two of them for protection?

Yeah, and they kicked their asses pretty well twenty-five years ago, I told myself. *So I doubt you have much to worry about.*

Thus comforted—sort of—I nodded. After that, the group pretty much broke up, with everyone heading out to their cars so I could lock up the place and go with my parents in their Mercedes.

As we pulled out of the driveway, I couldn't help but look back at the house and wonder if I'd ever live there with Raphael again.

———

My parents insisted on having me sleep in my old bedroom in the main house, not out in the casita.

"I just feel better knowing you're right down the hall," my mother said, and I didn't have the heart to argue with her.

One bed was pretty much the same as another, if Raphael wasn't there in it with me.

The world had already become surreal, and even more so as I set down my weekender bag and surveyed the room. Why, I wasn't sure; my parents still hadn't touched anything, and it was exactly the same as when I'd moved into the casita a year ago. I supposed I could have been thinking in the back of my mind that they might have finally realized I wasn't coming back, that purchasing a house with Raphael had the sort of finality that living in the casita definitely didn't.

Apparently not, though. Or maybe they just hadn't gotten around to it yet. After all, Raphael and I had only been living together for a couple of weeks.

Thinking of him—of the quick flash in his dark eyes when he smiled at me, of the warm timbre of his voice, the way he could distill the essence of someone who annoyed him into a single sarcastically pithy comment that would invariably send me into a fit of the giggles—all those memories brought a sudden, sharp ache to my chest and stinging tears to my eyes. Everyone had seemed so sure that the Reptilians would be contacting me again soon to let me know what they really wanted...but what if they didn't? What if this really was about revenge? Anyone as cold and calculating as they were must know that the best way to hurt me was to hurt Raphael.

My fingers wrapped around the back of the chair that sat in front of the computer desk. The carved wood bit into my flesh, but strangely, I welcomed the pain. It seemed to help with grounding me in the here and now, and not some horrible possible future.

A soft knock at the door, and my mother stuck her head inside. "I know you probably don't feel much like eating, but we were going to order some pizza. Any special requests?"

"Hawaiian," I said promptly. It was my favorite, but I almost always got overruled because neither of my parents liked it.

My answer earned me a lifted eyebrow. "Trying to take advantage of the situation?"

"Of course."

She chuckled. "All right, Hawaiian. Although

don't blame me if your father sneaks in a second one with pepperoni and olives."

"I won't say a word."

Smiling, and looking faintly relieved that she hadn't discovered me sobbing uncontrollably on the bed, she headed off down the hallway.

I'd actually contemplated breaking down and having a fit of hysterics, but I realized indulging that kind of weakness wouldn't help the situation any. Besides, if the Reptilians did decide to relent, the last thing I wanted was for Raphael to see me with puffy eyes and a red nose. Wishful thinking, I knew. I had the distinct impression that they were going to take their time contacting me, just so they could drag out the torture a little longer.

The pizza came about twenty minutes later. Once I heard the doorbell, I knew it was time to head out to be with my parents, even though my mother had been right—with the way my stomach was churning, I didn't know how much I'd be able to even eat. I'd do my best, though, if only because I knew that otherwise my father would tease me about leaving him a bunch of leftover pizza neither he nor my mother would want.

A warm, friendly smell came from the dining room, where two boxes of pizza sat on the sideboard. And, bless her, my mother had just opened a fun straw-wrapped bottle of chianti and was pouring some for all of us.

"Thank God," I breathed, reaching for my glass before I was even fully in my chair.

"We thought you might need a little fortification," my mother said.

"You could say that." I swallowed a mouthful of chianti and waited for the warm rush of it to flow down my throat and hit my stomach. Where it would mix with the martinis I'd had a few hours earlier, but right then, I wasn't too worried about blending two different kinds of alcohol. What with all the shocks I'd experienced earlier that afternoon, most of those martinis had probably worn off anyway.

From where I sat at the table, I was able to see that the television in the living room was turned on, but the sound had been muted. It was a twenty-four-hour news channel, the sort of thing Raphael loved to mock. I lifted an eyebrow at my father, since I assumed he was the one who'd turned it on.

"I figured it couldn't hurt," he said. "There haven't been any new developments, but that could change."

"And in the meantime, all they're doing is speculating and making fancy graphics to illustrate those speculations," my mother put in as she took my plate and deposited two slices of pizza on it. "I wanted to turn it off, but—"

"It's all right," I said, taking the plate from her. "Since there's no sound, it's really not that big a deal."

Her shoulders lifted, but she picked up my father's plate and dished up a couple of slices without comment. Then she got her own food—magnanimously taking one slice of each kind of pizza—and sat down.

For a minute or two, none of us said anything, only drank our wine and made some good inroads on our pizza. After all, what was there to say? None of us knew anything, not really. In that way, we were just like those talking heads on the news station. All speculation and no facts.

All right, I did know one thing. I loved Raphael, and I would do anything to get him back. Until I'd met him, I hadn't even known I was capable of such a fierce devotion. I'd thought I was doomed to be one of those people who drifted from short-term relationship to short-term relationship but who never met anyone who inspired love, *real* love. Maybe it was silly of me to have felt that way, since at barely twenty-two, I hadn't exactly put in much time in the salt mines, so to speak. But I'd seen people my age and younger fall in love, and I never had. Even losing my virginity had been a calculated act, not something that happened in the heat of the moment.

Now, though, I knew all that early detachment had only existed because I hadn't met Raphael yet. There wasn't something intrinsically wrong with me, as I'd begun to worry. I was only being true to my Pleiadian blood and waiting for my soul mate. And if I couldn't have him…

…then I would have no one. I accepted that realization with a strange level of equanimity, although I was feeling anything but calm at the prospect of losing Raphael when I'd just found him.

Terrified, more like.

I forced myself to eat pizza and drink wine, and I began to feel better. No, "better" was the wrong word. My thoughts were as worried and frenzied as ever, but my body relaxed just the slightest bit, as if it had realized it needed to take care of me at a time when my mind couldn't.

"...anything you need?" my mother was saying, and I blinked.

"What?"

"I was just asking if there was anything you needed. I hadn't checked the guest bathroom's toiletries and stuff lately."

"No," I replied absently, although I didn't know for sure if I'd really packed everything I required for a stay of indeterminate length. My mind hadn't been all that focused on the task. "I'm fine."

She shot me a troubled look, followed by a glance in my father's direction. Since he was in the middle of taking a large bite of pepperoni pizza, he couldn't really respond except to lift his shoulders. What could he say, anyway? I was sitting there and eating calmly enough. I hadn't dissolved into a big pile of blubbering goo. Right about then, that was the best either of my parents could hope for.

Even as I was looking over at my father, though, I saw his eyes widen. The half-eaten pizza slice fell from his fingers and landed with a thud on his plate, flinging bits of sliced olive in several different directions.

"Martin!" my mother exclaimed, then stopped dead, her gaze apparently following his. The color left her cheeks.

"What is it?" I asked, even as I swiveled in my seat so I could better see what they were both staring at.

Which seemed to be the television. Which was showing....

I blinked, certain that all the stress—on top of the martinis and the wine—had made me begin to hallucinate. Because I couldn't possibly be seeing what I thought I was seeing.

The setting was normal enough—dark blue curtains, a podium with the Presidential seal. I'd seen that sort of thing hundreds of times over the years, the typical setup for whenever the President wanted to address the nation.

There was nothing typical about the scene currently displayed on the TV, though. I saw the President, looking calm and focused enough, although something about the strained expression in her eyes reminded me of a horse that intended to bolt at any second. Behind her was a line of men and women wearing either business suits or military uniforms, and off to one side was the ubiquitous interpreter for the deaf.

Facing her, though....

I recognized them, even though I didn't know all their names. Tall, taller than any of the delegation who faced them. One almost human, except for his greenish skin and ruby eyes. One definitely not human, with coppery-brown scaled skin. Two more striped in green and black, and the last taller than all the others, the scales that covered his face and neck shimmering palest gold.

Lir Shalan. Along with the rest of the delegation who'd confronted me back on Penalta.

CHAPTER NINETEEN

I HEARD THE SHARP INTAKE OF MY MOTHER'S BREATH, but I couldn't turn away from the television to see her expression. Likewise, my father's muttered "holy shit" reached my ears, but it seemed to be coming from very far away. Right then, I didn't think anything could have unglued my attention from the screen, except maybe Raphael appearing in front of me and pressing his mouth to mine.

That didn't happen, though. Instead, I realized as I watched that the Reptilians weren't alone, that the six astronauts from the Mars mission were ranged behind them. All of the astronauts wore varying expressions of confusion, as if they weren't quite sure what was going on.

Well, I totally understood that feeling.

"Sound on!" my father barked at the television, which was still muted.

At once, the President's voice came from the speakers. She sounded just about as strained as she looked, her Boston accent particularly pronounced. "...we must extend the world's gratitude to these brave visitors, who stepped in when *Venture's* life-support systems began to fail. Without them, all of our astronauts would surely have been lost."

"We could not let our fellow spacefarers perish," Lir Shalan said in his cold, hissing voice. "But we thank you for your gratitude."

My attention shifted from Lir Shalan and President O'Donnell to the astronauts, all of whom stood there in silence, not reacting, their expressions still faintly puzzled. "Why aren't they saying anything?" I demanded. "They know he's full of bullshit, that his people attacked them back on Mars. Why aren't they telling the President what really happened?"

"Because they don't have any recollection of any of that, Callista," my father replied. His blue-gray eyes glittered with anger and some other emotion I couldn't quite identify. Frustration? "When Raphael got them back on their ship and sent them home, he made sure they would have no memory of what had actually transpired. All along we've had to do everything we could to make sure the people of Earth had no idea there was sentient life beyond this planet."

"Well, it looks like Lir Shalan has totally blown that out of the water," I shot back. "Disclosure is here, even if it's something the Assembly was trying to avoid."

"I know," he said. Pausing, he reached over and laid a hand on top of my mother's where it rested on the table. She was still staring at the TV, face frozen in horror. "You okay, Kirsten?"

She blinked. "Sorry. I mean, yes, I'm all right. I guess it's just seeing them like that...." The words trailed off, and it seemed as if she had to make a conscious effort to turn away from the television and back toward us.

"You saw them at the base." My father's voice was very gentle, with only the slightest hint of a question in it.

"I know. But that all happened so fast. I didn't really get a good look at them." She glanced over at me. "You recognize him, don't you?"

"Yes," I said, then swallowed. "He was on Penalta when I had to go in front of the Assembly. He's called Lir Shalan." That was the first time I'd actually mentioned his name to them. Yes, I'd told them a little about what had happened in that star system so very far from here, and maybe Raphael had filled in some of the blanks. But I really hadn't wanted to linger on the memory.

"Who's the other one?" my father asked then. "The one who looks almost human."

"I don't know. I never heard any of them say his name. Actually, I never heard him speak at all. I thought he must be some new kind of hybrid."

"I've never seen a hybrid who looked like that." Judging by his darkening expression, I guessed my father was troubled by the presence of the young man.

"Neither had Raphael."

For the first time, a flash of anger crossed my father's features. "And you didn't think to mention it to any of us?"

"Sorry." I sounded defensive even to myself. "Things have been sort of crazy lately. I guess I figured if it was really important, Raphael would have said something to you. He knows a lot more about the Reptilians than I do."

"Raphael wasn't one for heart-to-heart talks, in case you hadn't noticed."

It was probably just a slip, but I hated that my father had referred to Raphael in the past tense, as if he was irretrievably gone. I couldn't allow myself to think that. I *wouldn't*.

I glanced back at the TV, where it looked as if the historic human/alien meet-up had turned into a mutual lovefest. The President must have had to work pretty hard to come up with so many different ways to thank the Reptilians, while Lir Shalan kept going on about how they only wanted to help, and how they'd reached out because the Mars mission had shown his people that Earth and its inhabitants were now ready to join in the culture of the greater galaxy.

If it had been the Pleiadians making such overtures, I would have been thrilled beyond belief. People would realize that those who'd believed in aliens weren't crazy crackpots after all, and humanity would enter a new golden age complete with faster-than-light drives, endlessly renewable cold-fusion energy, and scientific advances that would forever end hunger and disease.

I kind of doubted the Reptilians planned to offer us anything quite so appealing.

"What *is* their game, anyway?" I asked. "I mean, we all know they didn't bring those astronauts home out of the goodness of their hearts."

"Hardly." My father looked as if he'd intended to say more, but right then his cell phone went off, followed by my mother's a few seconds later. He smiled grimly. "So let's see—I'm guessing that's Paul calling me and Kara calling you, Kirsten."

"Probably," she said, then went over to the kitchen counter where they'd left their phones and handed his to him before putting her own phone to her ear. "Hi, Kara. Yes, we're seeing it."

My father mouthed *Paul* right before he said, "Yes, we already had the TV on. We're trying to figure out what their game is as well." He was quiet then, as if listening to what Paul was saying.

In the meantime, my mother seemed to be covering more or less the same ground, although it also sounded as if Kara was trying to convince her to come over for another council of war or whatever they wanted to call it. That was about the last thing I wanted to deal with at the moment, though. I doubted that sitting around and dissecting what Lir

Shalan was really up to would help to get Raphael back. If the Reptilian leader was preoccupied with playing kissy-face with the President, then I worried that he probably wouldn't be expending much energy on whatever leverage he'd intended by kidnapping Raphael in the first place.

I turned back toward the television. The astronauts appeared to have been handed over to a team of scientists and military personnel, probably to determine that they were physically all right. I supposed the confusion they still seemed to be experiencing could be blamed on confronting the reality of extraterrestrial intelligence, but I wondered how long that excuse would fly. After all, they were highly trained scientists and pilots and engineers, not a bunch of teenagers who happened to run into a UFO in a cornfield or something.

Unfortunately, I didn't think their real memories would ever surface. Raphael had been doing that sort of thing for hundreds of years. Those memories were gone, along with any witnesses to prove that the Reptilians weren't quite as nicey-nice as they were pretending to be.

"Well, we'll talk it over and let you know," my mother said, then ended the call and dropped her phone on the table. Immediately, she glanced over at me, and I shook my head.

"If you all want to head over there, be my guest. I'm staying put."

"I had a feeling that was what you would say."

She didn't sound annoyed, though, more like relieved.

Which was somewhat surprising, although maybe she was glad to be able to use me as an excuse for why we wouldn't all be trooping over to my aunt's house to try hashing this thing out. My father hung up then as well, looking very tired.

"Paul's going to monitor the chatter and keep us posted. As you can imagine, all the UFO and conspiracy-theory forums have more or less exploded."

I could imagine. And Paul must be feeling a wee bit vindicated right about now. It was far too late for him to get his old job at the university back—and I doubted he'd want it, even if someone decided to make him an offer—but he still had to feel better knowing that no one could ever call him a fraud or a crackpot again.

The TV was now showing the President and Lir Shalan shaking hands. How she managed to touch him without shuddering, I had no idea. She was a politician, though; she was probably used to dealing with some pretty slimy characters. Then the Reptilian leader and his delegation moved off to one side, while the President and her advisor disappeared behind the blue curtains on the opposite side of the platform. Immediately, the camera switched over to a shaken-looking reporter, who began spouting some nonsense about what a momentous occasion this was and how the entire world now needed to pause and take a breath, and absorb the realization that we were no longer alone in the universe.

My father let out a disgusted sigh, then said, "TV off."

The screen went dark, and my mother and I both looked at him expectantly. "Now what?" she said.

"I don't know." He rubbed his chin. "It's clear that no one from the government has made any move to detain the Reptilians. That was always one of our own fears when it came to disclosure—that we'd be held and subjected to all sorts of experiments."

"Why do you think the Reptilians were allowed to go?"

"I'm not sure, but I know the military has good enough instrumentation to determine that a Reptilian ship has sufficient firepower to reduce Washington, D.C., and the area around it to slag. I have a feeling they simply didn't want to take the risk."

Superior firepower did tend to make a good deterrent.

"Why now?" I asked. "The Reptilians could have come forward multiple times before this, but they didn't. And they have Raphael. I feel like there's a piece here we're missing."

My mother tapped her fingers on the tabletop, eyes narrowing as she considered the conundrum. "You know how we thought earlier that they'd taken him as a bargaining chip?"

"Yes," I said, fairly sure I wouldn't like where this conversation was about to go.

"Well, they must know we'd go to some fairly extreme lengths to make sure Raphael was safe. What if they took him to guarantee our silence?"

"Like blackmail?"

"Basically, yes," my father put in, understanding spreading over his features, although he didn't look very happy about coming up with a plausible solution to the puzzle. "They couldn't risk any of us trying to tell the truth about what happened on the Mars base. But with Raphael as their hostage, they know we'll keep our mouths shut."

It did make a sort of horrible sense. My spirits sank even further, because if keeping him as a hostage for our continuing silence truly was their game, then I didn't see how they would ever let him go. Unless…

…unless someone else offered to be their hostage in his place. And I knew who that person needed to be. I couldn't ask such a sacrifice of anyone else.

I'd have to give myself up to the Reptilians so Raphael would be safe.

CHAPTER TWENTY

Needless to say, my parents weren't exactly thrilled when I suggested that I sacrifice myself to save Raphael.

"You don't know if that will do any good," my mother argued. "They could take you and keep Raphael as well."

"Then at least we'd be together," I said. "You just said it yourself—they need one of us to make sure no one lets the world know what they're really like. Raphael and I are soul-bonded. It needs to be me. Not anyone else."

"He would never allow you to make such a sacrifice," my father said. The finality in his tone only made me grit my teeth.

"That's not his decision to make," I retorted. "It's mine." In a way, I was almost relieved to have pushed myself to this point. I hadn't accomplished a lot in my life so far, but I could save Raphael. Maybe that was the whole reason I'd been born—not just to love him, but to make sure he lived and continued with his work.

My parents looked at each other. I didn't see any lips moving, but I knew they were communicating in silence, sharing a discussion they didn't want me to hear. By then, I was more or less used to the practice. Even so, I couldn't keep myself from snapping, "And can you please stop talking about me as if I'm not even here?"

"Callista," my mother began, then paused, as if trying to gather her thoughts. "I understand how you feel about Raphael. I know, because it's the same way I feel about your father. But you need to think this through logically. All we're going on right now are educated guesses. We don't really know anything. At the very least, I think we should wait a few days—"

"A few *days!*" I couldn't believe she thought I'd be willing to sit around for a few days and twiddle my thumbs when the Reptilians could be doing *anything* to Raphael. "That's impossible."

"It's not impossible," my father said. "For one thing, we don't have any way of contacting the Reptilians. I wasn't allowed to keep any of my tech when I was exiled here, and anything Raphael might have had with him would have been taken when he was."

Oh. I'd been so fired up about making a swap for Raphael that I hadn't even stopped to think that getting a hold of the Reptilians wasn't exactly the same as picking up my cell phone and calling Taryn to see if she wanted to go to the movies. Then a thought struck me. "What about the base?"

My father's brows drew together. "The base?"

"The abandoned base," I replied, not bothering to keep the impatience out of my tone. "In Secret Canyon. Wouldn't there still be communications equipment left behind?"

Once again, my parents exchanged a glance. "Yes," my father said slowly—and, I thought, reluctantly. "A good deal of it probably has been damaged, but—"

"But some of it may still work." Now that I'd seized on a plan, I positively itched to go out there and take a look. "If we head out now—"

"No," my mother cut in. "It's full dark, and that place is creepy enough if you go there in the daytime. We'll check in the morning."

Protests rose to my lips, but I could tell from the sober expressions both my parents wore that my arguments probably wouldn't get me very far. In the first place, I'd never been to the abandoned base, and I couldn't rely on my instincts to guide me there the way they had Grace. She had hybrid blood in her, whereas I certainly did not.

"First thing in the morning," I said, and they both looked resigned.

"First thing," my father agreed, and that seemed to be the end of it.

Until the next morning, of course.

Being resolved on a course of action wasn't enough to calm my mind, though. I kept worrying about what was happening to Raphael, and wondering what the Reptilians' true reason was for revealing themselves now. Of course, the story was all over the internet, all over the news, everywhere I turned. Everyone was talking about how the world would never be the same.

I knew the feeling. My world most definitely wouldn't be the same if I couldn't somehow ensure Raphael's safety. In a way, it would have been nice to be as blissfully ignorant as the rest of the world, to think that the Reptilians were only here to help us out. Oh, probably if I'd had the energy to lurk in some of the conspiracy-theory and UFO forums, I would have found people saying we needed to be careful, that the Reptilians weren't to be trusted, but those worries would only be dismissed by the general population. After all, everyone already thought the people who believed in Reptilian aliens and conspiracies were crazy. It was only that this time around, people would think they were crazy for an entirely different reason if they tried to warn the world's governments about being too quick to accept the aliens' promises.

Then I got a text from Taryn as I was lying in my old bed and staring up at the ceiling.

You okay?

Mostly, I dictated into my phone. *What do you think?*

I'm not sure what to think. I guess we'll just have to wait and see what happens.

That was Taryn for you. Always careful, always cautious. But I supposed she had to be, considering how much more she knew about what people were thinking, what the future might hold. She probably had to weigh every word she said to avoid letting anything slip that could damage a relationship or cause undue worry.

We're going to the alien base tomorrow morning, I told her.

Why?

To see if we can communicate directly with the Reptilians. Some of their equipment must still be there.

A long pause. Then, *Can I come with you?*

That request seemed to come from nowhere. *Why?*

Because I think I need to be there.

When someone who can see into the future tells you she needs to be in a certain place and time, you don't really argue. *Okay. Can you be here early, like 7:30?*

No problem.

See you then.

We ended the exchange, and I put my phone back

down on the nightstand. For some reason, I felt obscurely comforted. After all, Taryn had said several times that she wished we could communicate better with the Reptilians. Maybe she'd caught a glimpse of our upcoming confrontation and had realized that things would go a lot more smoothly if she was there to help things along.

Who knows—with her assistance, I might be able to get Raphael back without having to sacrifice myself.

I had never been a morning person. Nevertheless, I dragged myself out of bed at six-thirty and took a shower and got dressed, then wandered into the kitchen so I could fix myself some tea. The thick scent of coffee filled the room, but I didn't see either of my parents. The next moment, I heard them talking out in the family room, though, so I grabbed a tea bag and a mug, then left my tea to steep while I went out to find them.

They were both dressed and ready to go, it looked like, in warm, sensible clothes and sturdy hiking boots. Luckily, I'd known that the base was out in some rough country even though I'd never been there myself, and I'd outfitted myself in pretty much the same way— after a frantic dig through my closet to find the hiking boots I'd left behind when I moved in with Raphael.

His description of going to gallery openings and restaurants and concerts had made me think I might not need those boots for much, so I'd left them back at my parents' house, along with an assortment of other odds and ends that I knew I'd need to move eventually.

"Taryn's meeting us here," I said without ceremony. "She said she thought it would be a good idea if she came with us."

My father's eyebrows lifted. "A premonition?"

"She didn't say it in so many words, but that was the impression I got."

"Does Persephone know about this?" my mother asked, her expression troubled.

"Taryn didn't say." Then, since I could tell my answer hadn't done much to mollify her, I added, "I suppose that's her business. She is a grown person, you know. It's not like she has to ask her parents' permission to do something. Well, not exactly anyway."

Taryn did still live at home, so I supposed she'd have to offer some sort of reason as to why she was leaving the house at a little past seven in the morning. When we'd texted the night before, though, she hadn't mentioned anything along those lines, which meant she'd probably already come up with some sort of excuse for today's excursion. Because she worked as a psychic part-time at several of the various shops in uptown, her schedule tended to be kind of screwy, although not screwy enough to justify an early-morning departure several hours before any of those shops actually opened.

My mother lifted her shoulders, then said, "I suppose you're right."

I relaxed a little, glad that she didn't seem too interested in pressing the issue. Noticing that both she and my father held mugs of coffee, I recalled my own tea, still steeping in the kitchen. I mumbled something about going to get it, then headed back so I could extract the tea bag and pour a little honey in.

While I was doctoring my tea, the doorbell rang. I knew it had to be Taryn; she was always on time, although I'd hoped she'd run a little late this morning just so I'd have enough time to get something to eat. Breakfast didn't seem to be in the cards, though, so I snagged an energy bar from the pantry and took it and my mug of tea out to the living room.

Taryn stood there with my parents. Like me, she was wearing jeans and hiking boots, and had a warm down-filled coat on over her denim shirt. She flashed me a quick smile, but I sensed something almost tentative about it, as if she wasn't sure exactly how it would be received.

I thought I understood her diffidence. We'd only texted the night before, so she hadn't had much of a chance to see me or hear the tone of my voice to gauge how upset I really was by the whole Raphael situation. As far as I'd been able to tell, her actual mind-reading talent only seemed to work if she was in the same room with someone. Besides, she wasn't the sort of person who'd go tromping around in your mind without asking permission. She'd told me once that she couldn't always keep out people's thoughts if they were upset and broadcasting everywhere, but that wasn't the same thing as sneaking a peek under cover of darkness.

My mother asked, "Does Persephone know where you're going?"

I wanted to make a face, but Taryn said quietly, "I told my parents I was coming over to help Callista with something. They didn't ask any questions. So it's not like I'm sneaking around or lying to them, but at the same time, they didn't have to know everything."

Whether that was really what either of my parents wanted to hear, I didn't know, but they didn't pry further. My father asked Taryn is she wanted a cup of coffee or some tea. She shook her head and said that she'd had some coffee before she left the house.

Apparently, that question had exhausted my parents' delaying tactics, because my father said, "Okay, then I guess we'd better get going."

I took a couple of large gulps of my tea before setting it down on one of the coasters on the coffee table. The energy bar would have to wait until we were en route.

Because it was only the four of us, we all piled into my parents' SUV. No one said much of anything as we drove through the town's quiet streets, heading out to West Sedona and the road that led toward the Secret Canyon wilderness area. On that weekday morning in early February, it was quiet enough, so we didn't have to deal with much traffic as we made our way to Dry Creek Road and began to wind our way through neighborhoods where the lots got gradually larger and larger until it was only open land on either side, snow still gleaming in the shadows of the juniper trees and in the leeward sides of rock formations.

Eventually, we came to the turn-off that led to one of Sedona's numerous trailheads, but a hiking trail wasn't our true destination. We bumped along on a rutted dirt road, the Mercedes managing mud, snow, and rocks without batting the proverbial eyelash. Judging by some of the signage, we really weren't supposed to be driving out this far, but I decided it was probably a good idea to hold my tongue and let my father do what he wanted. My guess was that he was trying to save us from having to do too much hiking.

But even the SUV finally met its match, coming to an area strewn with boulders that had probably rolled down from the hills above during that last big storm. Everyone climbed out.

"This way," my father said, leading us away from the car and off toward the northeast, where I could see a sheer cliff face rising right into the sky. Even though I knew it must be an optical illusion, that the clouds had only dropped low enough to obscure the top of the mesa, I still had to suppress a shiver that didn't have much to do with the brisk morning air.

We hiked along in silence, our breaths rising in little mist-white puffs. By some unspoken agreement, my parents were in the front, while Taryn and I brought up the rear. That made the most sense, since they'd been here before and of course neither Taryn nor I had.

As the cliff loomed closer, I began to sense a growing tightness somewhere in my midsection, as if my body was reacting to the growing proximity of the Reptilian base. I took in a breath and told myself I need to relax. The place had been deserted for years. Anyway, I'd stood in the same room with a bunch of Reptilians and lived to tell the tale. Friendly they most definitely were not, but I knew it was entirely possible to survive an encounter with them.

Beside me, Taryn was looking around with wide eyes, but she didn't say anything. If the place was giving me the willies, I could only imagine how it must have been affecting someone with her particular sensibilities.

"Here," my father said briefly, pushing past a gnarled manzanita bush, its pale twisted shape looking as if it had grown out of the sheer rock. Behind the manzanita was a metal door with a wheel set into the center.

Even though I knew that wheel had been turned recently, by my cousin Grace, I still couldn't help letting out a little shocked breath as my father grasped hold of it and began to rotate it. The sound of metal grinding against metal seemed to pierce my eardrums, but I clenched my teeth and endured. A few more turns, and then he was tugging on the door, opening it.

A black rectangle yawned in the hillside. Both my parents pulled compact flashlights out of their pockets. "There's emergency lighting once you're actually on one of the levels," my mother explained. "But the stairwells are dark, so we'll need these until we get where we're going."

Fair enough. As we all went inside and began to descend those stairs, though, I had to wonder how Grace had managed to cover this same ground all alone and with no real idea of what she was heading toward. I had people surrounding me, and I still wanted to turn around and run back to the safety of daylight and my parents' SUV.

I wouldn't do that, of course. This was for Raphael, and I'd gladly suffer a lot more than a creepy stairwell to make sure he was safe and far, far away from the Reptilians.

"Which level, do you think?" my mother asked. Her tone was hushed, as if she didn't want to raise her voice and possibly wake up something that had been sleeping here for more than a quarter of a century.

"I'm not sure, but probably the fourth or fifth," he replied. "The labs and hybrid training areas were deeper than that—they always tended to put the most sensitive stuff the farthest away from the surface, while transportation equipment tended to be closer up top. So let's stop on the fourth level and see what we can find."

She nodded, and another of those uneasy silences fell. We descended one more set of stairs, and then my father opened the door at the next landing and led us out into the hallway.

The place was eerily familiar, mostly because it seemed to be an exact duplicate, in design if not actual layout, of the Mars base. Or I supposed the base on Mars was the duplicate, since this one had existed first. Either way, the sensation of *déjà vu* that swept over me was as strong as it was unwelcome.

Swallowing, I followed my parents down the corridor, which was lit with the same reddish lights I'd seen at the Mars base. Taryn followed a pace or two behind me, her steps lagging as she kept glancing all around, taking it in. Had she seen this place in a vision? Was she now trying to match what she'd glimpsed with that strange inner eye of hers with the reality that surrounded her now?

I didn't have time to ask her, because my father's strides had lengthened as he hurried us toward a set of double doors at the end of the hallway. On the wall next to them was one of those flat panel-looking objects the Reptilians used as their biometric locks, and I wondered how my father planned to get past it. I knew he didn't have one of those jewel-like devices to open it the way Raphael had.

But then I realized that one of the doors was partly ajar. Only by an inch or less, as if someone had meant to shut it, but it hadn't caught all the way. No real surprise there, if the base had been evacuated as quickly as my parents had made it sound.

Without an ounce of hesitation, my father reached out for the door, then grasped it by the edge so he could pull it open all the way. We began to follow him into the chamber.

And stopped dead, because the room was far from empty. The Reptilian delegation stood there.

With them was Raphael.

CHAPTER TWENTY-ONE

WITHOUT THINKING, I BEGAN TO MOVE FORWARD, BUT my mother caught me by the bicep. "No, Callista," she whispered fiercely.

I almost wrenched my arm from her grasp. But then I saw Taryn staring at me, eyes wide, pleading. She gave an almost imperceptible shake of her head.

All right, I'd consider myself warned. I stopped where I was, my gaze moving across the room to meet Raphael's, relief sweeping over me as I took in his appearance.

He didn't appear to have been harmed. His clothes looked a little rumpled, as if he'd slept in them, and his hair was likewise messier than I'd ever seen it, but physically, he appeared to be more or less intact. But his dark eyes seemed to bore into me, worried, intense.

Callista, what are you doing here?

We came to try to save you. We thought we'd use the communications equipment to contact the Reptilians—

I stopped there, though, because my father spoke.

"Lir Shalan," he said. "That is your name, isn't it?"

"Yes," the leader of the Reptilians said in his hissing voice. In English, too, unless he had some sort of translator device stashed on his person. He glanced past my father to me, and I had to keep from flinching at being on the receiving end of that baleful, ruby-tinted stare.

"What are you doing here?"

Lir Shalan's mouth twitched. By that point, I'd guessed that the strange grimace was the Reptilian equivalent of smile. It just looked very different on someone who didn't have any real lips. "Why, making things easier for you, Martin Jones. You were coming here to contact us, were you not?"

My mother shifted her weight from one foot to the other, but she remained quiet. No one could have ever accused her of being a shrinking violet, but she also knew when she was out of her depth.

"Yes, we were," my father replied, tone steady. "We want to sue for Raphael's release. You had no right to take him—"

"We had every right," Lir Shalan cut in. "He was the one who orchestrated the attack on our base, even if it was your daughter who actually committed the act of murder."

"I told you, it was an accident!" I burst out.

My love, do not provoke him.

I wanted to retort that I wasn't going to keep myself from telling the truth, but the naked pleading in Raphael's eyes stopped me. The situation was already tense enough. I didn't need to make it worse by going off half-cocked.

Another one of those stretches of Lir Shalan's mouth that might have been a smile. "So you constantly assert. I see you have already conveniently forgotten that the Assembly ruled in our favor."

"So they did," my father said, still in that almost too-calm voice. I realized then that he was forcing himself to remain steady, that if he allowed his emotions even the tiniest rein, he could make matters far worse than they already were. "But I doubt the Assembly intended for you to make Raphael part of your reparations. Even if taking him hostage was what you eventually decided on, you would still have had to submit your request to the Assembly."

"A request that would have been denied," Raphael said, speaking aloud for the first time. "As our good friend here knows all too well. So he decided to take preemptive action."

I didn't think I could love him any more than I already did, but something about seeing him standing there, mussed and rumpled and yet with his chin high and his dark eyes flashing fire, made me ache for him with even greater strength. He'd done nothing wrong. He shouldn't be a captive.

Taryn had been hanging back a foot or so behind

me, but right then, she stepped forward so we stood more or less shoulder to shoulder. Her gaze seemed to be fixed with a kind of awful intensity on the Reptilian delegation. I supposed I couldn't blame her; she had to have seen them on television, but those images couldn't really communicate their size or the sort of suffocating dread that seemed to surround them. As I watched, she looked from Lir Shalan to the strange greenish-skinned hybrid—or whatever he was—who stood behind him and off to the left. Something flickered in her eyes, but I couldn't begin to guess what the emotion I glimpsed might be.

"You may remain silent, Raphael," Lir Shalan snapped. "You have been meddling in affairs that were none of your concern for far too long as it is."

"Indeed?" Raphael replied, his voice almost a drawl. "For I believe the Assembly has a strict policy of non-interference, and so the few times I have been called on to intercede, it was for a very good reason. But I will admit that your idea of a good reason and the Assembly's are probably quite different."

"All right," my father broke in. "I think we all have to agree to disagree on that point. But surely you have something you do want to discuss with us, Lir Shalan, or you wouldn't be here now."

"Perhaps."

Now he was just messing with us. I could see it in the glint in his red eyes. It wouldn't have surprised me if he'd confessed in the next moment that he planned to kill us all, right before his henchmen pulled out their blasters, or whatever it was that Reptilians used.

My father appeared to have thought just about the same thing. He didn't exactly step forward, but he shifted in such a way that he was partially blocking my mother, and Taryn and me as well. "You mind answering a question?"

"It depends on what it is."

"Why save the astronauts? What's in it for you? Just curious."

Lir Shalan narrowed his eyes. "I thought you might be. But I also thought it should be obvious."

My father's shoulders lifted. "Well, give us slower thinkers a clue."

Something that might have been a chuckle. To me, it sounded more like Lir Shalan was trying to cough up a hairball. "Gratitude is a powerful emotion. It can cause one to…overlook…certain things. Also, since the humans now view us as their saviors, let us just say that they are less likely to look favorably on any other aliens who might try to present themselves as being the ones in the right. I doubt very much if they'd be pleased to learn that other aliens had been living among them for years, gathering intelligence and sending it back to their masters. There could be unfortunate consequences of such information leaking to the general public, don't you think?"

So that was it. Blackmail. If we created too much of a fuss—if we threatened to expose him and the rest of the Reptilians for what they truly were—then he would make sure the identities of any benign aliens here on Earth would be released, with the addendum that of course they weren't the good guys, because otherwise wouldn't they have stepped in a long time ago to help cure some of humanity's woes?

My father. My mother. My grandfather Gabriel, one of the gentlest souls I'd ever encountered. Possibly Grace and Logan, although that might be dangerous, since their alien blood was hybrid and not Pleiadian. And of course, I had no idea how many more of my father's people might be here on Earth right now, whether gathering data, or acting as a guide the way Raphael had. What I did know was that all those people were good, and didn't deserve to be exposed in such a way.

There could even be others like me, children of Pleiadians who'd been stationed here. My father had never mentioned them, if they did exist, but I couldn't discount such a possibility. All of them would be vulnerable, unless we kept our mouths shut and did exactly as the Reptilians said.

They can't do this, I thought desperately at Raphael.

They can, and they know it. Why else would they force a physical confrontation such as this? They wanted to see your expressions as you recognized the extent of your defeat.

I can't accept that.

It is a difficult thing to accept. A pause, and when he

continued, his mental voice was heavy with sorrow. *It is a terrible choice, to weigh the safety of those you love against the greater good. Are you strong enough to go up against them in order to save humanity from their depredations, knowing that they will expose your family for what they are?*

Was I strong enough? I glanced over at my mother's pale face, at the taut set of my father's jaw. They knew exactly what was at stake.

And Taryn. She stood beside me, rigid, her body so still that I could barely tell if she was breathing. No, Taryn shouldn't be at risk, since she was one hundred percent human, but her family had spent decades fraternizing with us aliens. I sort of doubted that an angry mob would care much about her human blood, since she was already gifted with the sorts of powers that most people couldn't understand and probably didn't want to.

Then I looked over at Raphael. I wanted to memorize every detail of his face, the heavy lashes, the long straight nose, the mouth that had kissed me with so much passion. Lir Shalan had been right about one thing—Raphael had spent a lifetime working for the greater good. He needed to continue that work.

As for me, well, he'd seen something in me, loved me. But what had I ever accomplished, except to amass one of Sedona's larger shoe collections? My family would grieve, but maybe having me in his clutches would be enough to satisfy Lir Shalan, or at least make him back off a little on his threats of blackmail.

A girl could hope, anyway. All I knew then was that my entire body seemed to ache with the intensity of my love for Raphael, for what he'd suffered for hundreds of years, until he finally was able to understand that there was nothing wrong with him, that he'd only needed to be patient. My sacrifice would wound him, but at least he would be alive. I had to hope he would understand why I acted as I did.

I stepped forward. "Lir Shalan!"

His gloating blood-red gaze had been fixed on my father, but it immediately shifted toward me. "Yes, honored Callista?"

I knew he'd used the Assembly's form of address simply to mock me, but I brushed the sarcasm aside. "Back on Penalta, you asked for me. I am offering myself now in exchange for Raphael. Let him go, and you can have the thing you truly wanted."

His eyes flared wide in surprise—at least, I thought that was the emotion showing on his alien features—even as my mother burst out, "Callista, no!" and my father began to utter his own denial.

And Raphael's voice in my head, saying, *You cannot do this!*

I can, if it means saving you.

No—

Painful as it was, I shut down our mental communication. I'd already made the offer. Now it was up to Lir Shalan to accept the exchange.

For a long moment, he was silent, watching me. No, if truth be told, it wasn't so much watching as leering. My entire body went cold, and I was glad I'd never gotten around to eating the energy bar I'd stowed in one of my jacket's pockets, because otherwise I was sure I would have been sick as I realized what probably lay ahead for me. But I didn't say anything, only stood there with my heart pounding and the dim room seeming to spin around me. I'd made my move. The next one was on him.

Before he could speak, though, the green-skinned hybrid went up to him and murmured something in his ear. A long pause, and Lir Shalan shot something back in the sibilant Reptilian tongue. I had absolutely no idea what was going on—and, judging by the mystified expressions my parents and Raphael wore, neither did they.

Then the Reptilian tilted his head to one side, and his gaze moved from me to Taryn. She didn't move, although a small shudder rippled through her before she went still again.

"Not you," he told me, his tone dismissive. "The other one."

Before I could react, Taryn had taken a step forward, then another one. My father moved in her direction, as if attempting to stop her, but somehow she sidestepped him and continued toward the Reptilian delegation.

I found my voice. "Taryn, you can't!"

She turned toward me. The glassy look was gone from her eyes. They met mine, calm, unafraid. In that moment, I understood why she'd seemed so far away lately. Somehow, she must have known what was coming, had realized it was her sacrifice that would save Raphael, not mine.

My heart ached. I wanted to stop her...and yet, I didn't. Something in her expression told me that any of my protests would be ignored, that she had decided on this fate for herself, so Raphael and I might be happy.

She even smiled faintly at me as she said, "I think it's my turn to have an adventure."

Then she went to the green-skinned young man and laid her hand in his. I watched as he wrapped his fingers around hers, while Lir Shalan gave a nod of satisfaction.

A flash of harsh yellow light surrounded the Reptilians, and then they were gone.

The Sedona Files series concludes with Taryn's story in *Enemy Mine*.

Darknight

Darkmoon

Sympathetic Magic

Protector

Spellbound

A Cleopatra Hill Christmas

Impractical Magic

Strange Magic

The Arrangement

Defender

Bad Blood

Deep Magic

Darktide

Books 1-3 and Books 4-6 of this series are also available in two separate omnibus editions at special boxed set prices. Chronicles of Cleopatra Hill includes the series' two "back in time" novellas, *Bad Blood* and *The Arrangement*.

Or get the entire series in one enormous, specially priced boxed set! (Not available on Amazon.)

THE DJINN WARS

(Paranormal Romance)

Chosen

Taken

Fallen

Broken

Forsaken

Forbidden

Awoken

Illuminated

Stolen

Forgotten

Driven

Unspoken (June 2019)

Books 1-3 and Books 4-6 of this series are also available in two separate omnibus editions at special boxed set prices!

THE WATCHERS TRILOGY*

(Paranormal Romance)

Falling Dark

Dead of Night

Rising Dawn

The Watchers Trilogy is also available in a specially priced boxed set!

THE SEDONA FILES*

(Paranormal Romance)

Bad Vibrations

Desert Hearts

Angel Fire

Star Crossed

Falling Angels

Enemy Mine

Get the first three books of this series in an omnibus edition, or read the complete six-book series in one super-low-priced boxed set!

TALES OF THE LATTER KINGDOMS

(Fantasy Romance)

All Fall Down

Dragon Rose

Binding Spell

Ashes of Roses

One Thousand Nights

Threads of Gold

The Wolf of Harrow Hall

Moon Dance

The Song of the Thrush

Books 1-3 and Books 4-6 of this series are also available in two separate omnibus editions at special boxed set prices.

THE GAIAN CONSORTIUM SERIES*

(Science Fiction Romance)

Beast (free prequel novella)

Blood Will Tell

Breath of Life

The Gaia Gambit

The Mandala Maneuver

The Titan Trap

The Zhore Deception

The Refugee Ruse

Books 1-3 of this series are also available in an omnibus
edition at a special boxed set price!

STANDALONE TITLES

Hearts on Fire

Sympathy for the Devil

Taking Dictation

Night Music

Golden Heart

* Indicates a completed series

ABOUT THE AUTHOR

USA Today bestselling author Christine Pope has been writing stories ever since she commandeered her family's Smith-Corona typewriter back in grade school. Her work includes paranormal romance, fantasy romance, and science fiction/space opera romance. She makes her home in Arizona.

Don't miss out on any of Christine's new releases — sign up for her newsletter today!

Christine Pope on the Web:
www.christinepope.com

facebook.com/ChristinePopeAuthor
twitter.com/ChristineJPope

www.ingramcontent.com/pod-product-compliance
Lightning Source LLC
Chambersburg PA
CBHW070907260626
47162CB00007B/2588